CODE OF SECRETS

A Cass Leary Legal Thriller

ROBIN JAMES

Chapter 1

THERE WAS no other sound like it. The pulsing whip-whip-whip getting closer. You could hear it everywhere. I looked skyward; two giant mute swans flew right over me, their wings cutting through the air, flapping three times per second with tremendous force and velocity. Flying at speeds topping thirty miles per hour, they could get from one end of the lake to the other in a little over a minute. This afternoon, though, they descended with grace and precision, coming to a restful stop about ten feet from my pontoon.

The male swan honked at me, stretching out his wings. I called him Neptune. He was the elder statesman of the Finn Lake waterfowl. His wife, Salacia, floated behind him, the shier of the two. It was strange to see her out with him today. She had eggs in her nest. But an odd situation arose this season. A lone female gander had taken up egg-sitting duties after her own clutch had been eaten by raccoons last week.

"All right, all right," I said. "Keep your feathers on." I knew what Neptune wanted. I kept a plastic container of dog food under the seat for this very purpose. My two dogs, Marbury and

Madison, yipped from the shore. But years ago, they and the swans had come to a fragile truce. Which was fine by me. It was the geese I wanted chased off, not these two.

I tossed a few kibbles into the water near Neptune and a few more near Salacia. They stretched their long necks to scoop them up. I was ready to toss more, but they felt the vibrations before I heard the sound of Eric's truck pulling into the driveway. They liked him too. Hated cars, though. Both swans lifted off to look for more snacks down the shore.

The dogs barked with glee as Eric climbed down from the cab. He had a red-and-white rectangular box in his hand and a broad smile on his face. What he did not seem to have was the birdseed he'd gone after at the local farm store.

"Cass!" he called out. I shielded my eyes from the sun. Early May and it was still too cold to get in the water. But I'd taken to stretching out on the pontoon to tan my legs after my morning coffee. For the past six days, I'd done something I rarely do. Take a vacation.

Grabbing my sweatshirt, I carefully stepped onto the dock and walked up to the yard. Eric was already in the pole barn across from the garage, strange box in hand.

"What are you doing?" I asked. Eric was on a mission. He'd been like this a lot over the last couple of months. After retiring as a detective for the Delphi PD, he'd become somewhat of a man of leisure. His brief stint as my private investigator hadn't been good for him. I defended criminals. Though he respected the process, it had just been a bridge too far for him. Since then, the man had become flat out bored.

Last week, he planted trees and tilled an additional twenty square feet up the hill for more garden space. Before I could ask what new project had taken over his mind, he came down carrying my nephew Sean's pack 'n' play. He'd long since outgrown it.

"Uh ... you have something you wanna tell me?" I asked. With the playpen under one arm, the strange box under the other, he stood in the center of the garage. He pointed with his chin toward a back corner of the barn.

"There," he said. "Plenty of room. And two outlets where I can put the heat plate and the red light. They're in the back of the truck. Can you get them? I'll grab the horse bedding in a second."

"Horse bedding? Exactly what do you have in that box, mister?"

He set it down on a picnic table he kept near his tools. Then he set his mind to unfolding the playpen. There was no talking to him when he was like this. I went to the truck and pulled out two boxes, raising my eyes when I read the first one.

Chick brooder light.

"Uh ... Eric?"

Carrying the boxes, I headed back to the barn. Eric had the playpen set up. The box on the picnic table started to move.

"I'll get the pine shavings," he said.

"Uh huh," I said, setting the other two boxes down. I went over to the picnic table and picked the red-and-white box up by its handle. There were four round holes punched out of each side of the box. I held it up and peered into one of the holes. A wide, blinking, amber eye stared back at me and peeped.

Eric had a giant bag of pine shavings hoisted onto his shoulder. He set it down, pulled out his pocket knife, and sliced into it.

Within seconds, he'd filled the bottom of the pack 'n' play with about two inches of fresh shavings.

"Okay, bring them here," he said.

"Them?" But I did as he asked. Carefully, Eric set the box on top of the freshly spread pine shavings and opened the lid.

At his shoulder, I peered down. One by one he lifted eight baby chicks and set them on the bedding. They all seemed offended by the situation and raced to the corner of the pen, huddling together.

"Chickens," I said. "We're doing chickens now?"

"Pullets," he said. "Two Silver Laced Wyandottes, two Easter Eggers, one Barred Rock, one Golden Comet, and those two little black ones are Australorps."

"Australia-whats?"

"Australorps," he said. "They're supposed to be great for beginners. Though I'm not a complete beginner. My grandpa raised chickens. He'd pay me to muck out their coop during the summer and collect the eggs. They're little now, but we don't have much time. Before you know it, they'll outgrow this brooder and need a permanent coop. I've got a spot picked out up the hill. It's probably a good idea if I build them a run."

He was right about one thing: the little suckers were cute. I reached down and picked up a tiny, reddish-brown chick. It had strange markings on its back. It basically looked like a chipmunk with a beak.

"That's the Golden Comet," he said. "She's supposed to be sex-linked."

"Um ... what now?"

Eric smiled. He put an arm around me and kissed my cheek.

"Sex-linked. As in, her coloration is linked to her sex. So you can tell she's a girl right at hatch. The hatchery sexed the rest of them before they were shipped. Keeping a rooster would be sort of a problem. I mean, if we care about the neighbors."

"Of course," I said. The little gold fluff in my palm looked straight at me with intense yellow eyes.

"I'll set everything up," he said. "I've got an automatic feeder and waterer. You'll be surprised at how much they can scarf down in a day. So, what do you think?"

Before I could answer, my little golden whatever-she-was stretched her neck, rose up on her little legs, and promptly pooped down my arm.

I set her down. Eric handed me a shop towel. "She's just a baby," he said. "She can't help it."

"I won't hold it against her."

"I'll build them the best coop you've ever seen. I found some plans on the internet. I can make it look like anything you want. I was kind of thinking of a Wild West saloon."

I reached up and brushed a hair out of his eyes. He needed a haircut. But I kind of liked it long. It gave him a rakish appearance. He looked downright dangerous.

I kissed him. Smiling, he turned and went back to the truck. A moment later, he'd brought back chicken feed, some sort of vitamin powder, and the contraptions for their food and water.

"Probably shouldn't name them yet," he said. "The kid at the farm store seemed pretty knowledgeable. But just in case one of them starts crowing."

A second later, Marbury and Madison came scrambling in, their sniffers working overtime. Marby whined when he picked up the chick scent. He rose up on his hind legs and looked through the mesh. Madison sat back, curious, but not overly excited about this new development.

"They're not food," Eric warned the dogs. "These are your friends. Be nice. They'll make you eggs, not chicken tendies."

My phone rang. It was my law partner Jeanie's ringtone. Eric recognized it and frowned. "I thought she was under strict orders not to call you about any work stuff this week."

"Only unless it was urgent," I said.

"What could be urgent? You don't have any trials on deck. You pled out your last two cases. Your decks are cleared."

"Right," I said. "Which means I better take this. She's not one to call without a good reason."

Eric knew better than to argue. He knew Jeanie almost as well as I did. "Looks like you'll be busy out here for a while," I said.

He had already turned back to the chickens. I stepped outside the barn and closed the door.

"What's up?" I answered.

"Sorry, kid," Jeanie said. "I don't mean to bug ya. And I wouldn't have. Only ..."

I knew only one of two things could compel Jeanie to break her vow not to call with anything work related. Either there was a kid who needed us, or she was looking at a big fat check.

"How much?" I asked.

"Don't assume ..."

"How much?"

Jeanie laughed. "It's a lot, Cass. Enough so you probably wouldn't need to take anything else on for the rest of the year."

My heart tripped a bit. That would, in fact, have to be quite a lot.

"I tried to put them off," Jeanie continued. "But they insisted on coming in. I was just going to take the meeting and screen them. Then, if I thought it was something, I'd loop you in when you got back."

"They sucked you in," I said. Jeanie was as tough as anyone I knew. But she also had a soft, gooey center. That trait is what pulled her into my life when I was just a teenager taking care of my two younger siblings without parents to speak of.

"The Doyles," she said. "Bill and Jenny. Good people. He owns a farm and feed store outside South Bend."

"Jeanie, I don't have to tell you I'm not licensed in Indiana. What gives?"

"It's their son, Andrew. He's sitting in prison for a murder he didn't commit."

"How do you know that? Because his mother says so?" This didn't sound like Jeanie at all. Never mind her soft center, she was practical, skeptical, and suffered no fools.

"Just hear them out. That's all I promised. One hour. They drove all the way up here. Bill can't keep the store closed beyond today."

I checked the time on my phone. It wasn't even noon yet. I looked back at the barn. I could hear Eric hammering something. He'd be in his own zone for most of the afternoon.

"One hour," I said. "How many zeroes are we talking about?"

When Jeanie answered me, I got dizzy for a second. She was right. If this ended up being something I wanted to do, the Doyles would be the only clients I'd need to take on for the year. And it was only early May.

Chapter 2

WHATEVER I EXPECTED from Bill and Jenny Doyle, it wasn't this. First of all, they hadn't come alone. A young woman stood between them. Pretty. Thin brown hair, a soft smile. She held a baby carrier in front of her. A chubby blond baby boy, maybe six months old, kicked his toes in the air.

Whenever someone walked into my office looking for my help in defending a loved one, they shared something in common. They could never conceive of the fact their son, daughter, spouse could have committed the crime for which they were charged. Bill Doyle started our conversation saying the opposite.

"I'm not naïve," Bill said. He sat on the couch in my office against the back wall. It was usually better this way. Rather than the formality of sitting across a desk from new potential clients, I preferred a more casual, conversational posture. I had a sitting area with comfortable chairs, the couch, and nothing between us.

Bill and Jenny looked to be about fifty years old. She was pretty, with gentle curves and an unassuming face. She wore her gray hair in a thick ponytail. No makeup. Her weather-beaten face proudly showed the years she'd spent running a small farm with Bill, just outside of South Bend, Indiana.

"Andrew's not perfect," Bill continued. "I've always said he's one of the dumbest smart kids there is."

"Bill," Jenny cut in. "That's a terrible thing to say."

"It's not. Andrew agrees with it. He's got a quick mind. He never got less than an A all through high school and college. They gave him a scholarship to go to U of M Law School. That's not easy to do."

"No, it's not," I said.

"But sometimes he lacks common sense. He trusts people he shouldn't. He's gullible." Bill wore jeans and work boots. He was well-muscled with a hard look to him. Like his wife, his face had the rugged evidence of a life spent out in the elements, working his farm. He also had a bit of a twinkle in his blue eyes. I could imagine in his younger years, he might have been a bit of a heartthrob. Now, there was a sadness to his smile. Darkness behind his eyes that had settled permanently after the last two years.

The young woman with the baby kept her head down. When the baby started to fuss, she handed him a stuffed blue bunny that calmed him instantly.

"And who do we have here?" I asked, leaning closer to see the baby. He had the stuffed rabbit's nose crammed into his mouth.

"That's Beckett," Jenny Doyle answered. "And this is our daughter-in-law, Grace. Andrew's wife."

"It's good to meet you," Grace said. "I hope it's okay I brought Beckett. I didn't have anyone to watch him. My parents aren't around anymore. The Doyles ... they ..."

"We're her parents now," Bill said. "Andrew's our only child. Grace and Beckett are the only things that are making this whole thing bearable."

Grace blinked rapidly, holding back tears.

"Tell me what happened," I said. "And what you think it is I can do for you. I understand Andrew's already been convicted of murder. The trial's over. This isn't normally what I do. I don't take appeals."

"You have though," Jenny said. "We read about it. You helped exonerate that man who killed that college girl."

She was right. Years ago, I'd broken my own rule and looked into a wrongful murder conviction. Only the accused was the father of the woman my baby brother married. Those were different circumstances.

"Tell me what happened," I said. "As far as you know it."

Bill dropped his chin. He took a breath, then lifted his head to look me square in the eyes.

"We weren't happy when Andrew decided he wanted to go be a lawyer. I mean, we were proud of him. But I always thought he'd want to work with me. I guess that was shortsighted on my part. But he took that scholarship and moved to Ann Arbor. He thrived there. He was always kind of a loner back home. He was just wired different than the other boys his age. They were all farmers, too. A couple of cops. Andrew always had his head stuck in a book. So when he got to law school, he told us he felt like he found his tribe. Except for missing Grace."

Grace looked up. "That's not exactly how it was. Andrew and I were just friends by then. We dated a bit in high school. But we weren't by the time he left for Ann Arbor. We kept in touch."

"He was waiting for you, honey," Bill said. "No matter what else happened."

"He had a group," Jenny picked up the story. "They met in their first year. Kade, Marcus, and Daria."

Daria Moreau. Jeanie had filled me in that Daria was the murder victim in question.

"He lived with the boys," Bill said. "After their first semester they rented a house. I'm not sure how they all met. The four of them. But they were tight all the way through school. It's all he could talk about. Marcus this. Kade that. Wait until I tell you what Daria did, Dad. It was good. He'd never been social like that in high school."

"They were all at the top of their class," Jenny said. "Andrew and Daria were neck and neck to graduate number one. Daria ended up getting there. But Andrew wasn't jealous. I don't want you to think that. Not at all."

"Okay," I said. "It sounds like he really found his niche. I can relate to that. It's how I felt when I left for U of M." And it was. So far, Andrew's story sounded a lot like mine. Law school was the first time I felt like I had people around me who thought like me. Who were serious about their futures. And I also felt like I'd escaped the limitations of my small hometown. Now, after spending the first ten years of my career in a high-pressure law firm in Chicago, I was content back here in Delphi. I couldn't imagine being anywhere else.

"He did," Jenny said. "I actually think he was feeling pretty melancholy about graduating. So ... he was all set to take the bar exam. July. Going on two years ago now. He and the others, Kade, Marcus, and Daria. They rented this fancy house just outside of East Lansing. Williamsburg. Williamston. Something like that. They were going to stay there for the week to study together."

"Marcus paid for it all," Bill said, his tone angry. "Marcus Savitch. Maybe you've heard the name. His great-grandpa started a hot dog shop just outside Detroit after the war. Making coneys, hoagies. Now it's the Greyhawk Grille. They own everything. A minor league hockey team. A bunch of resorts throughout the Midwest. A casino."

"Savitch Arena?" I said. Located in Petoskey, the arena held concerts and sporting events in Northern Michigan. The Savitch family had to be worth hundreds of millions of dollars.

"So you've heard of them," Jenny said. "Andrew and the others just wanted to rent something small. So they wouldn't have to drive an hour and a half every morning to get to the testing center."

The Michigan Bar Exam was always held on the campus of Michigan State University at the Breslin Center.

"But Marcus always has to show everybody up," Bill said. "This is what I mean about Andrew. Gullible. He was impressed by Marcus and all his money. The couple times I met him, I felt like he liked lording it over Andrew. Like we're some hicks."

"I suppose we are," Jenny said. "To him anyway. But I always felt it's none of our business. Andrew's a grown man. He can choose his friends."

"Anyway," Bill said. "The weekend before the test, the kids threw this big party at the rental house. When I say rental house, you need to know what we're talking about. This place was practically a mansion. On something like fifteen acres with woods and a pond. Two swimming pools. One inside, one outside. Andrew told me Marcus just went on one of those short-term rental sites and picked the most expensive listing he could find."

"Fifteen hundred dollars a night!" Jenny said. "That's crazy. That's more than I made in a month working at the library before Andrew was born."

"Jenny, she doesn't need to hear all this. She wants to know what they said happened to Daria."

"It's all right." I smiled.

"We are not here to waste your time, Mrs. Leary."

"It's Ms.," I gently corrected him. Bill lowered his head in deference.

"The party," he continued. "It was on a Saturday night. The first night they got there. It was just supposed to be them and a few people they invited from their class. But somebody told somebody else and somebody else posted it on Facebook or somewhere and it snowballed. Andrew said he thought maybe fifty or sixty people showed up."

"Turned into a rager," Jenny said.

"There were drugs? Alcohol?" I asked.

Jeanie walked into the office. She'd gone out to get soft drinks for the Doyles. She handed them their drinks. Jenny immediately sucked half of hers down. Her husband gave her a look and set his on the side table next to him. Grace didn't open hers. She set it on the ground next to Beckett's carrier. Beckett had fallen asleep.

"Yeah," Bill said. "I can't say for sure about drugs. You have to know, Andrew never did drugs. Not that night. Not ever. He said he had a couple of beers and I believe him. But that's neither here nor there."

"They got into an argument," Jenny said. "Andrew and Daria. See ... this is the part that's kind of embarrassing for me. I'm sorry. I'm a bit ashamed of Andrew for this. I raised him better. But Daria, she wasn't just some ordinary girl. She was ... special. Like she could be in a magazine. Gorgeous blonde hair. Trim. Athletic."

"She was some kind of gymnast," Bill said.

"She was gonna go to the Olympics!" Jenny said. "For Canada. I think her mother's from Montreal or something. Anyway, I think she got hurt or something. She went to law school instead. And smart. Like we said. Top of her class."

"Andrew had a thing for her. I had no idea. He never told us. But like I said, he had a few beers in him. Decided it was a good idea to tell her. She didn't feel the same way. So they argued a little bit."

"I'm sorry." I stopped him and turned to Grace. "Were you married then?"

"Oh no!" Jenny answered for her. "Andrew never would have done something like that if he was married. I raised him better."

"No," Grace finally answered for herself. "I hadn't talked to Andrew in a while. We were still friends. But we didn't talk often. I just saw him sometimes when he came home for holidays and breaks. I was dating somebody else that spring."

"Grace saved him," Jenny said. "When he came home after this ... this mess happened, I couldn't get him out of his room. I hate to even put this into words. But I thought he was going to kill himself. I called Grace. I didn't know what else to do. Thank God he agreed to see her. Honey, you saved Andrew's life. I know you know that."

"Jenny, this doesn't matter. Grace isn't part of this," Bill interjected.

"She most certainly is," Jenny protested.

"I knew he couldn't have done this," Grace said. "I know him better than anybody. I knew whatever happened that weekend, Andrew didn't do this."

"You got close again," I said.

"Yes," Grace answered.

"Enough," Bill said. "It doesn't matter. Ms. Leary wants to know about Daria's murder. Here's what happened. Sometime later, either during or after that party, Daria went missing. Nobody knew where she was for almost a day. Then Kade, Andrew's other law school buddy, called the cops. They found her in the pond. Broke her neck. Since people saw Andrew arguing with her, and Marcus and Kade knew Andrew was pining for her, he got arrested."

"He wasn't pining," Jenny said. Bill shot her a look.

"There had to have been more than that," I said.

"There was." Jenny sighed. She reached into a leather satchel on the ground next to her. She pulled out three large binders and plopped them on the ground in front of us.

"We ordered those," Bill said. "Came last week. We wanted to have them for you before we came."

I could read the title on the first binder. It was part of a trial transcript. State of Michigan vs. Andrew Doyle.

"This is the complete transcript?" I asked.

"There're two more of those in the trunk," Bill said. "But yes. That's the whole trial there. They said Andrew couldn't prove where he was."

"They said she scratched him," Jenny said. "She had some skin under her nails they matched to a scrape on Andrew's neck."

"It looks bad," Bill said. "We know that. It took me a long time to get over being angry with my son. To be honest, I haven't all the way. But I really don't believe he's capable of it."

"He's never lied to us," Jenny said.

"He says he didn't do it," Jeanie interjected. She'd taken a seat on the edge of my desk.

"Yes," Bill answered. "But it's more than that. That's the reason we're here. Ms. Leary, something's wrong. Something never sat well with me when we were in that courtroom. We couldn't afford to hire somebody like you then. That's my biggest regret. Andrew went with a public defender out of Ingham County. He seemed nice."

"Russell Nadler," Jenny said. "I didn't like him. I'm sorry. He smelled like cheese. Not in a good way."

I couldn't imagine anything but a bad way, but kept the comment to myself.

"We want you to look at it," Bill said. "Nadler just didn't seem like he was interested in fighting for Andrew. He hardly objected to anything. You're supposed to do that, aren't you?"

"Usually, yes," I said.

"Well, he barely did. He just pretty much went by whatever the witnesses said. Andrew's friends, Marcus and Kade, turned on him. They were there that weekend too. Nadler just let them trash my son. Nadler kept saying he didn't have to prove anything."

"Well, technically, he didn't. The prosecution has the burden of proving your son murdered Daria Moreau. The defense only has to show reasonable doubt."

"Well, he didn't do that," Jenny said. "Obviously, the jury didn't think so either. They all voted against Andrew."

"Please," Bill said. "Right now, all we're asking is that you take a look at what happened at the trial. We're going to pay you good money to do that. We're doing what we should have done two years ago. We raised some money through one of those charity websites. I didn't want to. Grace, you were right about that. She told us. From the very beginning, Grace told us to get him his own lawyer. Not one the county provided."

"Don't blame yourself," Grace said, reaching over to touch her father-in-law's hand. "I blame *myself*."

"For what, honey?" Jenny asked.

"Maybe if I'd been there. In the courtroom. Maybe it would have made an impression on the jury or something."

"No," Bill said. "Your job was to keep my grandson safe. She was pregnant, Ms. Leary."

"Cass, please," I said.

"They put me on bedrest," Grace said.

"My husband is very proud," Jenny said. "And we never thought Andrew would end up in prison. That was our mistake. We trusted Nadler. Now, I don't even know where he is. He stopped returning Andrew's calls. My calls. When you call his office number, it says it's disconnected. There's something going on. I can feel it."

"What does Andrew think about all this?" I asked.

"That's the other problem," Bill said. "When this all started happening, Andrew was in the fight. Swearing he was innocent. Trying to help find other witnesses who were at the party. But something happened. By the time the trial started, the fight just went out of him. He just sat there, looking miserable. Defeated. And it seemed to happen overnight. I'm telling you. The man I've seen for the last year is not my son. I don't know if he got depressed or what. But it's like he just rolled over and let them do this to him."

"Does he even want me involved? Because you have to understand, if I do agree to take a look at this, you're not my clients. Andrew would be."

"We know," Jenny said. "And Andrew knows. The answer to your question is yes. He said if you're willing to help him, he wants you to."

"What do you think?" I asked Grace. "Where's your husband's state of mind?"

She had a pained expression, as if her answer physically hurt her. "Andrew has struggled with depression since this all happened. My mother-in-law is right. When I came back into his life, the fall after all this happened ... before he was charged, Andrew was just despondent. But then when he was arrested, it invigorated him."

"You did that," Jenny said. "You gave him something to fight for. You stuck by him."

"But yes," Grace continued. "By the time it got to trial, Andrew kind of gave up. I think he was trying to protect himself. Trying to prepare me for the worst."

I had real sympathy for this family. But I had far too many questions they couldn't answer.

"I don't know," I said. "I told you. I'm a litigator, not a private investigator."

"You look at that," Bill said, slapping a fist on the stack of transcripts. "You look at that and you tell me Nadler did his job. If you think he did. If you think Andrew should have been found guilty, we'll believe you. We'll focus on helping Andrew accept his fate."

"No!" Jenny shouted. "No. We aren't just doing this for Andrew. We're doing it for Beckett. He needs to know his father didn't do this."

Beckett started to rouse at his grandmother's voice. Grace pulled a pacifier out and stuck it in his mouth. Two sucks and he was fast asleep again.

"We're willing to pay you good money," Bill said. "And there's more in the fund we set up. If we have to go to court again."

"I can promise you we definitely will," I said. "Assuming there's something here."

"Whatever it takes," Jenny said. "I know it sounds hollow. I'm his mother. Of course I would say this. But I am telling you. Something else happened that weekend. Andrew didn't kill that girl."

"This is easy money for you," Bill said. "We pay you for your time. Whatever it takes for you to read through that trial transcript and see if you see what we see. If you're not convinced, you walk away and you won't hear from us. But you'll still get paid."

"I have a condition," I said. "I'm not reading a single word of that until I've met Andrew face to face. What you've told me is interesting. Of course, I have sympathy for what you're going through."

"We don't need pity ..." Bill started.

"Let me finish. This isn't about you. It's about Andrew. I'm not claiming to be a mind reader. I can't tell if someone's guilty or innocent just by looking in their eyes. Hell, I've been wrong plenty of times. I've staked my career on a client's innocence and been proven wrong. It's gone the other way, too. I've been convinced of someone's guilt only to find out the police got the wrong guy. But if Andrew's like you say he is. Disinterested in his own future, then there won't be much I can do, no matter what's in that transcript."

"We understand," Bill said. "And I had a hunch you'd say something like that. So I've already made the arrangements."

"What arrangements?" I asked.

"I had Andrew put in a request. You've got an appointment to meet him at the prison tomorrow afternoon."

"How did you know ..."

"I told them it was okay," Jeanie said, sheepishly. "I had my own hunch that you'd want to get into this right away."

So much for the rest of my vacation. It looked like I'd be spending part of it in Ionia. Andrew would be at the Bellamy Creek Correctional Facility. But I meant what I said. It *was* interesting. If only for the fact that Andrew's story felt a lot like mine. Save for the part of him being a potential murderer.

"All right," I said, instantly feeling I'd later regret it. "I'll meet with your son tomorrow. But I make you no promises beyond that. And I'm not taking your money until after I talk to Andrew. Then I'll have a better idea if I can help you."

"That's more than fair," Jenny said, rising. "We'll leave the rest of the binders with your receptionist downstairs." She extended her hand to shake mine. Bill did the same. Grace stayed a bit behind them, struggling to lift Beckett's carrier. Seeing her, Bill took his grandson from her. "Thank you," Grace said. She stepped forward and awkwardly hugged me. She felt thin and frail. Then they left my office. I stared at the thick binders Bill had stacked on the floor near my feet.

Part of me felt like I'd just made another deal with the devil. Andrew Doyle couldn't possibly be like they said he was.

Chapter 3

BELLAMY CREEK CORRECTIONAL FACILITY housed roughly two thousand inmates. Andrew Doyle, inmate number 209453, met me in a private lawyer's room.

If Andrew's parents and wife defied my expectations, Andrew met them to a tee. He was skinny. Good-looking, but haggard. Jenny and Bill Doyle had shown me a photograph of their son, taken at the family Christmas the year before Daria Moreau's murder. In it, Andrew appeared joyful with a handsome, broad smile. His thick blond hair was cut cleanly. He was laughing, with bright eyes, as he had his arms around his mother.

The Andrew Doyle of today was almost unrecognizable. His hair was now a dull, light brown. It seemed thinner, somehow, and it hung in strings down to his earlobes. He swam in his prison jumpsuit, birdlike wrists poking out of sleeves too wide. No glimmer or shine to his eyes. His face had broken out all over.

"I understand your parents filled you in on who I am?" I started.

Andrew nodded.

"They want me to review your court file and see if there's anything your public defender might have missed. Before I do that, why don't you tell me what you think? Did he miss something?"

Andrew shrugged. He'd yet to speak a word.

"You know," I said. "I'm not going to ask you. You probably assumed I would. But I won't. I'm not interested in what you want me to believe."

"I didn't kill Daria," he answered anyway. "But no, I don't know what to tell you about my court file."

"You're not a layperson, Andrew. You graduated at the top of your class in law school. You were on the mock trial team. You took two semesters of trial procedure. Criminal procedure. I think you know exactly what to tell me about your court file."

"None of it matters. Everybody got what they wanted. Daria's dead. Everybody thinks I did it."

I leaned back in my chair. "Ah. So you're a bullshitter."

For the first time since I sat down, that got a reaction out of Andrew. He sat straighter, lifted his chin.

"You've given up," I said. "That's the thing that troubles your parents the most. They said at the start of all this, you were angry, desperate to clear your name. You were in the fight. But by the time the trial started, you turned into this guy. I mean, I get it up to a point. Nobody's ever accused me of murder. I've never had to face going on trial for my freedom, for the rest of my life. And you had to sit there for days on end, listening to people condemn your actions. No real way to stand up for yourself. Because despite whatever other failings your public defender may have had, he made the smart choice by not having you testify."

Andrew narrowed his eyes. "How can you say that? You don't know me."

"I don't have to. I know they're saying you killed Daria because you were in love with her and she didn't love you back. That's probably true. Isn't it?"

He pursed his lip. "It all got so blown out of proportion."

"Your friends didn't think so. Daria didn't think so. I haven't looked at your file yet. Haven't read a word except the case caption. But your folks said your friends turned on you."

Whatever animation I'd sparked in Andrew, the light went out again. He slumped in his chair.

"Do you want me to look at your file?"

"I know who you are," he said. "I know my parents were lucky to get you to meet with them. But I didn't ask them to."

"Why not?"

"What?"

I leaned forward. "I mean, why not ask them to? Why not keep fighting if you really didn't do this? What do you have to lose? It's not like you're going anywhere. And your parents have raised the funds to pay my bill."

"I don't want them to risk their own security for me."

"They're not. They raised enough online. People out there care what happens to you. Strangers. Your friends, neighbors. Your wife."

"Whatever they raised, they should use it for Beckett."

"Your son," I said. "He doesn't know you, right? You've been in here most of his life. He's never going to know you as anyone other than this guy he visits a few times a year behind bars. Until someday he's old enough and decides he doesn't want to come anymore. Because it's too depressing."

"Is this supposed to be a pep talk? If it is, you're pretty bad at it."

I smiled. "No. It's not a pep talk. I'm really just sitting here trying to decide if you're worth my time. Your parents think you are. But I'm not getting any passion from you. If you don't care, it's because you've just been beaten down enough you don't think it's worth the effort getting your hopes up again. That's legitimate. It's understandable. Or ... it's because you've decided you deserve to be here. To me, it doesn't matter which thing is true. If it's either, this is the last time we'll meet. I don't do this sort of thing normally. I don't get involved in appeals. But I don't know. I'm getting a vibe. Like maybe you really don't have any other shot at a different life except through me. Like it or not, I've been told I'm a sucker for lost causes. Which is true, but I'm not a sucker for apathetic causes."

"I didn't kill Daria," he said. "But I've stopped believing there's any way to prove it."

"Why don't you start by telling me what happened? I got the highlights from your folks. But they only know what you've told them. What they saw at trial. You tell me. What happened that weekend? Why did you lie to the police about it?"

"I never lied."

I raised a finger. "Stop. Think about what you just said to me. Tell me if that's really true."

He shook his head. "I thought you said you haven't read my file."

"I haven't," I said. "But I know how this usually goes. If you talked to the police, and I understand you did, you probably said something that made them think you were guilty. Lying is almost always why."

"Do you want my side of this or not?"

"I want the truth. All of it. Not just what you think helps your case. That's my main rule. Whatever you tell me has to be honest. No secrets. No lies. The reason your parents found out about me is because I *am* good at what I do. Every time I've had a client lie to me, I find out the truth on my own. Every time. Even if you killed Daria, I might be able to help you. But in that case, I'll need a strong reason why."

"I didn't kill her," he said again, more forcefully. It's what I wanted to elicit from him. I couldn't care about him if he couldn't care about himself.

"Okay, so tell me what *did* happen. I know you were at a rental house. I know you got into an argument with Daria that got intense enough you walked away with a chunk taken out of your neck. So give me the context."

He pressed his fingers to the bridge of his nose. "It all went so sideways. But it was nothing. Yes. We had a party that Saturday night the weekend before the bar exam. Yes. It got bigger than we wanted it to. That was all Marcus's fault. He's got a big mouth. Loves to impress people with who he is. How rich his family is. But we were used to that. It's what he does. And I had too much to drink. I've been honest about that."

"You didn't know what you were doing?" I asked.

27

"Yes. No. I mean, no, I knew what I was doing. Yes. I had a crush on Daria. I misinterpreted some signals. I thought she had feelings for me, too. And I got bolder than I would have normally. Because of the beer. But also because I knew it was a now-or-never kind of time. We'd spent three years as friends. Seeing each other almost every day. That was going to end. So I thought I'd take my shot. And I was clumsy about it. When she said she wasn't interested, I got angry. Not violently angry. But I got in her personal space. She pushed me back. She scratched me. But that was it. I swear. I got the message. I walked away. I never laid a hand on her."

"That's what you told the police?"

"Yes."

"But it's not all you told them, is it?"

He let out a hard breath. "No."

"Then what?"

"I was dumb, okay? When we found out Daria was missing. Then when they found her dead, I was in shock. I never thought for a second anyone was going to think I did it. We all loved Daria. Kade, Marcus, me? We were tight. We had each other's backs. For three years. You know. You made it through that same pressure cooker. We were like war buddies or something. I knew I didn't kill her. But I knew Kade and Marcus didn't either. So when the cops asked ... I told them we were all together that night."

It was my turn to sigh. "You gave them alibis. Kade and Marcus?"

"Yeah."

"You assumed they were going to have your back the same way?"

He hesitated before he answered. "Yes. Okay. Yes. I assumed they would say the same thing."

"Did you talk about it beforehand? The three of you? Did you promise to get your stories straight?"

"Sort of. Yeah."

"Who started that conversation? Was it you?"

"I don't remember."

"I don't believe that," I said.

"I can't control what you believe."

"Andrew, look. This isn't hard. There are three of you. You all knew you were about to be questioned about the murder of your friend. It would be natural to talk about that among yourselves. If you were as close-knit as you say you were."

"We were."

"Were," I said. "Not are. Do Marcus and Kade think you killed Daria?"

He didn't answer. Which was an answer in and of itself.

"What am I going to find in that trial transcript? What did Marcus and Kade tell the cops?"

He hung his head. "They told the cops they hadn't seen me after about eleven o'clock that night. But that they'd been together."

"They threw you under the bus. Why?"

"I don't know," he shouted. "I really don't. But I was stupid. I was also in shock. I wasn't thinking about trying to save my own ass. I was thinking somebody I cared about was dead."

"Except five minutes ago you told me the three of you were supposed to have each other's backs. That's not something you say if Daria was your main concern."

"I know. I know. See? This is what happened. I was bad at it. I'm bad at this. I know how I sound. But I didn't kill her. I regret not being totally honest with the cops. The truth is, I went to my room after Daria and I got into it. I was upset. Hurt. I just figured I'd sleep it off. I came downstairs to get something to eat in the middle of the night. Maybe four in the morning. The house was empty by then. Trashed, but empty. I should have just told the cops that. Because it was the truth."

"I don't get it, Andrew. Like I said before. You're not a layperson. You knew exactly what that was going to look like if Marcus and Kade didn't say the same thing when they were interviewed."

"I don't know," he said, slapping his hands on the table in defeat. "I really don't. I didn't kill her. That's what I know. I never would have hurt her. Or anyone."

"So if you didn't kill her, who did?"

He blinked. He opened his mouth but said nothing.

"Andrew?"

"Nobody's ever asked me that. Not once."

"So I'm asking now. If you didn't kill her, then somebody else did. You were at that party. You saw Daria at least within a couple of hours before she died. You're not a layperson on the events of the night either. You have to have thought about it. If you're truly innocent."

He stared at me for a few seconds longer than felt comfortable. He finally looked skyward, then back at me.

"I don't know."

"Rather anticlimactic as answers go," I said.

"There were dozens and dozens of people at that party. Most of them I didn't know. I knew the four of us. I knew maybe five other people we *actually* invited. The rest were students from other law schools. Their dates. Their other friends. Maybe even some randos that saw something on social media and decided to crash. It could have been anyone. I don't know if Daria tried to hook up with someone. I don't know if there just happened to be some psycho in the mix. I just don't know. I just know it wasn't me. So yes. Yes. If you're willing to look into my file, I want you to. If my lawyer did something he shouldn't have, or didn't do something he should have, I'd like your opinion on it. I just don't think any of this will work. You're right. I'm not a layperson. I know my best chance at beating this ended when that jury voted to convict me. I know my son, at this point, is going to grow up being told I'm innocent, but always have that question in the back of his mind. So for him, yes. I'll do what you ask me to do."

"Good," I said. "That's what I wanted to hear."

"Does that mean you'll help?"

"Probably not," I said. "I told you I expected honesty from you. You'll get it from me. The only promise I'm going to make you today is that I'll look at your file. If I find anything off, we'll talk again. If I don't? We'll talk then too."

He seemed relieved. I gathered my things and promised Andrew I'd be in touch next week.

As I walked out into the parking lot, I truly didn't know what to think. My finger to the wind, I'd say it was fifty-fifty. He might be guilty. But something about the case still intrigued me enough to keep going. I pulled out my phone and sent a group text to Jeanie, Emma, and Tori.

> Met with Andrew Doyle. Odds are he did it. I'll probably regret it. But let's dig into the transcript. Have Miranda make copies and start reading. Meet first thing in the morning.

I immediately got three thumbs up emojis from my whole team.

Chapter 4

IT HAD BEEN a while since we'd all been in a room like this. My whole team. Jeanie, my mentor, surrogate mother, and legal partner. A few years ago, I had plucked her out of retirement (she claims forced) and had her start this firm with me.

She brought Miranda Sulier on board. While her technical title was office administrator, Miranda kept everything running for me. She'd been in the legal business for close to fifty years, just like Jeanie.

Now, I had younger brains on my side and got to keep it in the family. Tori came to me as a paralegal, got her law degree, and now worked as my top researcher. She also snagged my little brother, Matty, and gave me a nephew along the way. She was pregnant again, but hadn't told us. But I knew the look. She had circles under her eyes and certain smells sent her out of a room.

Our newest addition, my niece, Emma, was just about to finish her first year of law school.

"Who has what?" I asked.

"I've got the timeline," Miranda said.

"I'll get us through the prosecution's case in chief," Tori said.

"I'm on defense witnesses," Emma said. "But spoiler alert, there weren't any."

"That's stunning to me," I said. "On a murder charge?"

"Put a pin in it," Jeanie said. "I've been making a list of all the things that might be able to sustain an appeal."

"What was your read on Andrew Doyle?" Emma asked.

"I'm still trying to figure that out," I answered. "He's sympathetic, sort of. But more for who's fighting for him. He says he's innocent. I don't know if I believe him."

"Well, the Doyles' check cleared this morning," Miranda added, always keeping track of my bottom line.

"Then they've bought themselves today, this meeting," I said. "Tell me the story, Miranda."

She stepped up to the plate. Behind her, she'd pulled out my giant whiteboard. She had four colored dry erase markers on the table.

"What the Doyles told you was the gist of it," she started. "Your four principals, Marcus Savitch, Kade Barclay, Andrew Doyle, and the star of your show, Daria Moreau all rented this house at 1535 Fairfield Road in Williamston. They had it from Saturday July 23rd to Wednesday, July 27th, checking out right after they finished day two of the bar exam at the Breslin Center."

She picked up a piece of paper and stuck it to the board. She'd printed off the Zillow listing for the rental property. It was a giant Tudor estate.

"Twelve acres," Tori said. "Six bedrooms in the house. A game room. Indoor pool. Outside there was a huge flower garden with a patio." She posted another photo. This one also from the Zillow listing showing the backyard. She put a big red circle around a built-in barbecue and pizza oven. Beside those, there was a long, cement ledge.

"According to Marcus and Kade's testimony," Tori said, "this is where the drinks were set up. They had pizzas and other food delivered throughout the night. They weren't expecting all those people. So several of the guests started ordering from MealHopper, a food delivery app local to the East Lansing area."

"Do we have their names? The guests? The delivery drivers?"

"Nope," Jeanie chimed in. "Call that screw-up number one. There's nothing in the police report about the identification of every partygoer. They have statements from one kid. Jason Lin. He was the boyfriend of one of the other law students from a different school. He claims he saw Daria and Marcus having an argument here, around eleven thirty."

Jeanie posted another photo. This one also from the backyard, but more toward the woods. The pavers extended beyond the patio just to the edge of the woods.

"Any testimony on what it was about?"

"No," Emma said. "Russ Nadler is your public defender. He's old. Has a bar number starting with a 4."

I raised a brow. "Careful who you're calling old."

She was right though; bar numbers were issued sequentially, starting sometime in the late fifties, early sixties. Someone with a bar number that low would likely have been admitted in the late eighties, early nineties.

"Anyway," Emma continued. "Nadler didn't call anybody on defense. Just relied on presenting his defense in his cross-examinations and objections."

"Which were few and far between," Jeanie said. "He just sits there most of the time. Doesn't challenge much. But Marcus was asked about this supposed argument Lin reported. He downplays it. Said she was angry that all these people showed up. It wasn't supposed to get out of hand and she blamed Marcus for bragging online about it."

"That's consistent with what Andrew and his parents said," I confirmed. "But we're taking Marcus's word for the substance of the argument?"

"Nadler presented no alternative theory," Jeanie said. "He didn't bring anyone forward to refute it."

"Andrew said there were maybe fifty guests by the time the party reached its peak. You're telling me the only attendees called at trial were Marcus, Kade, and Jason Lin?"

"No," Tori said. "There was one more. A classmate of Andrew's claims he saw Andrew and Daria arguing in roughly the same spot, out past the garden, at about twelve forty-five. Nobody testified they saw Daria after that. So the prosecution sold the theory that Andrew was the last person to be with Daria."

"That's ludicrous," I said. "What's the timeline on when she died?"

"ME says anywhere from midnight to eight the next morning," Jeanie said.

"That right there should have blown the timeline," I said. "You're telling me the prosecutor got away with just proving a negative? Just because nobody saw Daria with anyone else after 12:45 a.m., doesn't mean she *wasn't* with someone else. Tori, who was the lead detective on this?"

"From the Ingham County Sheriff's Department," she said. "A Tim Messer. Sounds like he's getting ready to retire. He put out a Crime Stopper number. Asked the public at large to come forward. Lin's the only one who did."

"That's it?" I said. "Were there security cameras?"

"Nope," Emma answered. "The property owner didn't install them. She said her lawyer told them there would be privacy issues he wouldn't want to deal with. But that's just from the property owner's statement. She was never called at trial."

"And I'm assuming Nadler didn't bother to do any of his own investigation into that?"

"He didn't call any witnesses," Jeanie said.

I had about a dozen ways I would have tried to run down more witnesses. Some more tedious than others. But for Nadler to not have even tried?

"I read the autopsy summary," I said. "Daria died from blunt force trauma after hitting her head on a birdbath?"

"That's here," Miranda said. She pulled out another photograph and posted it on the board. A little further beyond the paved trail, you could see a fairly large and ornate cement birdbath among the trees. "It would have been partially obscured from anyone up at the house due to the tree cover. And that's how Lin testified. Kade and Marcus too. Plus, in late July, the woods were lush with greenery. Nobody actually saw Daria fall."

"She broke her neck," I said. "Then got dragged from that site to the edge of a pond."

"About three hundred feet away," Jeanie said. "Through some pretty thick brush. They found some footprints in the mud on the shoreline. But they were never positively identified."

"Testimony and coroner's report estimate Daria died sometime between midnight and eight the next morning," Miranda repeated. "She was found partially submerged in the pond. From mid-torso down, she was waterlogged. They found her lying face down in the mud."

"Okay," I said. "Keeping this all straight. The last time anyone reports seeing Daria alive is 12:45 a.m."

"Right," Jeanie said. "Lin reported seeing her arguing with Marcus at eleven thirty. This other classmate ... uh ... Henry Barber, says he saw Andrew and Daria arguing at twelve forty-five."

"Kade and Marcus say they didn't see Andrew after that time either," I said.

"And that's the problem," Tori chimed in. "Andrew told the police that he was with Kade and Marcus well past midnight. He thought the three of them would alibi each other."

"He told me that," I said. "Though he didn't say it in so many words, I got the impression he thought the three of them were going to have each other's backs. How did Nadler handle cross-examining this Henry Barber?"

"That's a tricky one," Tori said. "Henry Barber got diagnosed with a rare, aggressive form of leukemia that preceding spring. Didn't respond to any therapy. They took a trial deposition a few weeks before the trial. Nadler attended, but didn't really challenge much of what he said. Then Barber passed away two weeks later. He didn't testify in person at the trial because he'd already passed."

I kept shaking my head. "Number one, that sounds awful. Number two, it just feels like every single thing broke against Andrew in this case."

"I watched the recording of Andrew's statement," Emma said. "Aunt Cass, you should have a look at it." She tossed a flash drive across the table.

"She's grabbing my headline," Jeanie smiled. "I spliced a section I want you to see."

"Spliced?" I said. "You know how to splice?"

"Oh, shut up. I can work a computer."

"You can also work microfiche," I teased. Jeanie flashed me a well-deserved bird. She opened her laptop and turned the screen so all of us could see it. Andrew sat in the corner of an interrogation room. Detective Tim Messer sat with his back to the camera. Jeanie hit play.

"They're not saying that, Andrew," Messer said. "Your friends don't know where you were after about midnight. Now you're telling me something different. Are they lying, or are you?"

On screen, Andrew sat straight up in his chair. "Don't say it," I whispered. "Don't say another word."

"Am I under arrest?" Andrew asked Messer.

"We're just having a conversation," he responded.

"I don't know if I should tell you anything," Andrew said. "I have rights."

"Sure you do," Messer said. "And you're a law student. Actually, a graduate."

"I'm not a lawyer," Andrew said.

Messer paused.

"Is that enough?" Emma asked. "I mean, he's not coming out and saying it. Not explicitly. But ... I mean, as soon as the person questioning mentions the word lawyer, doesn't that raise some flags?"

"It does," I said.

On screen, Messer crossed his legs. "Do you want to keep talking to me, Andrew? I suggest you do. I think it's in your best interests to tell me everything you know about what might have happened to your friend. She was your friend, right? You cared about Daria. At least, you said you did. Only, you left her to rot in that swamp for over twenty-four hours."

"I didn't do anything." On screen, Andrew buried his face in his hands.

"What's the timestamp on this?" I asked.

"He's almost two hours into it," Jeanie answered. She hit pause.

"Was he ever read his rights?" I asked.

"Nope," Jeanie answered. "Messer tells him it's voluntary, him sitting down with him. A couple of times early in the interview, Andrew tells Messer he knows his rights. But Messer never expresses them. He never gives a proper Miranda warning."

I shook my head. "Did Nadler, Andrew's lawyer, file a motion to suppress his statement?"

"He did not," Emma said. "That interview was played in its entirety to the jury."

I couldn't believe it. "What *did* Nadler do?"

"Six main witnesses," Emma said. "Detective Messer, a crime scene analyst from the Michigan State Police, the ME. Then the lay witnesses were Kade, Marcus, Henry Barber by trial dep, and Jason Lin. That's it. Nadler didn't call any of his own. And he barely cross-examined any of these people. I've highlighted a few things in the transcript. He did get Marcus and Kade to admit they could have been fuzzy on when they last saw Daria or Andrew. But it wasn't bombshell-type stuff. We're talking maybe fifteen minutes one way or the other. Nothing that would have disputed the prosecution's timeline. And Lin was specific. He said he saw Marcus and Daria arguing right around eleven thirty because the wings he ordered came a few minutes before that.And Barber in his trial dep was specific about the twelve forty-five argument between *Andrew* and Daria because he said the reason he didn't go see if anything was wrong was because his girlfriend called him on his cell. He walked to the front of the yard so he could take the call. Detective Messer had Barber's phone records to back up that claim."

"Do you think it's appealable as is?" Tori asked.

"I don't know," I said. "Probably not on the weak cross alone. But this issue of suppressing Andrew's statement. I need research on it. Is it enough that Andrew said he knew his rights? Can we find case law? Does the fact that he's a law school graduate mitigate any of it? My hunch is no. But I'd like to talk to Russ Nadler myself. I'd like to hear it from his own mouth, why he didn't move to suppress that statement. Even if he lost, he'd have preserved the issue for appeal. That's what might screw me."

"He had scratches on his neck," Tori said. "Messer didn't realize it the first time he interviewed him. Later, they matched blood and tissue under Daria's nails to Andrew. That, more than anything, is what nailed him.

"Messer didn't photograph Andrew the first day he questioned him. And they were there for a long time. He had Kade and Marcus in separate interview rooms. It was only Andrew that Messer hammered like that. A little with Marcus about the substance of their argument, but it really feels like Messer was zoning in on Andrew from the get."

"He had scratches on his neck," I said.

"Right," Tori said. "But it's the second time Messer went to question him, after the DNA came back on the blood and tissue samples from Daria. He *did* read him his rights then. Andrew chose to talk to him anyway. That's when Messer saw the scabs on his neck."

"That should have been a point of contention for Nadler," I said. "The prosecution couldn't prove beyond a reasonable doubt that those scratches were inflicted during some death struggle."

"Come on. Really?" Miranda said. "That's a stretch. Even you know that. Unless Daria just *happened* to scratch Andrew the day before. Nobody is saying that. I don't think that alone gets his conviction overturned or even an appeal granted."

"Probably not," I said. "But it's something Nadler should have pursued."

"There's something else," Jeanie said. She had her phone out. She was reading something on screen and it made her slowly rise to her feet.

"What is it?" I asked.

"I looked up Nadler, the public defender. I don't know why I didn't think to do it right off the bat. We've just had full-enough plates sifting through this file. But Russ Nadler was disbarred a few months ago. For embezzling client funds."

"Embezzlement," I said, disgust in my tone. "I don't want to prejudge anyone, but most of the time that stuff is due to drugs or gambling. If Nadler was intoxicated during the trial, that's definitely something I need to know."

Jeanie had her phone to her ear, then brought it down. "His office phone number is disconnected. My guess is his office is shuttered. But give me a little time. I'll track him down."

"He probably won't talk to me," I said. "But thanks."

"So, are we doing this?" Miranda asked.

I looked at my team. "Let's put it to a vote. It would require us coming at this from the ground up. Starting fresh. We'll pretty much have to reinvestigate the entire murder. That's not what we really do. And right now, I don't have a good private investigator on staff. So what do you think?"

Miranda turned so she was standing with her back to the whiteboard. "Like I said, the Doyles' check cleared. As long as they don't do anything stupid, they can afford your fee. I personally think Andrew is guilty as sin. But if they're paying for us to basically prove it, I'm game."

"I'm in," Tori said. "This thing is already sucking me in."

"Same," Emma said. "I don't have an opinion on Andrew yet. But I'm kinda dying to figure out what happened to Daria."

"Jeanie?" I asked. Everyone here had an equal voice, but Jeanie's opinion mattered to me deeply.

She smiled. "You only live once. Let's get after it. Nadler botched this. I feel it in my bones. But like Miranda said. Doesn't mean the bastard's not guilty."

I felt a familiar buzzing in my head. The kind I always got when a case took hold of me. "Okay. Then it's unanimous. Emma, Tori, you two keep digging through that file. Flag every single missed objection. Find the answer to whether Nadler violated Andrew's due process rights."

"We're like the Justice League," Emma said.

I shook my head. "One thing at a time. We very well may have a guilty client."

It was true. And yet, something in the back of my mind told me there was something much worse going on.

Chapter 5

"IT SOUNDS GOOD TO ME!" my brother Joe shouted over the boat engine. It was running, but docked. The other day, Eric didn't like the way the motor sounded. Now, Joe, my other brother Matty, and Eric were all leaning over the back of the pontoon, fiddling with its innards.

I walked out with a tray of lemonade, sidestepping the two dogs and a three-week-old baby chick right before it dashed under one of the porch chairs.

"Don't squish it!" Jessa shouted. She ran up in her red swimsuit cover-up, her hair flying behind her. Also behind her was Cameron, her new boyfriend. Vangie kept a watchful eye on the two of them. So did Matty when he wasn't being distracted by small engines.

A month ago, Jessa had her fifteenth birthday. It really felt like overnight, she'd gone from a sullen teen in an awkward phase to this more confident, vibrant young woman. It was currently terrifying her mother and uncles.

She scooped the chick up in her arms and held it close.

"I'm calling her Tootsie," she said, kissing the top of her head.

"Uncle Eric says we're not supposed to name them yet," Vangie called out. "He doesn't know if that one's a pullet or a cockerel just yet."

"She's a baby!" Jessa protested. "And she's perfect."

Cameron so far had little to say. He clearly sensed the testosterone from the alpha males out in the yard. I'd mouthed him a "good luck, kid" when he first showed up. Matty had immediately started grilling him on his future plans. Poor Cameron was only two weeks older than Jessa. They were just about to finish the ninth grade.

Eric walked up the dock. He came to my side and put an arm around me. "That one's an Easter Egger," he said. "Kind of a chicken mutt. If she's a she, she's supposed to give us blueish-green eggs."

"When will we know?" I asked. Over the last two weeks, Eric had become mildly obsessed with determining their sexes. Tootsie was a cute little chocolate brown creature. Hence, Jessa's choice in names.

"When she either starts to crow or lays an egg," Joe said, wiping his hands with a shop towel as he came to join us.

"What will you do if it's a rooster?" Jessa asked, concern in her voice.

"There's a horse farm next to my grandpa's," Cameron said sheepishly. "The lady who owns it has a wild flock. I'm sure she'd probably take him. She's a little chicken crazy."

I suppressed a chuckle. Vangie caught my eye. Cameron's face turned beet red. But so far, Eric hadn't taken offense.

Marbury sniffed Jessa's leg. So far, the dogs had pretty much left the chickens alone. They'd taken direction well that these chickens weren't like the kind I sometimes chopped up and put into their bowls.

Eric scooped up two more chickens before they darted under the porch. Then he and Jessa walked them back to the barn to place them safely back in the brooder.

"It's a good hobby," Joe said, grabbing a beer from the cooler next to him. Cameron wandered off in Jessa's direction. He wasn't yet comfortable enough to leave her side.

"Seems like a good kid," I said to Vangie as she walked up and took one of the folding chairs.

"He's a basketball player," she said.

"No kidding," Joe said. "He's built like a sand crane."

"Take it easy on him," I warned my brother. "We're a lot and Jessa said he's an only child."

Tori poked her head out from the back slider. "How many are gonna want cheese on their burgers?"

We all raised our hands. "Eric too," I said.

"Jessa won't," Vangie said. "And Cameron's vegan. There's a veggie burger in the fridge."

Joe muttered something under his breath.

"How the hell do you grill a vegan burger? What even is it?" Tori asked.

"It's soy or something," Joe said with disgust.

"He said you grill it just like the other ones," Vangie said, shrugging.

My brothers looked dubious, but a stern look from me and they kept their further opinions to themselves.

"Good thing Dad's not here," I said. "He'd kick the grill into the lake before he'd let anyone put something that never had a face on that thing."

One stray chick waddled around from the side of the house. Joe picked it up. It was the black-and-white-striped one.

"She's a Barred Rock, I'm told," I said. Joe inspected the little bird and frowned.

"She's a he," he said.

"How can you tell?"

Joe tilted the chick's head toward me. "It's already got a pink comb."

"Since when do you know so much about chickens?" Vangie asked.

"Katie's dad raised them for a little while. When Emma was little, I'd take her over to play with them. He used to pay her ten cents for every egg she collected."

There was sadness in his tone. The subject of Katie, his remarried ex-wife, was still a raw wound for him. A little over a year ago, she'd hooked up with the local news sports anchor while she was still married to my brother. She was now Mrs. Sports Anchor and they weren't speaking.

"That's sweet," I said. "But maybe don't break the news to Eric just yet. He's kind of attached to that one."

Joe put the chicken down. It promptly wedged itself under Joe's chair and fell asleep.

From the pole barn across the driveway, I could hear Eric informing Cameron and Jessa about his plans for the coop he was still building.

"He's got a one-track mind lately." I laughed. "He's drawn a whole blueprint for his coop design. This week's project is figuring out how to get the best airflow."

"Good for him," Vangie said. "He's earned it."

"I know," I said, letting my voice trail off. A shout from Emma in the kitchen and Vangie and Matty headed in to help her. I sat on the chair next to Joe.

"What's the matter?" he asked.

I started to tell him nothing. The thing with Joe and me though, we could read each other better than anyone else on the planet.

"It's nothing major. I'm just worried about him."

"Don't. Chickens are a good hobby. Vangie's right. The man earned his free time."

"I don't argue that," I said. "It's just ... he's been restless. Like pent-up. And I know he's taken some phone calls he doesn't want me to know about."

"What kind of phone calls?"

I drank my lemonade. It felt a little strange talking about Eric while he was just across the yard. But I knew Joe wasn't about to let me off the hook.

"I think somebody at the sheriff's department is trying to get him to come work for them."

"As what?" Joe asked. "As a detective again?"

"Probably. I don't know. Maybe."

"How do you feel about that?"

"I guess I can't feel anything yet. He hasn't actually come to me and told me anything. I've just overheard a few things when he was talking."

"So ask him," Joe said.

"I will. Or he'll tell me when he's ready to tell me something."

Joe laughed.

"What?"

"You get that look on your face. The one you get when you want to tell me something but you want me to ask you about it. Then you tell me you're worried. Now, in the next breath, you're trying to act like you're not worried. So basically, you goaded me into asking you about something you're worried about, but want to pretend you're *not* worried about it."

I opened my mouth to protest, then clamped it shut. Arguing with him would only serve to dig my hole deeper. Because he was right. I was worried. I knew I shouldn't be. But the day Eric told me he was done being a cop, it lifted a weight off my shoulders I hadn't realized I'd been carrying. He was safe now. He was raising chickens and living on the lake with me. I wanted it to be enough.

"Emma seems pretty excited about this new case you guys are working on," he said.

I raised a brow. "What's she telling you about it?"

"Relax," he said. "She's not breaking anyone's confidence. I just know you're looking into the murder of that law student. And I know from the way she acts that she's excited. That's all."

"Oh. Well, good. And she's been doing great work. We're getting to the point where I don't have to tell her anything. She's starting to anticipate what I need before I even know it."

Joe laughed, nearly spitting out his beer.

"What?"

"Nothing," he said, smiling. "I just think she's more like you than you realize. I've always thought so."

"Well, I'll take that as the highest compliment."

Joe's face got serious. He looked out at the lake.

"What?" I asked.

"She just ... I guess it's like what you're worried about with Eric. Emma's in a good place. She's here. In Delphi. But in a couple of years she's going to graduate from law school. What if she decides it's too small for her here? Like you did."

There was more to his question than he said. He didn't have to say it. I'd wanted out of Delphi from the second I turned eighteen. Even earlier. I'd chased after the first big, shiny thing that came my way when I got my law degree. It took me to Chicago and down a dark path I barely survived. I ended up working for a law firm that represented one of the most powerful organized crime families in the country.

"She's not like me," I said. "Because she had what we didn't have. An actual father. A good one. And despite all her current flaws, Katie was a good stepmother to her, too. When she decides what she wants to do with her talents, it will be because of that. *Her* talents. Not because she's trying to run away from something."

"Yeah. Maybe."

I turned to him. "Not maybe. For certain. The other thing she'll have is me. Someone who can help her understand what's too good to be true."

Joe's face darkened again. "But Jeanie tried to tell you that too. You went headlong into that crap anyway."

My stomach twisted a bit. It was something I didn't like to think about. But he was right. Jeanie tried to stop me from taking the job with the Thorne Law Group. I'd been too stubborn to listen. She'd given me an ultimatum out of desperation. She said she didn't want to hear from me ever again if I chose what she called a devil's bargain. And I'd called her bluff. It led to a ten-year estrangement I will regret for the rest of my life. But we came back from it. And I was here. Happy. Doing work I was proud of.

"We're about ready in here!" Tori called out. Matty and Eric manned the grill. Matty did his best not to scrunch his face in disdain as he put Cameron's mystery burger into a bun and served it to him.

We sat at the long picnic table my grandfather had built fifty years ago. It was sturdy. Strong. Meant to last. Just like the family I had left.

LATER, after everyone else had gone home, I couldn't sleep. I padded down to my home office on the first floor off the living room.

I had a copy of Andrew Doyle's trial transcript in front of me. For the last few days, I'd pored through it. Getting the timeline and players of Daria Moreau's murder as deep in my head as I could.

I still had no answers. I still hadn't decided who was telling the truth. But the more I read, the more I believed Andrew's public defender had been incompetent. Whether Andrew still would have been convicted without him, I couldn't yet say. But it bothered me he'd never been given a chance.

"You okay?" Eric poked his head in. He was scruffy-looking. Shirtless. Wearing boxers. The sight of him like that always gave me a little thrill.

"I'm okay," I said.

Eric came fully into the office. I closed the binder as he perched himself on the edge of my desk.

"You should come to bed. It's still the weekend for another twenty-four hours."

"I know," I said. I reached up as he leaned forward to kiss me. "I'm sorry if I woke you."

"You didn't. I was having trouble sleeping, too."

"Any particular reason?" I asked. He was getting good at reading me just as well as my brother could. There was weight to my question and he knew it.

"No," he said. "Not yet."

"Okay," I said. "But when you want to talk about it ..."

"Shh," he said. "There's nothing. I promise. You wanna talk about your case?"

I leaned back. "I thought you wanted to be out of the business of my private detective."

"Doesn't mean I don't want to know what's got your brain all in knots. I can give you an unbiased ear. Plus ... I just want to be sure you're not about to jump headlong into something dangerous. Again."

Like with my brother, I opened my mouth to argue, but found I had nothing. He was right. I'd jumped into danger for clients plenty of time. More than once, Eric had been the one to step in front of the bullets for me. Both literally and figuratively.

"I'm not. I promise."

"And if that changes, will you also promise to come to me? Somebody got murdered in your case. If it wasn't your client, there will be someone out there who might be willing to kill again to keep you from finding out."

"I know. But seriously. This is paperwork. Dry legal procedure." I held up the binder, then put it back down.

"Okay. I trust you. But I'm serious. Is there anything I can do?"

I smiled. "Right now, you can hand me that big white book on the shelf that says Bar Directory."

I was old-fashioned. I liked to keep a physical copy of the yearly directory, preferring it over PDFs.

Eric grabbed the book and put it in front of me. I flipped through the pages, getting to the Ss. I ran my finger down the page until I found it. His name. His bar number. His place of employment.

Eric followed my finger and read the name upside down.

"Marcus Savitch. Corporate Division," he said. "Carter and Baldwin. Bloomfield Hills. Hmm. Fancy. Those are where the big civil firms live, right?"

"Yep," I said. "See? Told you. Nothing dangerous. Just boring. I just need to go pay Mr. Savitch a visit."

"Savitch," Eric said. "As in Savitch Arena. As in owners of the Petoskey Greyhawks and about fifty resorts?"

"And a casino," I said. "Yes. Marcus Savitch and this other guy, Kade Barclay, rented a house with Andrew and the murder victim before the bar exam two years ago. It's where the murder happened. Savitch paid for everything."

"He could definitely afford it," Eric said.

I wrote down the address. Carter and Baldwin were one of the most prestigious firms in the state. A classmate of mine landed there. If he was still there, he had to have made partner by now.

I flipped to the Bs in the directory. I ran my finger down the rows, but couldn't find Kade Barclay anywhere.

"Hmm," I said.

"Hmm, what?"

"Hmm ... it doesn't look like my other witness is licensed in this state. Which means either he never took the bar here, failed it, or he's lawyering or doing something else or *somewhere* else. If only I had a private investigator on staff who could track these things down for me."

Eric smiled and shook his head in defeat. "Write his name down."

"I'm just teasing," I said. "I can handle a google search, Eric."

He leaned in to kiss me again. "How about handling coming to bed with me? Carter and Baldwin aren't open right now. I don't need to be a detective to tell you that."

He took the directory from me and closed it. He had that twinkle in his eye that meant something irresistible. So I decided *not* to resist and followed him up the stairs.

Chapter 6

CARTER BALDWIN P.C. encompassed the top two floors of a ten-story building overlooking Square Lake in Bloomfield Hills. A million years ago, the firm was one of the most coveted summer internships a law student could get. I suppose it still was. I took the elevator up to the tenth floor and checked in with reception.

"Is Mr. Savitch expecting you?" His nameplate read simply, Rowlf. I did a double take. He seemed like a nice kid. Clean-cut. Wearing an expensive suit and yellow tie. But I wondered if anyone ever told him he had the same name as a Muppet.

"I believe so," I said. "I cleared it with his assistant yesterday morning."

"Great!" Rowlf said. Behind his desk and the glass doors, I watched two lawyers, their clients, and a court reporter head into the conference room with the downtown view. It brought back memories. I once had a corner office overlooking the Chicago river on one side, Lake Michigan on the other.

Everyone ran around that top floor as if their rear ends were on fire. All the time. Including me.

I liked things better now. And there was a time the thought of ending up back in Delphi working with and for people I went to high school with would have me breaking out in hives.

"Ms. Leary?" Rowlf said. He'd come out from behind his desk and I hadn't even noticed. He held the glass doors open for me.

"Sorry, thanks."

Rowlf showed me down the hall. Marcus Savitch didn't have a corner office, but he had a pretty good view of the lake. As Rowlf let me in, Marcus had his back to us. He wore tan chinos and a blue polo shirt. He cast a casual glance over his shoulder and held his index finger up.

"Have a seat," Rowlf said. Not before I caught him rolling his eyes at Savitch.

I sat for almost a full minute while Savitch finished up whatever call he was on.

"I can't take that to him," he said to his caller. "I don't even know why we're having this conversation. Call me next week. I won't have a different answer. But maybe you like the sound of my voice."

He hung up abruptly, turned, and plastered on a smile.

"Ms. Lowry," he said, extending his hand to shake mine.

My skin prickled. He couldn't be serious. "Leary," I said. "But feel free to call me Cass."

"I'm so sorry, of course," Savitch said. "Please, Marcus."

He sat down behind his desk but leaned comfortably back in his chair. I expected him to put his feet up on his desk. "Did you need something? Water? Coffee? Rowlf should have offered."

"I don't need anything. And I'll try not to take up too much of your time."

"Great," Marcus said, leaning forward so he could rest his elbows on his desk. "I do have another meeting in about twenty minutes."

I bit my lip past the retort in my mind. Then why the hell did you take a meeting with me now? I'd actually arrived ten minutes early.

"Then I'll get right to it. You should know I've agreed to take a look at Andrew Doyle's appeal."

Marcus's face never changed. "How do you think I could help you with that?"

"I wanted to get your version of events."

He let out a haughty laugh. "My version is already on record several times. I gave a lengthy statement to the police. They questioned me for hours. I fully cooperated. Then I testified for half a day at Andrew's trial. Surely you have access to all of that."

"Of course. But I find it helps me if I talk to witnesses myself."

"Fine," Marcus said. "What is it you'd like to know?"

"Tell me about your relationship with Daria. With Andrew. That weekend. I'm just trying to get a sense of who saw what."

Marcus shrugged. "I didn't have a relationship with Daria. Not in the way you appear to be implying."

"I'm not implying anything. My understanding is that you were all friends. You. Andrew. Daria. Kade Barclay."

"We were."

"Do you still talk to Kade?" I asked.

"No. I mean, we're friends on social media. But I haven't talked to him since just before the trial. It was a difficult time for all of us. I can't speak for Kade, but it's not one I particularly enjoy reliving."

"That's understandable. But how did it end up being the four of you?"

"We were in Professor Sinay's first term Research and Writing class. She was a terrible teacher. Totally unapproachable. Obtuse. It was one of those things where we bonded over dislike of a common enemy. I half wonder if that was Sinay's plan all along. We got grouped together for a project. After that, we stuck together."

"And you were the one who arranged to rent the house in Williamston? Before the bar?"

"Yes. As I recall, Daria wanted to stay in some ratty East Lansing hotel. I refused. My idea was better. The house would have been quiet. There was enough space for us all to claim our private spots and do whatever last-minute brush-ups we needed. Though I didn't need it. Not then. Andrew and Daria weren't as laid-back. Daria had all these color-coded notecards. It was pretty amusing. I took a couple from her stack. Just to try to get her to loosen up."

"How did she take that?"

Marcus laughed to himself. "Not well. She was pretty pissed at me."

"Is that what you were arguing about? The night she died?"

"What?"

"I mean, you're aware there were witnesses who saw you arguing with her the night of the party."

"You said you have access to the court file. I've already told this story a thousand times. I don't even remember what we were arguing about. Daria was wound tight. That was her baseline. I was worried she was going to worry herself into a heart attack or a panic attack. Something. It never took much to set her off. My general memory was her just having a short fuse that night. She wasn't happy the party got so big."

"She thought it was your fault?" I asked.

"Yes. She blamed me for telling too many people. But I didn't. I couldn't control who other people told about it. But yes. That was the source of whatever friction there might have been the night we lost her. And it wasn't directed specifically at me. She was just stressed out about the whole situation. And she was stressed out about Andrew."

"The prosecution entered some texts she sent to Kade. That she was uncomfortable with Andrew's crush on her."

Marcus exhaled. "Yes."

"Were you aware of it?"

"I was. Yes. Daria mentioned it once or twice."

"How? What did she say?"

"She said Andrew was giving her the ick. Her words. He was like a lost puppy in those final couple of months of law school. Like he was afraid he was going to miss his chance. My only regret is that I didn't take it more seriously. Her concerns."

"So you think Andrew killed Daria over this?"

"I really hate this question. I hate this whole subject. It's been almost two years. I've moved on."

"Andrew hasn't. He insists he's innocent. He has some rather valid concerns about how his public defender conducted himself during the trial. How the police did leading up to his arrest."

"Look," Marcus said. "I don't talk to Andrew anymore. Not since after they found Daria."

"A day and a half after the party," I said. "See, that's the part I'm struggling with. You know the police struggled with it too. You're right. I've read your statement. That's one of the things they were pretty concerned about. That none of you reported her missing for more than a day."

"That was Kade's doing, not mine. He told us she was sleeping in. That she'd locked herself in her room. I'll regret that I accepted that from him. But it tracked. I told you. I told the police. I told the jury. Daria was pretty angry that the party got so big. It stressed her out. Just her. The rest of us were a lot more chill about it. Did it end up being more people than I wanted? Yes. But under the circumstances, we *all* wanted to blow off steam getting ready for that exam. It was just ... Daria being Daria. Or that's what I thought."

"But you liked her. I mean, everything I've heard is that the four of you were joined at the hip for three years."

"We were close. Yes. We relied on each other to get through that slog. Surely you understand that. You graduated from U of M Law yourself, right?"

So he knew where I went to school. But he'd tripped over my name at the top of our meeting. I didn't like the guy one bit. He was like every jerk in Delphi who'd ever looked down their noses at me because I lived on the east side of Finn Lake. Times a thousand. But the moment I thought it, I knew that was the problem. Maybe I was making assumptions about the guy based on my own baggage.

"Yes," I said.

"Okay. Then you know. And how many people are you still friends with from law school now?"

I chewed the inside of my lip. "None. But I wasn't there when any of them got murdered."

His face darkened. "I wasn't there."

"What?"

"I wasn't there. I mean, yeah. It happened on the property. But it had nothing to do with me. Andrew didn't turn out to be the person I thought he was."

"What person was that?"

Marcus shook his head. "I thought he was just this serious, geeky, but good-hearted, harmless guy. Someone who'd led a pretty sheltered life up until then. He'd only been to two states his whole life. Indiana and Michigan. I didn't know the deep shit he had swirling in his mind. And I never thought he'd hurt Daria. If I would have sensed that, I would have ..."

He trailed off. "You would have what?"

"I'd have broken his damn neck, that's what." He rose from his seat. "Look, I really don't have anything else to tell you. You're just going to have to rely on everything I've already told everyone who's asked. I'm on record. This part of my life is over. I'm gonna need you to leave now."

"Right," I said. "Your meeting. I'll get out of your hair."

Marcus didn't say anything else to me. But he followed me to the door and pretty much slammed it behind me. Hard enough, the noise of it got the attention of his colleagues in the adjoining offices. Most of them stared at me as I made my way back to the lobby. I got halfway there before someone called my name.

"Cass? Leary? Is that you?"

I turned. I almost didn't recognize him. Funny how I'd been in the trenches with people for three years. Now that so much time had passed, I'd forgotten most of them. But Brian Sweeney was a standout. Not for how well he did in tort law, but for his six-foot-four stature and booming voice. At twenty-four, he hadn't been able to grow a beard. He had perpetually red cheeks that earned him the nickname Rosey from some of the wise asses in our class.

"Brian!" I said. "I heard a rumor you landed here."

He came up to me and enveloped me in a crushing bear hug.

"What are you doing here? I heard you were only doing criminal defense these days."

"Mostly I am. I just needed to talk with one of your colleagues."

"Get the hell in here," he said, gently guiding me into his office two doors down the hall.

He shut the door behind us and gestured to the leather couch he kept along the wall. He sat beside me, resting one ankle on the opposite knee, a giant grin on his face. He'd figured out how to grow a beard, but his cheeks were still apple red.

"It's damn good to see you," he said. "You keep in touch with anybody else from school?"

"I'm afraid I don't. I don't even remember half of them."

"Me either." Brian laughed. "Man, you look so different. In a good way, different. You were like a deer in headlights that first year."

That's not how I remembered things at all. To the point I wondered if he was confusing me with somebody else.

"I was just serious," I said. "I had a lot riding on succeeding."

"Sure. Sure. I heard you were at some big firm in Chicago making a boat load. Which tracks. But now you're on the defense side?"

"I'm in Delphi. You've probably never heard of it."

The blank expression on Brian's face told me I was right.

"So, what are you doing here?"

"I had a meeting with Marcus Savitch."

Brian's face fell. He'd never had a good poker face but his expression was downright wary.

"That guy," he said. "What could he possibly have to do with anything you're working on?"

"He's a witness in a murder case where I'm handling the appeal. I'm surprised you haven't heard of it. It's exactly the kind of thing that would generate office gossip. He was hosting a party where one of his law school classmates got killed."

"Oh. Yeah. I did hear something about that. Some friend's girlfriend or something. Is he cooperating with you?"

"More or less. What can you tell me about him?"

Brian rolled his eyes. "He's a screw-up. Don't let him fool you. Let me guess, he was probably on some very important call when you walked into his office." Brian made air quotes around "very important."

"Uh. Yeah."

"Look, you didn't hear this from me. But we go way back. I trust you. The only reason that idiot is even here is because of his daddy's money."

"Lars Savitch. Yeah. I heard about that."

"The partners wouldn't let him near anything he could screw up. Which is just about everything. I mean, he's not an idiot. He can be charming. He's good at schmoozing some of the VIP clients and when they hear his last name, it earns us some cache. But that's about it. He's just part of the dog and pony show. To be honest, we have a hard time keeping him busy around here."

"Really? He shooed me out because he said he was late for some other meeting."

"Savitch isn't allowed to take client meetings solo anymore."

Brian's desk phone buzzed. "Mr. Sweeney? Your two o'clock is here. I've got the Moores set up in the conference room."

"I'll let you get to it," I said, rising. "It was good seeing you, Rosey?"

Brian laughed at the nickname. "Haven't heard that one in what, seventeen, eighteen years?"

"Ouch," I said. "That physically hurts. How have we gotten so old?"

"Beats me. My oldest got married last summer. She called me two days ago. She's twenty-one!"

"Well, congratulations. She'll probably be calling you Grandpa next."

He put his hand over his heart and staggered back a step.

"You let me know if you need anything," he said. "If Savitch is a problem for you in any way, I know how to light a fire under him. I have my ways."

"Thanks," I said. "I'll keep it in mind."

We said our goodbyes. I saw four missed texts as I made my way to the elevator. They were all from Emma. She'd tracked down Kade Barclay. He worked at a small firm near Columbus, Ohio. She'd talked to him and he could see me tomorrow afternoon. As I pressed the lobby button, I texted her back.

> Thanks. Looks like tomorrow's going to be another road trip.

So far, Marcus Savitch had wasted my time. Hopefully Barclay would be more cooperative.

Chapter 7

KADE BARCLAY reluctantly but surprisingly agreed to meet with me. His only condition, he wanted to be nowhere near his office. So we met at a coffee shop right off the highway. He was waiting for me when I walked in, seated at a booth in front of the window.

He stood up when I came to the table, amicably shaking my hand. But his expression read pure suspicion, narrowed eyes, a hard set to his jaw.

"Thank you for your time," I said. "I would imagine this isn't a very comfortable subject for you."

"How's Andrew?"

The question surprised me. Marcus Savitch never asked it.

"He's breathing." I gave him an honest answer. "I suppose I'm supposed to say he's doing as well as can be expected. I'm just not sure what's supposed to be expected in his situation."

Our server brought coffee. Kade gave her a tight-lipped smile and waved off ordering anything else. So did I.

"I'm not sure what I can do for you. Or him."

"Just meeting me is one thing. But do you want to do something for him?"

Kade considered my question. "I don't know. I guess not. This was ... not a good time in my life. Even saying that makes me sound selfish. Daria's dead. I still miss her. But I've tried to move on. I'm getting married in two weeks."

Once again, I was struck by the contrast between Marcus and Kade. Marcus didn't really talk about Daria as a person. He only spoke about how everything affected him.

"Tell me about her," I said. "I've read your testimony. Your statement to the police. The entire trial transcript and police report. I still don't have a sense of her."

Something changed in Kade's face. There was sadness still, but as he looked out that window, I saw a slight smile.

"She was ... everything. Whip smart. Beautiful. Driven. We all kind of got thrown together the first few weeks of law school. That whole time, I knew we were the lucky ones that she put up with us. Marcus was just a complete screw-up. Andrew was really introverted. Me? I don't know what I was. Scared out of my mind, I guess. Of all of us, Daria was the one who belonged there the most."

"You loved her," I said.

Kade whipped his eyes back to me. "No. It wasn't love."

"But you dated her."

"For about ten minutes," he said. "Beginning of third year. We both realized it was a bad idea pretty quickly."

"Why?"

Kade ran his finger around the rim of his coffee mug. "Because Daria was ... I don't even know the right way to describe it. She was just bigger than we were. Brighter. She was always going to blast past us. We knew there was never any real future for us. She wasn't supposed to end up with me. And I certainly wasn't supposed to end up with her."

"That had to have been hard," I said. "For you, I mean."

He shrugged. "I don't know. It was enough that we were friends. That relationship mattered more to me than anything else. But I knew what was going to happen."

"What do you mean?"

He regarded me. I had the strangest sense that in the last five minutes, he'd gone somewhere else in his head. He was just now realizing he'd said all those things out loud.

"We weren't going to keep in touch. We were going to say we would. But she was going to end up somewhere big. New York. LA. Maybe even Toronto. That would have been the most natural fit. Eventually, she would barely remember being friends with me. And that was okay with me."

"And you have to know what that sounds like," I said.

That anger came back into his face. "I know what the cops thought it sounded like. Like maybe I decided if I couldn't have her, no one would."

"Did you decide that?"

He laughed. "Are you really sitting there accusing me of hurting her? Of killing her?"

"I'm just sitting here," I said.

He shook his head. "You haven't asked me what I know you want to."

"And what's that?"

"You want to ask me if I think your client killed my friend. Our friend. The answer is yes. Yes. I didn't want to believe it back then. I still don't. But yes. Andrew had something wrong with him. I know now he felt like I did. That Daria was just ... above us somehow. And it's nothing she ever said or did. She was a good friend. Hell, there's no way Marcus would have made it through school without her. Sometimes I thought the same thing about me. But Andrew? It got all twisted up for him. He knew that week was really going to be the last time we saw her."

"You think he planned to kill her?"

"No," he said. "That's not what I mean. I mean he knew as soon as we took the bar, Daria would be gone. First, back to Montreal. Back home. Then it's like I said. She would have landed in some big city. Andrew had a job offer in Eau Claire and some dinky town right over the Michigan border from Indiana. He was lying to his family. They thought he was gonna go back to Walkerton, where he's from. He had no desire to. I had a hunch he was gonna try to follow Daria."

"Did he say that?" I asked.

"No," Kade answered. "I'm just guessing. Turns out he couldn't handle losing her like that. Turns out he couldn't handle that she didn't feel the same about him."

"You testified about some texts you had from her," I said. "She expressed some concerns about Andrew's attention."

"Yeah," he said. "And I blew her off. I didn't think Andrew would hurt a fly. None of us did. But Daria started feeling uncomfortable about the attention he paid her. Following her around like a puppy. Calling her. She was trying to be polite. She didn't want to hurt his feelings."

"So she asked you to talk to him," I said. Daria's texts to Kade were one of the most damning pieces of evidence the prosecution entered. It established Andrew's motive loud and clear. He loved her. She didn't love him back in the way he wanted. He snapped.

"Yeah."

"But you never did."

"No. Look, I don't want to talk about this anymore."

"You were at the trial," I said. "You know what happened."

"I was there the day I testified. That's all. I didn't sit through the whole thing. I took the stand. When I stepped down, I left."

"Come on," I said. "You're not some newbie off the street. You're a lawyer, Kade. Since then, you've tried your own cases. I understand you've even taken some public defense work in Franklin County."

"So?"

"So." I leaned forward. "You know how incompetent Andrew's lawyer was. You know he barely cross-examined you. You know he let the prosecution allow you to give hearsay testimony. Speculate about what happened that night. He didn't object. I know how this works. You had to have been thinking about it while you were in that witness box. We can't go back to thinking like regular people. You can't shut off the lawyer brain. Ever."

"I wasn't thinking about being a lawyer," he snapped. "I was thinking about Daria. I was thinking about the fact that I was forced to explain myself ... again ... about the worst day of my life. I was thinking about how much it sucked to be grilled in open court about how maybe if I'd have done something different, Daria might still be alive."

"What could you have done differently?"

"Just stop," he said. "You're right. I can't shut off my lawyer brain now. You're asking questions you already know the answers to."

"I want to hear them from you, Kade."

"It's not a secret. I've never lied about it. I should have realized Daria was missing a lot sooner. I should have called the police a lot sooner. I didn't call them until twenty-four hours after she didn't come back."

"You told the cops and the jury you didn't realize she was missing."

He squeezed the handle of his coffee mug so hard I thought it might pulverize.

"We'd all been drinking, okay? We were up until something like four or five in the morning. Daria was mad about the party getting so big so I assumed she just locked herself in her room. That would have been like her. And when she got like that, you couldn't talk her out of it. You just had to let her blow off steam in her own way and give her space. I thought that's what I was doing."

"But she didn't answer when you knocked on her door."

"She was mad at me. I've said all of this. I made a stupid comment to her earlier the night before. I told her to unclench her ass or something. Lighten up. I was crude and a little drunk and I goddamn didn't know somebody was going to kill her a few hours later."

"Of course not," I said.

"So yeah. She'd told me in no uncertain terms to leave her the hell alone. So I did. But then she never came out. So I broke into her room and everybody knows the rest. Andrew did this. I don't know that he planned to. I can believe it was sudden. That he snapped. Got angry and took things too far. But then he lied about it. He let her rot out there in that pond for over a day and said nothing. So no, back to your original question, I really don't want to help him. I shouldn't have agreed to meet with you. I did it because I figured you'd keep hounding me if I didn't. Or you'd slap me with a subpoena. Maybe you still will. And screw you for stirring all of this up when I'm about to marry a wonderful woman who doesn't need to be mired in this crap."

"I didn't know about your wedding. I'm sorry for that part of it. But you know Andrew wasn't convicted of a heat-of-passion murder. He was convicted of premeditated murder."

"And I know that's not my problem. If it's yours, find somebody else to tell you what you want to hear."

He rose and threw his napkin on the table.

"Kade, I ..."

"I'm done. There aren't any more stones to turn over. Not even for you. I know you're supposed to be one of the best in your state at what you do. Good luck with it. But don't call me again. This is the last time I talk to you voluntarily."

I let him storm off. There was no point in chasing him down. He was probably justified in every emotion he was having. Even as part of the system himself, it made sense that he'd view me as the enemy.

But as Kade Barclay stormed back to his car, I had the strongest sense he still wasn't telling me something.

Chapter 8

LATE THE NEXT AFTERNOON, just before the end of the workday, I gathered the team, save for Miranda who was handling payroll downstairs. I filled Tori, Emma, and Jeanie in on the highlights of my conversations with Marcus Savitch and Kade Barclay.

"So you didn't get the sense either of them was lying?" Tori asked.

"Not exactly. Both of them want me to believe Andrew's guilty. Marcus would barely talk to me at all. Kade seemed the most genuine of the two in the sense he seemed to still be grieving the loss of his friend."

"I don't know," Jeanie said. "I don't like it. Barclay doesn't report Daria missing for over a day. If he was that worried about her, that makes no sense to me. What makes more sense is that he or all three of them knew she was already dead and spent that day trying to get their stories straight."

"Which would be great," Emma said. "But Nadler never made an issue out of it at trial. He never even raised the question."

"How's my research going?" I said. "Can you give me a definitive answer on whether Andrew's statement rose to the level of invoking his Miranda rights?"

Emma shook her head. "It's not a slam dunk. It's a big old fat it depends."

"On what?" I asked.

"The law is clear. It has to be an explicit request for a lawyer. On the face of it, Andrew didn't really do that. He said maybe I should have a lawyer. Then Detective Messer says, I thought you were a lawyer. Then, Andrew kind of leaves it at that."

"If it's not really a slam dunk," I said, "then Nadler should have at least raised it. He should have filed a suppression hearing. That could be enough to get my foot in the door with the appellate court."

"I don't know," Jeanie said. "You know the appeals court will give deference to the trial court. If they're not convinced Andrew raised the question explicitly, it's just smoke and mirrors."

"Maybe," I said. "I still say it's incompetence that Nadler never even filed the motion."

"Which means he also didn't preserve it for appeal," Tori said.

"We're banging our heads against the wall," I said. I reached toward the center of the conference room table. Emma had made copies of each section of the police report as well as the trial exhibits. Tori had summarized the witness testimony. I grabbed one copy of the fat purple binder from the stacks. Emma had gotten busy with her label maker. This one read "Autopsy."

Jeanie grabbed her copy. We opened them at the same time. Though I'd skimmed it before, we needed to have a real discussion. Tori and Emma grabbed the other two purple binders.

"Cause of death wasn't disputed," I said. "Fracture of the cervical vertebrae between C-2 and C-3. Consistent with a fall backward onto a hard surface."

"Death by birdbath," Emma said. "They call it a hangman's fracture."

"No defensive wounds," I said. "She was pushed or fell and that was pretty much it."

"That's one thing that should have been in Andrew's favor," Jeanie said. "If she had Andrew's skin under her nails, why didn't she have any other defensive wounds? To me that's consistent with his story that he didn't fight back. He just took his licks from her and walked away."

"If he pushed her quickly," I said, "it was over quickly. This wasn't a prolonged struggle."

I flipped through the binder. The medical examiner had been thorough. There were dozens of full-color photos of Daria Moreau's body on his examination table. She was pretty, even in death. True platinum-blonde hair. No dark roots. Well-muscled from her years as a trained athlete. Her face was perfect, almost like a wax figure, unblemished. High cheekbones, full lips. Five foot one, one hundred pounds on the dot.

"What's toxicology say?" I asked.

"Low BAC," Emma reported. "The theory was she probably drank two beers the whole night. Lin said he saw her grabbing one earlier in the night. No illicit substances. Positive for over-the-counter inflammation medication. Naproxen sodium. She was on levothyroxine for low thyroid. The only really interesting thing was she was on an SSRI. Fluoxetine."

"That's an oral antidepressant," I said. "Prozac."

"Yep," Emma said. "I've taken that in the past myself. After um ... my bad breakup."

Everyone in the room lifted their eyes. We shared an uncomfortable silence. Emma's bad breakup had been very bad indeed. Her boyfriend had been accused of murder. The outcome of all of that wasn't something I liked to think about. I knew Emma didn't either.

"Therapeutic levels though," Jeanie said.

I flipped through the binder. "We don't have any medical records on Daria?"

"No," Emma answered.

"I think that's strange," I said. "Yet another thing Nadler should have ordered. If she was on antidepressants, I'd like to know why or who prescribed them. If she was seeing a therapist, that could be huge. Can we find that out? Tori, do you think you could get her medical records?"

"Getting a court order for that as things stand right now would be impossible," Jeanie said. "There's no open case. Maybe when you're ready to file something."

"There's another way," I said. Though it turned my stomach thinking about it.

"Ugh," Tori said. "Please don't make me do it."

"I wouldn't," I said. "But if Daria's next of kin would grant us permission, I wouldn't need a court order."

"Ooof," Emma said. "How would you even approach them? We're talking about her parents, right?"

"Right," I said. "The last thing I want to do is bring them more pain. But I would think if there's even a chance the full story didn't come out at trial, they might be willing to work with me."

"I'll figure out where they are," Emma said. "If they're in Montreal, that's a whole other kettle of fish. Unless you wanna take a little vacation, we might see if we could set up a teleconference call or something."

"Just get me their contact info," I said. "We'll go from there."

I went back to the autopsy report. It boggled my mind why Nadler didn't run down Daria's medical records. The police would have had no need for them. Neither would the prosecutor. Daria's overall health wasn't in question at the murder trial. Still, her use of antidepressants could open a potentially interesting lead.

"She had a bad knee," Emma said. "The coroner found evidence of an old injury. Torn ACL. She had a prior surgery, total reconstruction. She had titanium pins and screws. Post mortem showed evidence of chronic joint instability. Degeneration of the medial meniscus, synovial scarring consistent with repeated trauma."

"Her father testified she blew her knee out during a floor routine at a national competition when she was sixteen. They were afraid it was career ending. But she worked her way back after the surgery," Tori said.

"Tough kid," Jeanie said. "She had to have been in constant pain while she was still competing. And for the rest of her life."

"Then she blew it out again at an NCAA competition her sophomore year of college at the University of Florida," I said.

"I just wonder," Emma said. "If she hadn't. If she'd been able to continue competing. Maybe her life would have taken a different path. Maybe she never would have ended up in law school at all."

"We'll never know," I said. "I didn't think to ask, but I haven't heard Andrew, Kade, or Marcus say anything about Daria complaining about pain."

Tori combed through the witness summaries Emma wrote. "You know," she said. "There isn't a single mention of Daria's knee injury in the entire trial. It's just part of the autopsy report."

"Why would that make a difference?" Emma asked.

"Even if Andrew's lying and he did kill Daria," I said. "If it were me, I would have probably used that information to support an accident. If she was pushed hard enough to fall backwards, what if her knee failed her again? I don't know. Maybe that's a stretch, but once again, it just makes me want to shake Nadler. This guy completely phoned it in. He failed Andrew."

"Unless the kid really did it," Jeanie said. "Then what are we even doing here?"

"I like making payroll!" Miranda called from downstairs. The walls were thin and Jeanie's voice carried.

Smiling, I closed the autopsy binder. "It's more than that. Nadler's incompetence is one thing. I just have the strongest sense that those three men are leaving something out. It's like you said, Jeanie. Why weren't they more concerned Daria was missing?"

"But Daria's not our client," Tori said. "Andrew is. Whatever we're doing, we're doing it for him, not Daria."

"Maybe it's both," I said. "I know it was Andrew's family who came to us. They care about their son. But if I keep digging at this and find out he's guilty but didn't act alone, I think that's a worthy pursuit."

"That's the cops' job," Jeanie said.

"What if they didn't do it?" Tori said.

"And this is exactly why I don't normally do this kind of work." I sighed. "I don't know. This thing is keeping me up at night."

Jeanie took her readers off and tossed them on the table. "Yeah. Me too. Dammit."

Emma and Tori exchanged a look. "It's keeping us up too," Emma admitted. "Tori and I were texting each other about it until about four in the morning."

"Couldn't sleep," Tori said. "But that's not completely Andrew Doyle or Daria Moreau's fault."

She was blushing. She patted her stomach. Jeanie's eyes lit up. Emma just gave Tori a knowing smile.

"When?" Jeanie asked. "When do I get to be a grandma again?"

Jeanie really was the closest thing my nieces and nephew had to a grandmother. She was a good one, too. When they were with Nana Jeanie, she had no rules.

"Six months," Tori said.

"Did you know?" Jeanie turned to me.

"I suspected," I answered. Then I looked at Emma. "You knew?"

"Tori told me last night," Emma said.

"Fantastic!" Jeanie shouted. "We really needed some good news around here. Something to talk about besides all this." She gestured toward the stacks of binders on the table.

Jeanie got up and wrapped her arms around Tori. Tori kept her eyes on me and I saw something serious behind them. When Jeanie sat down, I guessed at what it was.

"You're leaving us, aren't you?"

Tori clenched her teeth. "Not forever. But when this one comes, I was thinking I might step back from work for a while. But let's not worry about that now. I want to focus on this case. I want to know what really happened. We *need* to know what really happened."

"Okay," I said. "Then it's settled. Full steam ahead."

"What's next?" Emma asked.

"Find out how I can get in touch with Daria's parents," I said. "And I want to have another talk with Andrew about what I've heard from Marcus and Kade."

"We'll get on it," Tori said. She and Emma rose and walked out of the conference room together.

"I've got a couple of divorce judgments to review," Jeanie said. "You let me know what you need from me. I'll be in my office."

As she shut the door, I sat alone with the increasing piles of documents on the Doyle case. Tori had blown up a picture of Daria's law school class picture and put it on the whiteboard.

"What did they do to you?" I whispered. I knew I should probably go home. It was past five o'clock. Eric was on a fishing trip with a couple of other retired cops. The dogs needed letting out. I sent a text to Vangie to have Jessa do it for me. I added a second text, asking her to check the chicks in the brooder. They had an annoying habit of kicking pine chips into their food and water.

I stood and surveyed my mess. Open binders. Case law books. Scattered pieces of paper. If I couldn't get any further on Andrew's case tonight, I could at least do some organizing. I reshelved a few law books. Those were Jeanie's. Like me, she still liked reading from physical books rather than online.

I got a text from Jessa a few minutes later with a picture of one of the chicks staring at her phone camera. She'd named that one Marge on account of a strange crest that had sprouted on top of its head that reminded her of Marge Simpson's hairdo.

I pocketed my phone and grabbed the last book off the table. It was another copy of the bar directory. Emma used it to fill in part of a short bio sheet she was making for each trial witness. She had Marcus Savitch's name highlighted in pink. I stared at the entry for a moment. I pivoted, meaning to reshelve that book too. Instead, I froze. I ran my finger down the page and tapped the data entered right next to Marcus's name. My whole body flooded with heat. For a moment, I couldn't breathe. I couldn't be reading what I thought I was reading. I must have lined something up wrong.

I ran my finger down one more time then sank slowly to my seat. I carefully put the book back on the table, keeping it open to that page. Then I dove for the blue binder where Emma had made copies of the witness statements. Heart racing, part of me said I had to be wrong. Except I knew I wasn't. I knew what I was about to find could be a motive for murder.

Chapter 9

"Cass. Cass!"

I sat upright, nearly falling off the couch. I had a second of disorientation as I realized where I was.

"Did you sleep here all night?" Jeanie said. She surveyed the chaos of the room. I had books strewn everywhere. Pages I'd printed off the internet. My copy of the Daria Moreau police report was taken out of the binder and piled all over the floor in front of me.

"What time is it?" I asked. The adrenaline of last night ramped up again.

"It's seven thirty," she said.

"Okay. Okay. Damn. I'll have to wait another hour and a half before I can get anyone on the phone."

Jeanie sat down in the chair opposite me.

"What's going on?"

I touched my hair. Rising, I went to my desk and picked up a small handheld mirror I kept in one of my drawers. No wonder Jeanie was so concerned. I looked awful. I tied my hair up while working last night. Half of it had sprung loose and hung every which way. My mascara ran down to my cheekbone. I had dents in my face from the seams of the couch.

"I'm glad you're here," I said. "I've got a lot to explain."

"I would say so."

"Give me five minutes to change and grab a toothbrush. Is Miranda down there? Has anybody started coffee? I can do that too."

"It's taken care of," she said. "Of course Miranda's down there. She's the one who sent me up here on a search and rescue mission. She brought pastries. You wanna set everything up in the conference room?"

Jeanie peered behind me. The door behind my desk was my separate entrance into said conference room. It wasn't nearly as destroyed as my office.

"Sure," I said. I grabbed my toiletry kit out of my desk. I kept a change of clothes, one suitable for court, the other suitable for days like this ... a pair of yoga pants, a sports bra, and a tee shirt. I grabbed all of it and headed to the bathroom.

My hair was a rat's nest when I pulled it down. I ran a quick brush through it and found some dry shampoo under the sink. I probably wouldn't be going anywhere I'd be seen. I washed my face, brushed my teeth, slipped out of yesterday's skirt and blouse and got changed. As I walked out, Miranda stood there holding a plastic bag open. I gave her a sheepish grin and tossed my dirty clothes into it. She'd have it sent to the dry cleaner before the morning was over.

"Better get in there," she said. "Jeanie's climbing up the walls. Sean woke up with a cough so Tori's taking him for a quick checkup. Emma's got a dentist appointment until one o'clock."

"It's okay," I said. "I won't need either one of them today, I don't think."

Miranda gave me a stern, motherly look, but let me pass. I caught Jeanie reaching across the conference room table for a blueberry scone. My stomach growled and I grabbed my own. She put a steaming mug of coffee in front of me that I felt like swimming in.

"So what's the Eureka?" Jeanie asked, wiping a crumb from her shirt. "I've only ever seen you go beautiful mind like this when you're on to something."

"I am," I said. I walked back and picked up the bar journal where I'd left it on the floor. I set it in front of Jeanie and pointed to the entry I'd highlighted several times over.

"Okay? Marcus Savitch. Works for Carter Baldwin in Bloomfield Hills. We already knew that. Why's that got you drooling on your couch?"

"Look closer," I said.

She read off his P-number. His law license number.

"Yeah, and?"

"Jeanie," I said. I put my index finger over the entry I found most interesting.

"Admitted to practice November 2022. Okay. So what?"

She didn't see it. It made me feel a little better that it had gone right over my head the first time, too.

I pulled one of the green binders off the table. This was Emma's copy of the police report. I tabbed through it until I got to Marcus Savitch's statement transcript. I took my yellow highlighter and circled the beginning of the page where Detective Messer had recorded the length of the interview.

"Cass, it's early. I'm gonna need at least two cups of coffee before my brain kicks into high gear. What am I looking at?"

"November 2022. Marcus, Daria, Andrew, and Kade graduated and got their JDs in May of 2022."

"Right. So?"

"So ... look. I know it's been a looong time since you took the Michigan bar. But that entry in the bar journal says Marcus was admitted in November of 2022. The exam is offered exactly two times a year. It was like that when you took it too, wasn't it?"

"It was. Yes."

"So, Marcus Savitch couldn't have taken the February 2022 bar. He wouldn't have been eligible. Because he hadn't graduated law school yet."

Jeanie sat back, her mouth slightly open. She was starting to get it. I kept going.

"Daria's body was found Monday late in the day. Detective Messer takes Kade, Andrew, *and* Marcus down to the station and puts them in interview rooms at one a.m. Messer's at the scene all through the evening. He doesn't get to Marcus's formal interview until almost three in the morning. He keeps him there until 9:08 a.m. Tuesday morning. Six hours. He was questioned for six hours."

I slid the transcript back in front of her. I'd highlighted the times.

"Son of a bitch," Jeanie says.

"What's the issue?" Miranda asked. She must have heard the last thirty seconds of my speech as she was walking up the stairs.

"The issue," I said, "is that Marcus Savitch can't be in two places at once. I double- and triple-checked online. That July and every July for the last forty-plus years, the bar exam started promptly at nine a.m. They don't allow late entrants. You have to be checked in at least fifteen minutes prior to start and in your seat at nine a.m."

Jeanie picked up the thread. "You get your results about three months later. Then either you find a local judge to formally swear you in or head back up to Lansing for a more formal group swearing-in. Doesn't matter which one Marcus did."

"Right," I said. "The point is, if he was admitted in November, the *only* time he could have taken that year's bar exam was July."

Miranda slumped against the door frame, the weight of my revelation hitting her. "Which is impossible because we know he never made it to the Breslin Center that morning. He was at the police station."

"Right!" Jeanie and I shouted in unison.

"Somebody took it for him," I said. "I see no other possibility. Kade Barclay didn't sit for that exam. Neither did Andrew.

Kade went back to Ohio and took the February exam there. He didn't come back to Michigan until the trial. Andrew obviously never took it. And yet somehow Marcus did."

"Why didn't anyone pick up on this before?" Miranda said.

"Why would they?" I asked. "By the time whoever impersonated Marcus for that test would have gotten results, it was three months later. Andrew had already been arrested. Marcus wasn't a suspect. He was a witness. He got his results. He got sworn in. Daddy got him a job at Carter Baldwin and he went on with his life. Nobody would have had any reason to question it."

"It was obviously already in motion," Jeanie said. "In order to pull something like that off, you'd need money."

"Exactly," I said. "Which we know Marcus Savitch had plenty of. We also know from Andrew and Kade that Marcus was barely making it through school. Kade told me without Daria's help, he'd have flunked out first year. It tracks."

Miranda sank into one of the chairs. I couldn't sit. I started to pace. "You have to present a picture ID when you check in," I said. "I think you probably also have to provide your driver's license number on the application. That's easily checkable."

"I'll get a hold of the current application," Miranda said. She reached for a piece of paper and started taking notes.

"He'd have needed a fake ID," I said. "A good one. I don't see that as having been a problem for someone like Marcus with the means. Detective Messer took all three boys' phones that night. They all consented to that search."

"Kade and Andrew did first," Jeanie said. She studied the police report. "Then Marcus did. Detective Messer wrote down that Savitch was reluctant at first."

"He had to have known that would make him look suspicious when the other two handed their phones over," Miranda theorized.

"Yes," I said. "It also means Marcus probably wouldn't have had any way to call off his imposter test taker. The guy probably just showed up as planned and did the job he was paid for."

"Wow," Jeanie said. "Savitch had to have been sweating bullets. If he's sitting in an interrogation room while somebody else is across town pretending to be him."

"Or he was cold as ice," I said, finally taking a seat. "If his father was paying for all this ... I mean, he may have even known all of it ... been in on it. I get the strong impression that Marcus Savitch is used to having other people cleaning up his messes for him."

"What if she knew?" Jeanie said. "What if Daria Moreau found out what he was planning?"

"That's what I'm thinking," I said. "I have no way of proving it yet. But if she found out. Maybe she confronted him. Maybe that's what they were seen arguing about earlier in the night. Marcus claims it was over the size of the party. Everyone has just taken his word on that. But now I know he was keeping a secret. A big one. It can't be a coincidence."

"So now what?" Miranda said. "This is all well and good. But cheating on a bar exam makes him a liar and a fraud. It doesn't make him a murderer. And you don't even have solid proof yet. I get the issue with the admission date."

"I'm going to need more," I said. "I want to find the guy he hired. I want to try to piece together Marcus Savitch's movements that whole day."

"Where do we start?" Miranda asked.

The office phone rang. I looked at the caller ID and my heart skipped. Late last evening, I'd left a message for someone at the Board of Law Examiners. This was my return call.

"Put it on speaker," I said. Miranda reached forward and pressed the button.

"Leary Law Group," she answered. "How may I direct your call?"

A woman's voice responded. "I'm returning a call to Cass Leary?"

"I'm here," I said. "This is Cass. I'm assuming you're calling about the message I left."

"Yes," the caller said. "My name is Maggie Charles. I'm the executive assistant for the BLE. I think I have the information you requested. I've called our members. You stumped the band a little. Nobody's ever asked for this information before. They want me to get a FOIA request before I can release the records you want. And I'm to make sure you keep the scope narrow. But I can tell you we do, in fact, keep that information on file." Miranda gave me an okay sign. I knew she'd have the FOIA request typed up within the hour.

"Tell me what you can," I said.

"We do indeed keep records of our seating charts for each bar exam," she said. "So I'll be able to tell you where your applicant was seated. If you give that formal request."

"And who he was seated by?" I asked.

"Yes. I can give you the names of those sitting on either side of your applicant. I can't give you the entire roll call of everyone who took the test. I'll send what I can over as a PDF. Once you send me the FOIA, I can shoot your documents over. As far as the check-in information. I've looked up your applicant. Marcus Savitch was checked in at 8:47 a.m. for the first session of testing. Our records show he presented a valid Michigan driver's license."

"Do you have the number of that license?" I asked. "Is that something you record?"

"Generally, no. There's just a check box that indicates what form of ID was used. We don't make a copy of it. The only time something like that would be recorded in more detail is if the applicant standing in front of the examiner didn't match the ID."

"So in this case," I said, "you can at least tell me that nothing would have raised any suspicions about that applicant."

"That's correct."

"But you'd expect the same driver's license number presented on the day of testing would also appear on the written application."

"That's correct. So that we do keep on file. The examiner has access to that information and it's cross-checked when the applicant shows up on the day of testing."

"That's great," I said.

"Once you get me that FOIA, I can send it on right away. I've got the document pulled up right now. I've got to be honest, this is intriguing. It feels like a caper. I don't get many of those."

I smiled. "Fantastic, you've been so helpful, Ms. Charles."

"It's been my pleasure," she said. We hung up.

"I kind of think she's bending quite a few rules," Jeanie said.

"Probably," I admitted. "But we could use a break. I think she would have handed everything over without the FOIA. I don't even know if those records are considered public. Let's just hope she gets this through before anybody over there changes their mind. I'd like to do this quietly. Before someone figures out they should probably get consent from the applicant."

Both Miranda and Maggie Charles were efficient. An hour later, I had the seating chart. It showed Marcus sitting at a table ten rows from the north wall. Two women sat on either side of him. Lenora Tackas, Brianne Folger. Miranda read over my shoulder. She immediately noted the names and pulled them up in the bar journal.

"No entry for Tackas," she said.

"She might not have passed," Jeanie offered.

"But Brianne Folger," Miranda said. "She's in Ann Arbor. Folger and Associates. They do social security disability work. I actually know one of the paralegals who works there. She's an old friend. I can get her on the phone right now. If this Folger woman is in the office, I bet I can even get you an appointment to see her by the end of the day."

"Fantastic," I said. I felt that familiar buzzing in my brain. Something was about to happen. A break. A turn.

"You're going to need to know Marcus Savitch's actual driver's license number," Miranda said. "Give me an hour. I can get a hold of someone with the state police. I've got a few contacts there myself."

Miranda was already on the phone. Whoever was on the other end made her laugh. She nodded at me and gave me a thumbs up. She wrote something on the pad in front of her and slid it across to me.

"Brianne Folger. She'll meet you at two o'clock in her office."

I ripped off the piece of paper and blew a kiss to Miranda.

Chapter 10

FOLGER AND ASSOCIATES was a small boutique firm in Kerrytown, near downtown Ann Arbor. Brianne Folger had joined her mother's practice, specializing in family law and estate planning. They'd converted a two-story Victorian home in the commercial district and painted it white with purple trim. It reminded me a little of Rainbow Row in Charleston.

Miranda's friend Betty, the firm's office administrator, greeted me at the door with a bright smile.

"Thank you so much for helping arrange our meeting," I told her.

"You tell Miranda she needs to come down here and take me to lunch. You know, we used to do a Tuesday ladies who lunch every month. I think Randy and I are the only ones not retired. That should tell you something."

I'd never heard anyone refer to Miranda as "Randy." She and Betty must have known each other far longer than I realized.

Betty showed me to an office down the hall. It was a small sitting room with four mauve upholstered overstuffed chairs around a low table. It was bright, inviting, designed to put new clients at ease. A smart strategy since most people didn't want to talk about divorce or planning for the day they die.

"Bri will be right in," Betty promised. I declined her offer of refreshments and stood by the window looking out at Depot Street.

Not a minute later, Brianne Folger walked in. I tried to keep my reaction to myself. She was pretty. Blonde. But what struck me was how young she looked. She had to be twenty-seven or twenty-eight, but to me she looked barely old enough to babysit. Which only meant I was getting older. My twentieth year practicing law wasn't too far off.

"Ms. Leary?" she said.

"Cass. Please."

"Cass then. Please, have a seat. I have to admit I'm curious about what I can do for you. I don't handle criminal matters. I know you're becoming sort of a Michigan legend in that arena."

"Oh, I doubt that," I said, then realized legend didn't necessarily mean something good.

I pulled a small thin file out of my beat-up messenger bag. The thing was unwieldy, heavy, far too big for anyone to mistake for an actual briefcase. But Jeanie had given it to me in law school and it was my good luck charm ever since.

"I don't want to take up too much of your time. I'm afraid I can't get too detailed due to some confidentiality issues, but I need to ask you what is probably gonna sound strange."

Brianne took the seat opposite me. I held my file folder on my lap. "Well, now I'm *really* curious."

"I need to ask you what you remember about sitting for the bar exam."

Brianne let out a sharp laugh. "What? That's just ... random. But sure. I'll do my best. Don't most of us try to block that day from our brains?"

"Usually, yes. Look, I'm trying to find someone who might have sat near you during the test. I was able to get a hold of the seating chart for the 2022 July exam. It shows you sitting next to a gentleman I am trying very hard to find."

I took the blown-up photograph I'd snagged of Marcus Savitch off his social media but kept it face down for the moment.

"Who I sat next to?" she repeated. "Well, obviously you know they space people out fairly far. So I wasn't *right* next to anyone. But it's funny you should ask. I actually do remember quite a bit."

"Oh?"

"Yeah. I don't remember much about who was seated to my right, but on my left, I very much remember the guy."

I relaxed into my chair. "That's great. May I ask why?"

"Sure. Because he was cute. No. Not cute. Gorgeous. But serious. Almost a little rude. You know, you kind of smile at people. Give that unspoken encouragement as you climb into the foxhole together. I just remember that guy was just as hard as granite. Not engaging with anyone. But again ... gorgeous. In a kind of heart-fluttering way."

"Did you introduce yourself?" I asked.

"Not as such. I was planning to. After everything was done on the second day, I'd sort of worked up the courage to say hello. If we walked out together, I might have even asked him to grab a coffee or head over to a bar with some friends I was meeting. I was feeling pretty bold and exhilarated since we were getting to the end of a very long journey."

I laughed. "I remember that feeling."

"Well, I never got the chance. Both days of testing, the guy finished up earlier than most of us. Come to think of it, on day one, I think he turned in his exam first. And on the second day, he was done almost a full hour before me."

"That's something," I said. "I think I was one of the last people finished on both days. It messes with your head."

"Yes, it does."

"Brianne, if I showed you a picture, do you think you might recognize him now?"

"Maybe," she said. "But I have to ask, why are you so interested in this? To go to the trouble of looking up a seating chart from a two-year-old test seems pretty ... um ... granular. And if you had his name like you have mine, wouldn't a simple google search be more efficient?"

"If you could just indulge me. Like I said, it's to do with a case I'm working on and I'm afraid I can't break confidentiality more than that."

I took out the photograph of Marcus Savitch and handed it to her. Brianne held it up and cocked her head. Then she handed it back to me.

"That's not him," she said.

"You're sure?"

"I'm sure. Whoever that is, he's cute, too. But that's not who was sitting next to me. You must have the wrong name."

"Can you describe the man you *did* sit next to?"

"Well, he sort of looked like that guy. Same basic coloring. But my guy had thicker, wavier hair. And had this cleft in his chin. That was just, chef's kiss, you know? He was what you'd call ruggedly handsome. Your guy isn't like that at all."

Not a word of what she said surprised me. But I was relieved anyway. I wasn't losing my mind. The further I went down this road, the more sure I was that Marcus Savitch had a pretty big secret to hide.

"I really appreciate this," I said. "You've saved me quite a bit of work."

"Did he pass?" she asked.

"What?"

"Did he pass the bar? If you have my name, you've got his."

"Yes," I said. "He passed with flying colors."

"Damn," she said, rising. "Not that I'm disappointed. It just means he's got brains as well as good looks. You wouldn't mind sharing his name with me, would you? Is he local?"

"Sorry," I said. "I can't. Not yet."

"I get it," she said. "Wishful thinking."

"Brianne, there's something else. Do you feel confident enough about your memory that you'd be able to testify in court if I called you?"

"I would. Yes. I mean, if you're asking me again if your guy in the picture is the guy I sat next to. My answer is gonna be no for sure."

"Okay. Great. I'm not certain if it's going to come to that. But I'll let you know as soon as I do."

"Great! You know, I've never actually been to court other than for filing. I don't do trial work. I do client work. My mother does all the litigation."

"I'm sure your mother loves being able to work that well with you," I said as we walked toward the front door.

Brianne leaned in and whispered in my ear. "Don't tell her I said this, but I kinda can't stand it. She's a horrible boss. She owns this practice. I'm actually low-key looking for something else. You wouldn't happen to have any openings for estate work, would you?"

I extended a hand to shake hers. "Not at the moment. My partner handles that end of things. But if it changes, I can let you know that too."

Brianne thanked me, and we said our goodbyes. She'd make a good witness if it came to it. But I still had a few more things to tighten up before any of this was solid enough to use for Andrew Doyle's benefit.

Chapter 11

I WENT straight home from Ann Arbor. Eric and I had been ships passing in the night for the past few weeks. He'd been doing some freelance work with the DNR. Just basic hunting and fishing license enforcement. The kind of thing that allowed him to spend his day on a boat or out in the woods.

I found him pounding nails into the roof of the new coop he was almost finished building. I stopped for a moment to enjoy the view. He was shirtless, sweating, with three chicks grazing at his feet. They had officially reached their fugly stage of development. Gangly legs, big feet, uneven tufts of hair mixed with wacky feather patterns. Still, they were cute little buggers in their own way.

As I approached, I picked up our friendliest one so far. A Golden Comet we'd named Gertie, after Eric's maternal grandmother. Gertie's little squawk drew Eric's attention. He had two roofing nails in his mouth.

"You're early," he said through gritted teeth.

"Looks good," I said. It did. He'd built the coop to look like a small barn, matching the green and white paint on my actual barn down by the lake.

Eric slipped the nails into his back pocket and climbed down from his ladder. Gertie let out a strangled little cluck. Eric scratched her under her beak. Two seconds of that and her eyes started to close. I set her gently on the ground.

"I tried to call you," he said. "You spent the night in your office, didn't you?"

We walked down the hill together. Eric took a porch chair and sat under the shade. He waited for me while I walked inside, kicked off my heels and took off my blouse. I had a cami underneath. I grabbed two glasses of cold lemonade and brought them out.

"Good thinking," Eric said, grateful for the beverage. I took the chair next to him.

"Sorry," I said. "I should have texted you. Things took a bit of a left turn on the Doyle case. I actually wouldn't mind running it by you."

"What about confidentiality?"

"I don't think this falls under that. It's not directly about my client and I haven't even discussed it with him."

I quickly filled Eric in on my suspicions about Marcus Savitch's bar exam fraud.

Eric let out a whistle when I got to the end of it.

"Do you know anything about stuff like that?" I asked. "Have you ever worked on a case like it? Maybe on one of your task forces?"

"Not really," he said. "I've done some work on identity theft. I suppose that's adjacent. But how does any of this tie in with your case? You're trying to prove your guy didn't commit murder."

"It's a stretch," I said. "But Marcus Savitch was a material witness. If Daria Moreau found out about his scheme, what if he decided to silence her?"

"It'd take money," Eric said. "A lot of it."

"Which he has."

"And arrogance."

"He has that in abundance," I said.

"It's just ... dumb. I mean, I get how he wouldn't have had an opportunity to call it off in the moment. But you said that bar admission date shows up for every lawyer licensed in the state?"

"Yep."

"And he voluntarily had to file a motion to get sworn in. It doesn't happen automatically."

"Nope."

Eric scratched his head. "So why wouldn't the idiot just wait a few months and file his motion the following spring or something? I mean, sure, the court and the bar examiners would know when he passed. But nobody else would. That's definitely not the kind of thing I'd have thought to run down if I were lead detective on that girl's murder."

"Exactly what I was thinking," I said. "And who knows why Marcus didn't try to cover his tracks a little better? Other than what you said. Arrogance. And the fact the odds were with him that nobody was ever going to piece it together."

"You think that's enough to get your guy a new trial?"

"Not even close," I said. "But it does cast a more suspicious light on Marcus Savitch's version of events. As far as I'm aware, and I could be wrong, neither my client nor the other material witness, Kade Barclay, knew anything about it."

"And they weren't part of it," Eric said. "You're sure."

"I guess I can't say that. I can only say that Andrew and Kade didn't sit for the bar that week. Andrew never did. And Kade took it in Ohio the following year. So if they were part of this fraud scheme, they managed to call it off in time."

"Except that doesn't make sense either because their phones were confiscated too, right?"

"Right."

My phone rang. Jeanie.

"Hey," I answered.

"Hey, kiddo, how'd it go with Folger?"

"Good. She confirmed Marcus Savitch wasn't the guy she recognized as sitting next to her. Her story was pretty compelling. She noticed him. She's willing to provide a description and testify to all of it if I need her to."

"Good. Good. You with Eric?"

"I am."

"Put me on speaker. I have a question for him."

I did as she asked and set my phone on the arm of my chair.

"Hey, Jeanie," he said.

"So ... here's what I've got," Jeanie said. "Tori got a hold of Savitch's bar exam application. She has the driver's license number that was used. I had some help from state police getting Savitch's actual DL number. Three guesses as to what it showed. The first two don't count."

"No match," I said.

"Bingo."

"That's what I would have expected," Eric said. "It means whoever Savitch or his old man hired to take the test for him was probably part of a larger ring. These guys are smart. And the rich guys who hire them usually aren't. They use a fake driver's license number and fake ID so that it can't be traced back to Savitch. He's somewhat protected."

"Unless somebody realizes the guy sitting at the test table isn't the same guy whose name is on the application."

"Right. If you're asking me ..." Eric started.

"We are," Jeanie and I said in unison.

"Eric, I need you," I whispered.

He reluctantly nodded. "If you ask me what your next step is, Cass, do you still have your contact at the Bureau?"

"Lee Cannon," I said. "I haven't spoken to him in a long while. But theoretically, yes."

"Then I'd give him a call. Like now. Have him run that fake driver's license number. Sometimes these guys use the same ones from a pool. It's usually someone deceased. Then they mix and match the IDs to photographs of the imposters."

"That's a great idea," Jeanie said. "When are you gonna tell Doyle all this?"

"Let me talk to Lee first," I said. "See if there's any there, there with the ID. Ultimately, if we can find this imposter, I'd sure like to have a conversation."

Next to me, Eric scowled.

I clicked off with Jeanie and pulled Lee Cannon up in my contacts. I said a silent prayer that he'd answer the phone. We weren't on the best terms.

Miraculously, he answered almost immediately.

"Leary?"

"Hi, Lee," I said.

"Am I hearing the voice of a ghost?"

I detected no animosity in his tone. I briefly explained my purpose in calling him.

"Hey, Cannon," Eric chimed in. "It's Wray."

Lee paused before answering. "You on this too?"

"Sort of," I answered. "I'm picking his brain. It was Eric's idea to call you."

"Gotcha," Lee said. "Yeah. Send over what you've got. I know they were running a sting out of the Chicago Field Office a year or so ago. Same kind of thing. People hiring ringers to take SATs, ACTs, Medical Boards. I don't know about bar exams specifically but it would stand to reason. I'll reach out to some agents I know who were part of it."

"I really appreciate it," I said. As we spoke, Jeanie sent me images of both Marcus Savitch's bar application and his current driver's license. I forwarded them to Special Agent Cannon. I thanked him again and clicked off.

Eric was still scowling.

"What is it?" I asked, though I could already guess.

"You know I don't love the idea of you interviewing some guy who makes his living taking tests for other people."

"Relax, he's probably some harmless nerd," I said.

"It's not the harmless nerd I'm worried about. If Cannon's right and this is part of a more sophisticated ring, it's the nerd's bosses I'm worried about. You're gonna hate me for suggesting it. But if and when you find the guy, I wanna go with you."

I smiled up at him, then rested my head on his shoulder. "I don't hate it. I don't mind getting the band back together. Even if it's a one-night-only performance."

He kissed the top of my head and let out a growl I'd come to know as his way of giving into me, but protesting anyway. As I craned my neck and kissed him back, Gertie, the chick, hopped onto the porch and promptly shat on it.

Chapter 12

"I THINK DELILAH MIGHT BE A DANIEL," Vangie said. After a bit of a foot chase, she'd caught the little Barred Rock chick. She was one of my favorites. She'd become somewhat of a flock leader and tended to break up squabbles between the rest of them.

"Don't tell Eric," I said.

"A million years ago I lived with this guy whose mom lived on a small farm. They had chickens. She had some like this one. But look, see how its comb is getting pinkish here? And put your finger under its beak."

I did as she asked. I felt fleshy little nubbins.

"Wattles," she said. "This bird's what? A month old? Too red, too prominent, too fast."

She set the chicken down and she ... he ran off to join the others currently seeking shade under a large bush in the side yard.

Delilah/Daniel's father was currently out in the fishing boat with my brother Joe. Vangie cupped a hand over her brow to try and spot them.

"They're in the north cove," I said. "That's where Joe said the crappie are bedding down."

"He likes it here," Vangie said. I walked out on the dock with her. We stepped onto the pontoon and settled on the long leather seats. It was pure sun today. Eighty degrees on Memorial Day. But there was already a frost warning for tomorrow night.

"Who likes it here? Joe?"

"No, silly. Eric. You know, I didn't take him as much of a fisherman in the beginning."

"He's lived in Delphi his whole life," I said. "Just like we did."

Vangie gave me a sidelong glance. "*We* haven't lived here our whole lives. We're the only ones who haven't. Joe and Matty? I don't think they've ever been west of Milwaukee, or south of Florida."

For the early part of her adulthood, my sister had been somewhat of a vagabond. She wanted to be anywhere but Michigan. I suppose that had been true for me, too. For a time. Now, I couldn't think of being anywhere else.

"I wish he would," I said. "Joe. He's been different since Katie left him. Quieter. I think it might be good for him to just go on a trip somewhere. Clear his head."

Vangie rolled her eyes. "I think his head's clear enough. Or would be if he wasn't letting his you-know-what do his thinking for him." She gestured in a circle between her legs.

"What now? What are you talking about?"

She reached for the cooler between us and pulled out a hard lemonade. It was just the two of us today. Jessa was spending the weekend with friends. Emma and her new boyfriend (the older man Joe didn't like) had gone to visit his parents in Traverse City. Morning sickness hit Tori hard and Matty stayed home to take care of her. I couldn't remember the last Memorial Day weekend I didn't have a houseful.

Vangie twisted off her bottle cap. "I thought you knew. I figured he would have told you."

"He hasn't, but it sounds like you'd better."

Vangie put her drink in the holder next to her. "I don't know exactly how long it's been going on. Or how many times, but Joe and Katie hooked up again."

My jaw actually dropped. "What do you mean, they hooked up?" Though I knew it was a stupid question. I knew exactly what she meant.

Vangie shrugged. "I don't know. I think it was a month or so ago. She just showed up on his doorstep, crying her eyes out. Telling him maybe she made a mistake."

"And he didn't throw her off the porch?" I said. I didn't know if I'd ever forgive my former sister-in-law for cheating on my brother.

"Guess not. Anyway, I don't know if it was that day, but they hooked up sometime after that."

"He's sleeping with her? Our brother. Is sleeping with his ex-wife. His very married ex-wife. What the hell is he thinking?"

"That's my point," Vangie said. "He's not."

"And how do you know all of this? There's no way he confided in you."

"He didn't. But Matty knows." Though they weren't officially twins, Matty and Vangie had always been extremely close. It was like that for Joe and me as the two oldest. At least up until now. Though it would make sense he'd want to keep something like this from me. He knew what I'd say.

"And how does Matty know?"

"He saw them together. He showed up early at Joe's house sometime last week. He needed a tool or something. He just went to the garage, figuring Joe was already at work. Well, he heard them. Laughing. He recognized Katie's voice and went to see what's what. He said he never made it past the kitchen window. They were ... uh ... at the table."

"So?"

"Cass," my sister said, lowering her eyes. "Don't be dense. I mean they were *on* the table."

"Great," I muttered. "I've had lunch with him at that table. Did Matty confront him?"

"Not then. He said he tried a couple of days later but Joe told him to mind his own business. So he has."

"Except for telling you. And you're telling me."

"You wish I hadn't?"

I shook my head. "Of course not. At the same time, Joe has to know if Matty knows we all know. This is a bad idea. It won't end well. Do you think Emma knows?"

"Katie's not her mother," Vangie said.

"But there's no love lost between them. You're the one who helped her vandalize Katie's car last year."

Vangie waved me off. "We were just blowing off steam. Emma earned the right."

I wanted to ask her more. But Joe and Eric were just pulling into the dock.

"We limited out," Joe said. "Guess what we're having for dinner."

Eric opened the live well. It was teeming with very angry fish. I couldn't help it. I glared at my brother. He caught my eye and knew immediately what had me ticked off. As Eric shut the well, he saw the exchange between us.

"I don't wanna talk about it," Joe said gruffly.

"Well, apparently we all know about it now," I said.

"I don't," Eric said. "Do I want to?"

I said yes at the exact same moment my brother said no.

Eric lifted his hands in surrender. "Okay. Sibling stuff. Just let me get outta the line of fire." He stepped onto the dock and holstered both his and Joe's fishing poles. Then he headed back up to the house to corral the chickens back into their brooder. One more week and the coop would be ready.

"Don't," Joe said as he stepped off the boat.

"Joe, she's married. I mean, that's number one. Numbers two through one hundred are also pretty bad."

"Stop!" he said. "It's nobody else's business. I don't get in the middle of your love life."

Vangie and I both laughed. "Joe, you've pretty much planted a flag and set up lawn chairs in the middle of my love life," I said. "Who are you kidding?"

He didn't argue. But he didn't give me any other answers either. He walked up the dock to help Eric with the chickens.

"Let it go, Cass," Vangie warned me. She stood up and stepped off the pontoon. I got up with her. "He doesn't want us telling him I told you so. I know you're right. He knows you're right. This will end in disaster. But when's the last time Joe did anything just because you told him to? Let's just enjoy the day. I'm gonna go help clean the fish."

I slammed the pontoon door shut behind me as I followed her up the dock. Eric was just putting Delilah/Daniel in the brooder.

"He's a dude," he said. "Damn. How much would you hate me if I kept him anyway?"

"It's not me you need to worry about, it's the neighbors. And if he cock-a-doodle-doos all hours of the night, maybe we can make some really delicious soup."

I was kidding, but the look on Eric's face told me just what he thought of that idea.

Joe walked past me, holding his electric filet knife and a grudge. I wasn't in the mood.

"Don't look at me," I shouted at his back. "I'm not the idiot."

Joe flipped me a middle finger behind his head.

"How about neutral corners?" Eric said. "He was in a good mood. So were you."

We walked up to the house together. "You wanna tell me what it's about though?"

As we walked into the kitchen, I turned to him. "Oh, just your average train wreck. He's apparently been sleeping with Katie again."

Eric's face didn't change. Didn't register the hint of shock.

"You knew?" I asked.

"Not officially. No. He didn't confide in me. But I had a feeling. I saw her pulling out of his driveway the other day when I passed by his house."

I threw my hands up, then planted them on my hips. "So he's not even being remotely discreet? How long do you think it's gonna take to get back to her husband, Tom? If he doesn't know already."

"He's right. It's Joe's business. Let it go for now."

I had a million other things to say on the subject, but my phone started ringing on its charger. Eric was closer to it. He looked at the screen.

"Lee Cannon," he said, pulling it off the charger and handing my phone to me.

"On Memorial Day?" I said. I put the phone on the counter and clicked the speaker button.

"Hey, Lee," I said. "Shouldn't you be enjoying a cold one by the grill or something?"

"Ha," Cannon said. By the staticky sound behind him, I guessed he was driving. "No rest for the wicked, or something like that."

"Don't suppose you're calling just to wish me a peaceful holiday or some such," I said.

"Sure. All that. But I've got some interesting news on those IDs you wanted me to run. You have a second?"

I looked out the window. Joe and Vangie were wrangling the fish. I couldn't hear what they were saying, but by Vangie's posture, she was giving him crap. Joe's face turned redder by the second.

"Of course," I said to Cannon. Eric settled himself on the counter stool, ready to listen with me.

"I'm here too, Cannon," Eric said.

"Okay. Good. So the one number traces to Marcus Savitch. I think you already knew that."

"Yes," I said.

"The other popped up in that sting operation I was telling you about. It's been used four other times in the last five years. The bar exam you're asking about, two in Illinois, one in Ohio."

"How is this guy passing bars in multiple states, aren't they different?" Eric asked.

"Not exactly," I said. "Not all of it. Most states use the UBL now. It's a multi-state portion of the exam. It's going to cover mostly the same material no matter what state you take it in. Then there's generally a state specific section, but if a person does well enough on the UBL portion, they can probably pass overall without too much trouble. In Michigan, it used to be that if you hit a certain score on the multi-state portion, the examiners wouldn't even grade the state essays. They didn't grade mine."

"Okay, nerd," Cannon said. Eric stifled a laugh. "Anyway, it was a pretty big operation. A lot of high-profile clients got into some serious trouble. Though, for the most part, the clients were pretty well shielded. That's why it's so expensive and why the clientele were pretty elite. But these guys know how to hire contractors who will keep their mouths shut. So if any of the imposter test takers were to get caught, they wouldn't say anything that would implicate who paid them to do it."

"How much?" Eric asked. "Just out of curiosity?"

"A lot," Cannon answered. "Around a hundred grand."

I whistled. "Well, that would have been chump change for the Savitch family. From what I understand, Marcus himself doesn't have that kind of bankroll. So I think it's fair to conclude his father was in on the deal."

"He might have even insisted on it," Eric said.

"Were any arrests made?" I asked Lee.

"A bunch," he said. "The Bureau pretty much shut down the arm of this thing here in the mid-west. But this particular hydra has many heads."

"I'm sure," Eric said.

"Thanks," I said. "I don't suppose you have any good ideas on how I might go about finding Marcus Savitch's test taker? I'd really like to talk to him."

Eric gave me that concerned look again.

"I'm working on it," Lee said. "It's gonna take some time to match the ID numbers to the actual people who took these tests. We've got several in custody, but they all have at least a dozen aliases between them."

"Anything you can find out would be great," I said.

"No problem. I'll say you always seem to have something interesting going on, Leary."

"We'll talk soon," I said, thanking him again.

"Well," Eric said. "Looks like you've got a real goose to chase with this one. What's your next move?"

"I think it's well past time I pay a visit to my client."

Chapter 13

SOMETHING HAD CHANGED about Andrew Doyle when I sat down with him for our second face-to-face meeting. He looked hopeful, meeting my eyes, even smiling when he saw me.

"You look well," I said.

"I feel better. Grace just brought Beckett for a visit. I'm surprised you didn't run into them on your way in."

"I'm glad. And I'm glad you're in a good mood. I've brought some news that might brighten your day even more."

Andrew's expression froze, as if he knew my next words had the power to shatter him or change his life forever.

I'd brought a few documents with me and spread them on the table. A photograph of Marcus Savitch's driver's license. The front page copy of his bar exam application. The exam seating chart. A blown-up copy of his entry in the bar journal showing his date of admission. I put my finger on that date and tapped it.

"See anything interesting about this?"

Andrew leaned forward, still keeping that guarded expression on his face.

"I don't know what I'm looking at."

I had one more document to pull out. I'd made a copy of the front page of Marcus's written statement, showing the start and ending time of his interview the night Daria's body was found. Andrew picked up my documents, one by one, studied them, then slowly placed each face down on the table between us. He folded his hands and sat back, not saying a word.

"I can prove Marcus Savitch had an imposter take the bar exam for him two days after Daria was murdered. Did you know?"

Nothing. No change in his expression. Silence.

"Andrew, do you understand what this means?"

"What does it have to do with me?"

"It means he lied. Marcus Savitch is a liar and a fraud. He's been holding himself out as a licensed attorney, practicing law for two years. That's a crime. He could go to jail for it."

"I still don't see what it has to do with me?"

I reared my head back as if he'd slapped me. It kind of felt like he had.

"You haven't answered my question. Did you know he was planning this? That he did it?"

Everything changed about him. The bright eyes he had when I first walked in. His upright posture. I watched him crumple in front of me, becoming the beaten-down pessimist he'd been the day we first met.

"No," he said. "I didn't know."

"What if Daria did?"

"She never told me."

"Marcus admitted to arguing with her that night. Witnesses saw him with her, just as they saw you with her. A witness, one of your party guests, Jason Lin, testified it was a heated exchange between them. Marcus claimed it was about her anger at how big the party got. I think he lied. My hunch is that she somehow found out he was planning to cheat on that test. You tell me. How do you think she would have reacted to that news? How would you?"

"I don't ... I don't know." He slumped in his chair.

"She'd be angry. I know I would if I found out one of my study partners ... one of my friends ... was planning to scam the exam while I busted my butt studying and worrying about it. If she knew ... if she threatened to expose him, it changes everything."

He gave me that stony silence again. Why? It made me suspicious he was the one lying now. If he knew, why in the world wouldn't he have told me? Or more importantly, told his lawyer during the first trial. Unless ...

"Was this your plan, too?" I asked. "Did Marcus rope you into something? Was there someone else waiting to take the bar on your behalf?"

"No!" He slammed a fist on the table. "I would never do something like that. Neither would Daria. Neither would Kade."

"But Marcus would and did."

"So what? What does it matter now?"

I couldn't believe what I was hearing. "It matters because it gives Marcus a motive for silencing Daria Moreau."

"You can't prove she knew."

"I wouldn't have to prove she knew. Neither would have Russ Nadler. Don't play dumb. You understand the burdens of proof. You have a basic understanding of trial practice. Marcus took the stand against you. He basically told the jury Daria was afraid of you. He called you a liar, saying you weren't with him later that night. And I strongly suspect he told you what to say to the cops. I think it was his plan to have you all give each other an alibi. But he sold you out. Betrayed you. He knew you'd be the one to follow his direction. Then he could throw suspicion right at you by telling the cops otherwise."

"No."

"No? No, what? Good lord, Andrew. At a minimum, this would have been enough to impeach Marcus's testimony at trial. His credibility. He is a liar and a fraud. And I think everything he's done since the minute Daria died was aimed at covering his own tracks. This was a loose end."

I picked up the seating chart. "I have a witness who sat at this table with the man pretending to be Marcus. She is willing to go on the record that Marcus Savitch, the real Marcus Savitch, wasn't the person taking that exam along with her. He's caught. I think this could be enough of a wedge to at least get you a new trial. Nadler never pursued it. It only took me a day to put it all together with solid proof. He had Marcus on the stand! The prosecution didn't bother asking him when he was admitted to the bar. Nadler never followed up on it. This would have been reasonable doubt. You know it."

"I don't know anything. And I can't let you do this. We're not going down this road. I'm not going to destroy Marcus's life."

Never mind feeling like I'd been slapped. I now felt like he'd blown a hole straight through my chest.

"I'm telling you I think he might have murdered Daria. Are you telling me that doesn't matter to you?"

He clenched his jaw so hard I thought his head might crack like a walnut.

"This is what you hired me to do. You asked me to review your file. See if there was anything Nadler screwed up that would have made a difference. Well, he resoundingly did. This is what you paid me for."

"No. My family didn't hire you to go after Marcus Savitch."

"Why are you protecting him?"

As soon as I asked, the answer seemed to creep up my spine like a snake. I felt like I was choking on it.

"You're afraid of him," I said. "He's got something on you. What is it? Andrew, for god's sake, what really happened that night?"

"Find another way," he said.

"I don't think there is another way."

"There has to be. Because I didn't kill Daria. Maybe there was something wrong with the way they tested the physical evidence. Maybe there was another witness who can say I wasn't out there when Daria was supposed to have been killed. Because I wasn't. You said Nadler or the cops didn't do much to track down any other people at that party. There were dozens. I don't know how many for sure. It was a lot. I was in the house most of the night after I talked to Daria. I was trying to clean up the house. I was feeling pretty bad about myself. Somebody had to have seen me."

"And you still aren't giving me honest answers. You think Marcus killed Daria? Don't you? So why are you taking the fall for it?"

"I'm not taking the fall. If I were taking the fall, why would I have even hired you?"

I gathered my papers together and stuffed them into my bag. My head started to pound. Probably because I felt like I was banging it against the wall.

"You didn't hire me," I said. "Your family did. They're more invested in proving your innocence than you seem to be. Maybe they should know about this, too."

"You can't," he said, with fear back in his voice. "You absolutely can't. You have a fiduciary duty to me. Not them. It doesn't matter who's paying your fee. Everything we say here is confidential. I don't want you telling anyone about what you think Marcus did. I'm serious. I'm not willing to buy my freedom by destroying someone else. I won't do it. I couldn't live with myself."

"But you can live with yourself, letting a possible murderer go free. You cared about Daria. You still care about her. What happened to that? You're worried about protecting Marcus when you should be worried about getting justice for your friend."

"I've said all I can say. Not this way. You do not have my consent to report Marcus to the bar. Are we clear?"

I wanted to strangle him. I took a breath, fighting to keep my temper from taking over.

"Fine," I said. "But right now, I don't know if I can continue to represent you."

That got his attention. "Then I'm sunk. It's over."

"So let me do my damn job!"

The door buzzed behind him. A guard walked in. "Time's up, Doyle. I need to get you back."

Andrew rose. "We're done here. And Cass, it's not that I don't appreciate everything you're doing. I do. More than you realize. It's just ... I can't do it this way. I wouldn't be able to live with myself. I'm sorry. I mean that. I *am* sorry."

"Tell that to Daria," I muttered. "Tell that to your wife and son. Is covering Marcus's ass more important than they are?"

His face went ashen when I said it. But he didn't change his mind. He simply turned his back on me and walked out the door.

I was at a complete loss. Nothing Andrew said made any sense unless Marcus Savitch had some influence over him. To the marrow of my bones I knew that had to be the problem. But he was right about something. I couldn't act on my suspicions about Marcus without his permission. I couldn't report him to the bar. Yet. Only ... that didn't mean I couldn't try finding out who Marcus hired to cheat for him.

I gathered my things. I wasn't sure what I'd be able to do with Marcus's imposter if I could find him. If he told me anything at all. But I was determined to follow this thread and get to the truth. Wherever that might lead.

Chapter 14

"He's lying," Emma said. "I mean, he has to be lying."

It was just the three of us. Emma had found me staring at the whiteboard in the conference room. I'd blown up four photographs and taped them to the top of the board side by side. Andrew's mugshot, Marcus's headshot from the Carter Baldwin website, Kade's law school yearbook portrait. I'd drawn thick red lines from the bottoms of each to a point, like an upside down tree. At that point, I taped a photograph of Daria Moreau.

"One of them is lying," Jeanie said.

"Or they're all lying," I said.

"It has to be one of them," Emma said. "Right? Or do you think all three of them had something to do with killing Daria, but Andrew for whatever reason got set up to take the fall?"

I plopped down in a chair. My head was spinning from all of these questions. I'd asked them of myself over and over, barely getting a wink of sleep last night.

"He won't help himself," I said. "He's protecting Marcus. I can only think of two real reasons why that's true. Either Andrew really did kill Daria and he's got enough of a conscience not to want to throw him under the bus for his own crime ... or ... Marcus Savitch has something on him."

"Blackmail?" Emma said. "It would have to be something pretty big in order for a man to be willing to give up his freedom for the rest of his life rather than getting out."

"And I can't think of anything worse than murdering another person," Jeanie said. "But Andrew's already in prison for that."

"Which means it's got to be someone else he's protecting," I said.

"Kade?" Emma asked.

I shook my head. "That's not my sense of it. From everything I know, Kade and Andrew have barely spoken since the night of Daria's murder."

"We need to know who's been visiting Andrew in prison over the last two years," Jeanie said. "That's easy enough to find out."

"Put Tori on it," I said. "That's something she can do from home. I'm kind of hoping I can get her to realize she can still do plenty from the sanctity of her own living room and still be part of this team."

"You're in denial." Jeanie smiled. "She's moving on, Cass. But she's an amazing mom to your nephew and whoever else comes along. Not everyone wants what you do."

I waved her off. That was a bigger conversation for another time.

"So, where do we go from here?" Emma asked. "If Andrew won't let you use Marcus's lies to his own advantage, we're right back where we started. Empty-handed."

"I'm not giving up on changing his mind just yet. He told me not to disclose what I know about Marcus. He didn't tell me I couldn't try tracking down who took the test for him. I've got Agent Cannon looking into it. The fake driver's license number is all over that sting operation the FBI did. He should be able to track who it was used by. With any luck, he's in the system. Maybe even sitting in a prison cell."

"And if he *is* in a prison cell," Jeanie said. "Seems to me that might give you some leverage. Maybe if he cooperates with you, the US Attorney might look more favorably on him."

"Maybe," I said. "But Cannon says these guys get paid so well because of the known risk that they'll get caught. They don't give up the principals easily."

"It's still the best lead you've got," Jeanie said.

"Except even if you do find him and he's willing to talk, how much do you think this imposter will actually know about Marcus Savitch, let alone some woman he might have murdered?"

"I can't ..."

Before I could finish my sentence, Miranda poked her head in. "Sorry to interrupt. But Grace Doyle just showed up. I put her downstairs in Jeanie's office so I wouldn't risk her overhearing your conversation from next door."

"Good thinking," I said. "Did she say what she's here about? We don't have an appointment, do we?"

"No," Miranda said. "She said she got a babysitter. And Andrew's parents are at some small animal auction in Elkhart. She said this was the only window of time she could drive up here without either of them knowing."

Jeanie shot me a look. This was strange. And it had to be more than just coincidental since I'd only just talked to Grace's husband the day before.

"Use my office for as long as you need it," Jeanie said. "I'm going to get started taking a deeper look at Marcus Savitch. And if you don't mind, Andrew Doyle's family."

"Why?" Emma said.

"Because if Andrew's trying to protect anyone besides himself, someone he's willing to go to prison for for a crime he didn't commit ... betting odds favor people he loves."

"Maybe that's why Grace is here," Emma said.

It was on my mind, too. And there was only one way to find out.

GRACE DOYLE SEEMED SMALLER SOMEHOW from the first time I met her. Then, she'd been sandwiched between her in-laws with a baby carrier in front of her. In some ways, she'd hidden behind them. But now, all alone on Jeanie's couch, she looked straight-up terrified, wringing her hands on her lap.

"Good morning, Grace," I said. I reached out to shake her hand. She took mine with hesitation, then pulled back, clasping her hands in her lap. I took the chair opposite her.

"I know you've been to see Andrew," she said. "We talked last night on the phone. He told me."

"Good," I said. "Do you mind telling me what he told you about our meeting?"

"Just that you had it. He clammed up when I asked him what you said. And he ... I don't know. I could hear something different in his voice. Or rather, something familiar."

"What do you mean?"

"I mean, before you got involved, Andrew was just defeated. He had no fight left in him. It's like my father-in-law told you. Ever since the trial started, Andrew's just been passive. Then when he realized you could help him, everything changed. He's been animated. Hopeful. Like himself again. But last night, he was back to being a man who's given up on himself. It's breaking my heart and I don't know what to do. So I came here, because I'm hoping you still think you can help him. And I want to know if there's anything more I should be doing."

"I appreciate that," I said. "Does he know you're here?"

She shook her head. "And I hope you won't mention it. But Cass, last night Andrew told me he wanted a divorce. He said he never should have married me and dragged me into this. He said Beckett and I would be better off starting over and forgetting about him."

"That had to be hard to hear," I said. "I'm sorry. And I'm also sorry I can't tell you what we talked about. This is what I meant when we all met with your in-laws. Andrew's my client, even though your fundraising is paying his legal fee. If Andrew doesn't give written permission, I can't disclose our conversations."

Her face looked pained. "Please, I know it was something. Something that changed his whole attitude about his case.

Whatever it is, if you found something you think makes him look guilty, you have to know it's not true. Or it's wrong. It has to be. I know he didn't do this. I know he didn't kill that girl. It isn't in him. I know him. I've known him since we were in kindergarten. He wouldn't hurt anyone like that. No matter how mad he was. He's gentle. Caring. He doesn't have a temper or lose control. And even if it was an accident, even if she just fell and hurt herself ... there's no way Andrew wouldn't have called for help."

"Grace ..."

"No!" she shouted. When I reached for her, she jerked her shoulders backward, out of my grasp. "No. No. No!" She was on her feet. Her face turned purple as her emotions rose.

"Grace, please ..."

"He wouldn't just leave her without calling for help. He wouldn't leave her to rot in some scummy pond with fetid water like some rotting fish. God. That isn't my husband. That isn't the man I fell in love with."

I didn't know if she was trying to convince me, or herself. I couldn't begin to imagine what this whole thing had done to her.

"Grace, please, sit down," I said.

This time, she complied. I expected her to break down completely. She didn't. Though she trembled, she kept my gaze and her emotions in check.

"I have to ask you," I said. "How well do you really know Andrew? You'd been out of contact for a long time. Years."

She nodded. "While he was away at school. Yes."

"Did you know Marcus Savitch or Kade Barclay? Or Daria Moreau, for that matter?"

She shook her head. "No. We'd drifted apart while Andrew was in college. I found somebody else. I knew Andrew wanted other things. Bigger things. I like it in Walkerton. I like my small town. The farm. It's good there. Andrew didn't want that for himself and I understood. But when he came home that summer, he was just so ... I don't know. He was like the boy I fell in love with all those years ago. And he needed me. For the first time since we were eighteen years old, I knew he needed me."

"He does need you," I said. "More than you realize. Probably more than he realizes."

"So you have to change his mind," she said. "You have to convince him his life is worth fighting for. Beckett and I are worth fighting for. We're not better off without him."

"I wish I could, Grace," I said. "I wish it were that simple."

"You can't give up on him."

I wanted to yell from the top of my lungs that I wasn't the one giving up. He was. He was blocking me from doing the one thing that had the strongest chance of getting him a new trial. Only I couldn't breathe a word of it to Grace.

"I'm not giving up on him," I said. "But you're right that he's the one giving up. I'm not. I promise."

"What can I do?" she said. It was the right question and I thanked God she asked it. I tried to phrase my next question carefully. I couldn't tip her off about what I suspected. But Grace was probably much closer to the truth than she understood.

"Grace, is there anything you can think of that Andrew would keep from you? Or his parents?"

"What do you mean?"

"I don't know. Maybe money problems? I know your in-laws have struggled to make ends meet in the past. Do you know how their farm business is doing now? The actual farm?"

"Fine. Better than fine, I think. But it comes in cycles. Sometimes they're up. Sometimes they're down."

"But now they're up?" I asked. "Do you know when that turned around?"

"Why?"

"I'm just trying to get a sense of the timeline of events over the last couple of years. I didn't have the benefit of knowing Andrew when all of this went down with Daria. I'm just trying to piece everything together."

"I can't really speak to that. We weren't talking much that last year of law school for him. But when he came home, you know, after the murder. Jenny told you she thought he was going to kill himself. She called me. She thought maybe I could get through to him. So I did. Believe me, I wasn't looking for it. I don't know. Something just happened. We both realized how we used to be. And it seemed ... natural. God. So many people told me I was crazy. That Andrew had way too much baggage for me to hitch my wagon to him all over again."

"You loved him," I said.

"I guess we never stopped. Then Beckett came along. I know the timing wasn't ... um ... ideal. We didn't plan it. But when I found out I was pregnant, it was just a miracle. Andrew came to life again. I did too. Now ... he just seems willing to let the family we wanted to build float away."

"Has Andrew ever told you who he thinks killed Daria?" I asked. A risky question. I couldn't reveal Andrew's confidences, but I'd just asked his wife to reveal them.

She got quiet and still. I knew I'd hit on something. I felt acid in my heart. I'd just asked the million-dollar question. Part of me wanted to take it back.

"No." Her voice was so soft, I almost didn't hear it.

"No?"

She shook her head. "No."

"Did you ever ask?"

"No. Well, not in so many words."

"But if you knew it wasn't him ... Grace, I know I'm probably stepping over a line here. But I hope you understand I'm on your side. We both want to clear Andrew's name. Me, because I don't think he did this. You don't either, but your life is with him. I get that. So I guess I'm asking you to break whatever confidence he has with you. But it's to try and save him."

"I know," she said. "But no. We don't talk about Daria very much. I think he thinks I'll get angry. I'm not stupid. I know he had feelings for her ... or at least he thought he did. I know that's why people think he killed her. That she rejected him and it broke his heart. Maybe I'm naïve or delusional by saying this. But I don't think his heart was broken. I think he'd had too much to drink. He had a crush on this girl. And it was warranted. I get it. She was beautiful. Exotic in her way. So far removed from Walkerton. From ... me. She spoke French. She had this big life before she came to Michigan. I think she hurt Andrew's feelings. But he wasn't jilted. She wasn't the love of his life. Whatever happened out in that grotto, it wasn't something that would have pushed him to the edge."

"But somebody else was pushed to the edge," I said. "Andrew must have a theory about who that was."

She shrugged. "Not that he's confided in me. No."

"What about you? Surely you've got a theory."

"I really don't. I didn't know any of those people he was friends with. I didn't visit him at U of M. He's really walled off that part of his life from me. He never wanted to talk about the trial when it was happening. It killed me. I couldn't be there for him then. But the stress of it all, I went into early labor. That's why they put me on bedrest."

"Who do you think did this?" I wanted to scream. Was it Marcus? What does he have on your family?

"I really don't know," she whispered.

"Can you tell me what you know about his friendship with Kade Barclay and Marcus Savitch?"

She shrugged. "I told you. I've never met them. He talked about Marcus more than Kade."

"In what way?"

"He was intimidated by him," she said. "He had so much money. Andrew is trusting and loyal. He always has been. To be honest, it's one of the things I love about him. He just has this pure soul. But I don't think Marcus Savitch was a good friend to him."

"Why do you say that?" I asked.

"I don't know. Well, obviously, Marcus and Kade weren't loyal to Andrew after Daria died. It felt like they ganged up on him. But before that, the way Andrew would talk about him, it seemed to me like Marcus liked to brag about being rich. Looked down on Andrew for being from modest means. That's the impression I got."

She didn't say she thought Marcus was guilty. But I felt like we were having a different, implied conversation under the surface. She zoned in on Marcus, not Kade.

"You asked me if I knew who killed Daria." Grace paused. "I have no idea. Andrew's never given me a theory. It was probably somebody random. Some drunk. Maybe it was an accident. Maybe they didn't mean to push her. Who knows. I only know Andrew's innocent. You have to prove it. Can you?"

I wanted to tell her yes. I wanted to take the worry out of her eyes and her heart. I couldn't. Not if Andrew refused to take the chains off me.

"I can try," I said. "But the truth is, I really don't know."

"Not without Andrew's cooperation," she said, completing my thoughts. She rose to leave, slinging her purse over her shoulder. This time, she was the one to hold her hand out to shake mine.

"Talk to him," I told her. "Convince him that I know what I'm doing. Convince him to rejoin the fight. Use whatever you have to. Yourself. Beckett. His parents. Fight dirty. Do you know what I mean?"

She had a sad half-smile on her face. "I'll try again."

Then I hugged her. Part of me was furious with Andrew Doyle. He may not have killed Daria Moreau, but he was leaving a trail of victims in his own wake anyway.

Chapter 15

WHEN JEANIE CALLED me at five a.m. the following morning, I expected it to be an emergency. Jeanie Mills hadn't woken up earlier than eight o'clock in years.

"Sorry, kid," she opened with. "Nobody died. But I just got off the phone with Michael Moreau, Daria's father. They're apparently early risers. Anyway, they're in town. Ish. He's meeting with clients from Henry Ford Hospital, in Detroit. His wife's with him. She's also got some business at the Detroit Institute of Art. Anyway, he called to tell me that they'll both be done with their meetings by nine. He said they'd meet you for coffee. Nine thirty. Darby's on the River. I had Miranda clear your schedule. You're free and clear for the day."

I rubbed the crust from my eyes. Eric was already gone. He had one of his freelance gigs with the DNR this morning. I yawned.

"That's great, Jeanie. Thank you. Did he mention why he had a change of heart?" For the past couple of weeks, Jeanie had been trying to get the Moreaus to return her phone calls. So far, things had gone as we expected. Daria's parents wanted nothing to do with the team hired to defend their daughter's convicted killer.

"He did not," she answered. "He was abrupt in his call. And it was basically be there today, or never call him again. I have no idea what they'll be like. There's probably a good chance they won't even show. But it's the best shot we've got. If you really want Daria's medical records without a court order, it's now or never."

I thanked her again and hung up the phone. It would only take me an hour to get to Detroit. But I planned to get to Darby's a half an hour early. It was a popular lunch spot for anyone who worked downtown. If either Moreau showed up, then got cold feet, I could try to flag them. The trouble was, I wasn't sure exactly what to say.

I NEEDN'T HAVE WORRIED about getting stood up. But it was a good thing I showed up early. Darby's had an outdoor patio section overlooking the Detroit River. I'd asked for a bistro table where I could clearly watch the front door. At ten after nine, Jacqueline Moreau walked straight up to me.

She turned heads. She stood over six feet in heels wearing a sleek black power suit. Not a hair out of place, she pulled it back in a tight chignon that almost looked painted on.

She regarded me for a moment, not offering to shake my hand. Then, without a word, she sat down and held up two fingers for the server. She ordered black coffee. I detected the trace of a French-Canadian accent. Just a slight lilt on the end of her words. Though born and raised in Montreal, she'd spent a chunk of her adulthood in the same affluent suburb of Detroit where Marcus Savitch now worked.

Emma had found her CV online a few weeks ago. She worked at the Montreal Museum of Fine Arts as an assistant curator. Her husband, Michael, was a technical consultant for a biotech firm based also in Quebec.

"Thank you for meeting me, Ms. Moreau," I said.

"My name is Jacqueline." She said her name with the French pronunciation, emphasis on the first syllable with a soft J.

"And I'm Cass. Are we waiting for your husband?"

"We are not. Michael doesn't wish to join us. He changed his mind."

"Well, I appreciate your time. I won't waste it. First off, I need you to know how very sorry I am for your loss. I don't wish to cause you or your family any additional pain."

The coffee came. Jacqueline slowly raised her cup to her lips, holding it with two hands. When she set it back down, she left a fire-engine-red lipstick mark on it.

"You work for Andrew," she said.

"I do. He has some concerns about things that happened at trial."

"He is going to appeal?"

"Perhaps."

"He wants everyone to believe he didn't kill my daughter."

I didn't know how to respond to that. I knew any attempt I made to convince her Andrew was innocent would be an insult. And frankly, beside the point.

"Ms. Mor … Jacqueline. I think more happened that night than came out in Andrew's trial. I'm not sure justice was completely served."

She crossed her legs, stared at me, said nothing.

"There are aspects of this case I don't think anyone ever looked at. I'm trying to do that. I'll get to my purpose."

"Please do. What exactly is it you want from me?"

I reached into my bag and pulled out a blank medical consent form. Miranda had filled it out for both the Moreaus' signatures, but Jacqueline's alone would do. I slid the form across the table. She flicked her eyes downward, but never picked it up.

"I would like to see Daria's medical records," I said. I hated asking. I would have tried to soften my request, work up to it. But something about this woman convinced me all of that would be pointless.

"But before I explain all of that," I said, "do you mind if I ask you about your daughter instead?"

There was no trace of emotion on her face. She kept her armor up. I could respect that.

"Her dreams," I said. "Her goals. Her aspirations."

She took another sip of coffee. "My daughter would have accomplished anything she set her mind to. She already had. Did you know she was a gymnast?"

"Yes. And a very talented one. I understand she'd suffered an injury though. To her knee."

"An injury," she repeated with a half-smile. "That is a mild way to put it. She destroyed her knee during a floor routine when she was sixteen years old. She'd been working for over a year to perfect the Cheng vault. No one else in this country could perform it at a high school level. But she was going to. She had it. Gymnastics Canada had her on their radar. She could have made the Canadian Olympic team. She had dual citizenship. But something happened in the air during her last practice before one of her invitationals. When she landed, the doctor said it was like her knee blew apart. But ... she landed. She stayed upright. I've watched the tape a thousand times. She couldn't bear weight on that leg for months afterward. It took her a year and a half to rehabilitate it. But she never fell in competition again. Not until that last day when she was twenty years old."

"That's amazing."

"There was nothing amazing about it. It was Daria. If she wanted to do something. She did it. She never let obstacles stand in her way."

"And she was a star student," I said.

Jacqueline didn't answer. I had the sense she'd told me the only story she felt anyone needed to know about who Daria was. But there was something in the subtext. Daria could do anything she set her mind to. And one fatal night, a few tragic seconds, and none of it mattered.

"I truly am sorry for your loss. And for any additional pain my presence is bringing you."

"You think I'm afraid of you? You think anything in this world could hurt me again?"

"No."

"What do you think this will accomplish?" She waved a dismissive hand over the medical release.

"I don't know. What I do know? It's not just about mistakes Andrew Doyle's lawyer might have made. I think the police and the prosecutor settled on their suspect and that was it. I think something else happened that night. Someone saw something. The police didn't look hard enough. Didn't try hard enough to find other witnesses. There were dozens of people at that party. They only called four. Jason Lin, Henry Barber, Marcus Savitch, Kade Barclay."

There it was. Just a flicker in her eyes. Contempt. Disdain. I knew immediately she was no fan of Kade or Marcus.

"I agree with you," she said. "It was something I asked a hundred times. Those boys let my child rot in the woods for over a day. They didn't check on her. They didn't make sure she came back. That she wasn't out there somewhere."

"I don't understand that either."

"And you think looking at her medical records could help you solve that?"

"Maybe," I said. "Do you know if Daria was seeing anyone? A therapist perhaps?"

"I don't know. These records will tell you that?"

"Probably. Yes."

"Will I get a copy of them?"

"Of course."

"Maybe I don't want them. For me, it changes nothing."

I held my breath, expecting her to tell me to get out of her face. Expecting her to hurl the papers into the river beside us.

"They are liars," she said instead. "All of them. You may not believe Andrew Doyle killed Daria. I do. But you're right. There was more. I believe those other boys know more than they told. I believe the three of them conspired together somehow. I can feel it. Can't you?"

I wanted to tell her yes. Because it was the truth. I did feel that. But Andrew was still my client.

She reached into her purse and pulled out a pen. To my complete shock, she grabbed the papers and hastily signed them. She folded them and shoved them in my direction. I took them and slipped them into my bag.

"Thank you," I said. Though it seemed inadequate.

"Michael didn't want to come," she said. "He didn't want me to come. He's back at the hotel. Men aren't built the way we are. Do you have children, Cass?"

"No. I have brothers and a sister. The younger two I practically raised. I have nieces and a nephew that I would kill or die for. But no, I have no children of my own. And I cannot imagine what the last few years have been like for you."

"You do not know pure terror until you have children."

"I believe you."

"I don't know. If someone had told me what would happen before she was born. That I would lose Daria like this. I don't know. We went to grief counseling for a while. The doctor felt Michael needed it. Group therapy. They all said the same thing. That what brief amount of time they had with their sons and daughters before they were murdered ... thrown away like garbage ... that it made everything worth it. That they'd never trade a second of what they had. Me? No. I don't think so. If my choice was to never have had my daughter. Never have to live in this life knowing what she would suffer. I would not have had her. I suppose some people would call me a monster for that."

"I wouldn't."

"It's not me," she said. "Yes. It would spare my own pain. Yes. I will not apologize for finding that desirable. But it's Daria's pain I would spare. I would not bring her into this world if I had to do it all over again. Knowing how she suffered when she left it."

There were no tears in her eyes. No emotion at all. She was a strong woman. Cold, perhaps. But I would never judge her for it.

"So, consider yourself lucky," she said. "It isn't worth it. Children. They don't deserve the pain that comes with being in this world."

Again, I found myself not knowing how to respond. I realized it was probably better if I said nothing at all. She didn't expect me to.

"So yes. Do this. Find the truth. Marcus Savitch. Kade Barclay. They are not innocent. I know it. I feel it. They should pay for what they've done. You're not on Daria's side. Don't tell me you're on justice's side. It's hollow. I won't hear it."

She leaned forward, her face becoming a mask of rage, her eyes going red, her pupils to dots. "You find your witnesses. You go after whomever you must. I hope your efforts are what bring Kade and Marcus to their knees. I don't have the patience to wait for them to go to hell. I curse them now. Again."

She rose and spat on the ground. At that moment, I knew if Jacqueline Moreau was a witch, Marcus Savitch and Kade Barclay should fear for their health and their firstborn children. And maybe so should I.

Chapter 16

Two days later, I roped Eric into a road trip to East Lansing. Actually, Williamston, just twenty minutes further east.

The Colby House wasn't easy to find. My GPS took me down several wrong and unmarked roads. Finally, we found the long, winding, dogwood-lined drive off Fairfield Road.

"It's gorgeous back here," he said. To the west of the big house, we saw an orchard with at least two dozen fruit trees. White ducks, a pair of swans, and a flock of large gray geese crossed the drive in front of us, forcing Eric to stop and wait.

The house itself was grand, to say the least. Traditional Tudor with three stories and two separate wings. The For Sale sign out front threw me. I didn't know it was on the market.

"Why wouldn't they put that out on the road?" Eric wondered. It was a good point.

The property owner, Vivian Lanski, waited for us in the open front door. She was pretty. Smartly dressed in a yellow-and-blue-flower-print dress tied with a white sash. She pointed to the far end of the circular drive, directing Eric where to park.

I slipped on my sunglasses as we got out. The first week of June and we'd hit a heatwave. The forecast called for high eighties and no rain, all week long.

"Ms. Lanski?" I said, extending my hand to hers. "I'm Cass Leary. This is my partner, Eric Wray. I'm so glad you agreed to meet with us."

"Come on in," she said. "I'm afraid the air conditioner isn't working. I've got a guy coming out later this afternoon. But there's a breeze and the slate floors keep things pretty cool."

She led us to a sitting room off the main hallway. To my right, a winding wooden staircase went all the way up to the third floor with a landing on the second.

"You have a beautiful home," Eric said. I knew he was admiring what I called "wood porn." Every room had huge, six-paneled doors made of dark oak. We passed a study with eight-inch-wide hickory planks, the kind you couldn't find easily anymore, but a hundred and fifty years ago might have been common.

The sitting room was more of a solarium. Lead glass windows made up one wall and curved upward, covering half the ceiling. Vivian led us to a white wrought iron table. She had orange juice in a carafe, piping hot coffee, and freshly made fruit tarts on a tray.

"You didn't have to go to all this trouble," I said.

"I don't mind," she said. "Baking is a stress reliever for me. Lately, everything about this house causes me anxiety."

"Well, thank you for hosting me. I imagine you've been anxious to put this whole affair behind you."

She sat across from us, spread a cloth napkin over her lap, and reached for one of the tarts. Eric's stomach growled. Blushing with embarrassment, he grabbed his own tart and practically had a religious experience when he took the first bite.

"I'd like to ask you some questions about the weekend Daria Moreau was killed here."

Vivian winced. "It's been almost two years and every time someone says that, it's just a knife in the gut."

"I'm sorry."

"I worked hard," she said. "It took me almost ten years to fully renovate this place. I tried to restore everything as close to the original condition as I could. The previous owners had really let it fall into disrepair. The master bath upstairs was a tragedy. They'd ripped out all the original tile and replaced it with quartz and subway tile. Can you imagine?"

"Ugh," Eric said. "I don't know why people do that."

"I was able to put it back to the way it would have looked in the late nineteenth century. Of course, I added some modern amenities. It's got a heated floor. I built a wet room. But I found the original claw-footed soaker tub in the basement. I had it reglazed and it's a work of art."

"I'd love to see it," Eric said.

"But you're selling," I said.

Vivian's face fell. "I don't have a choice. I can't afford to maintain it anymore. Not since my rental income had dropped to a trickle. Ever since that horrible weekend, nobody wants to stay here. They call it the Murder House online now. You should see the comments under my Yelp listing. The short-term rentals I have managed to book in the last two years, a lot of them left reviews saying there's a ghost inhabiting the gardens now. It's ridiculous. But it's stuck."

"I'm really sorry. How awful."

"I have a friend who thinks I should wait it out. Lean into the haunted house angle. She says there are people who actually seek out rentals like that. I don't know. It just seems so morbid. It's not what was intended for this place. It shouldn't be some ghoulish attraction."

"Of course not," Eric said.

"Ms. Lanski," I said. "Do you mind if I ask you a few questions about that weekend?"

"Sure," she said. "Though I can't think of anything I haven't already been asked."

"The prosecutor came here?" I asked.

"I talked to her several times," she answered. "And a couple of the assistants she had working for her. And the police, of course, they took pictures all over the grounds."

"Did Russ Nadler ever talk to you? The lawyer representing Andrew Doyle?"

"No. I don't remember him."

Eric tossed a look my way. The news didn't surprise me. Just one more bit of sloppy defense work on Nadler's part.

"I regret ever renting to those kids," she said. "I went against my better judgment in doing it. I make it a policy not to rent to college kids. I mean, I know they were in law school or something. But it's pretty much the same thing. But I knew who the Savitches were. I figured it would be good business if one of their own enjoyed it here and recommended it to people in their circle. I thought that rental was going to pay dividends for a long time. It did. Just not the kind I expected."

"That's understandable," I said. "I'm sure you've been asked this before as well. But do you have any security cameras installed anywhere? I don't recall seeing that in the police report."

"I'm afraid not," she said. "The prosecutor asked me that, too. On the advice of my lawyer ... my real estate lawyer ... I never put them up. He was afraid the potential liability would outweigh any security benefit. He said privacy issues would be a problem."

"That makes sense, I guess," I said.

"Were you here at all that weekend?" Eric asked. I covered my mouth with my hand, concealing my smile. The whole drive here, Eric swore he only wanted to be an observer. I knew he'd never be able to shut off his detective brain. I was counting on it.

"No," she said. "I make a point of being scarce when new renters come in unless they ask to meet me here. I leave a binder on the kitchen counter with instructions on how to work the floodlights, turn the fountains on, little quirks with the fireplace and furnace, that sort of thing. And I've got a list of local attractions. Food delivery menus."

"May I see it?" I asked. "Are you using the same binder as you did three summers ago?"

She excused herself and disappeared into the kitchen for a moment. She came back with a small black binder. I flipped through it. It contained everything she said. I stopped at the food menus. She had a note written on the top with the number to the MealHopper delivery service.

"They're local," she said. "For a while, they were the only ones that would come out this far. The more known services like DoorDash tend not to want to come out here. It's too far out in the boonies for their drivers to make it financially worth it. Which is fine by me. MealHopper is local. I know the owners pretty well. Dick and Miranda Tindall. Though Miranda passed away last year. Dick's brought his son up to take over."

"MealHopper was the only delivery service that you know of who came out here that weekend? I understand from some of the testimonies several food deliveries had been made the night of the party."

"You'd have to ask the Tindalls to be sure. But probably."

Eric wrote down the MealHopper main number.

"They don't have an app," Vivian said. "I think the son is working with somebody to develop one. It might be too late though. Those other bigger-name places probably have the market pretty well cornered by now."

"I would imagine," I said.

"It just kills me," she said. "I was just starting to recover from the lean years of the pandemic. Bookings were starting to creep back up. Then bam. And I'm sorry if I sound callous. A girl died out there. And here I am whining about my financial bottom line. I don't mean to sound that bad. I'm sorry."

"It's all right," I said.

"Anyway." Vivian rose. "You said you wanted to have a look around. Please make yourself at home. My realtor scheduled a showing about a half hour from now. I don't mind if you're on the property when they get here. But there are a few things I want to finish staging if you don't mind."

"That's perfectly fine," I said. "You've been helpful. I hope your showing works out."

"Me too. It's the only one I've had in almost three weeks. At this rate, I may have to consider putting the place up for auction."

"Try to avoid that as long as you can," I said.

"That's what my lawyer says, too."

Vivian Lanski said her goodbyes and disappeared deeper into the house.

"Where do you want to start?" Eric asked.

"Let's go out to the garden. I'd like to see the crime scene."

I could see the pizza oven and brick barbecue Andrew and the other witnesses described the night of Daria's death. It was just across the patio, next to a beautiful rose garden. It was from there that some of the witnesses claimed they saw Andrew and Daria arguing.

Eric opened the door to the patio and held it for me as I stepped outside. I slid my sunglasses back on.

"This is really beautiful," I said. The stone pavers went all the way out. Vivian Lanski had cute little tables set up all over the patio. This would be the perfect venue for a wedding shower or a small party. In my mind's eye, I could envision the dozens of people Andrew described as they enjoyed their beer and wings out here.

Eric walked to the barbecue. A stone ledge beside it would have made the perfect spot for an outdoor bar. Which is exactly what Andrew said it had been used for that night.

"There's the trail leading to the birdbath, I think," Eric said. He pointed due east of us.

It was a small clearing through dense trees. As we walked down it, it felt like we were in a storybook. After a slight curve, we reached the cement structure. Just past it a large hill rose. One side of its base was carved out, a massive oak tree having fallen long ago. Its remaining root ball was covered in moss. The depression it left behind on the hill formed a tiny hollow. Someone had put a stone bench beside it.

"It looks like a fairy cove or something," I said.

But birdbath was an understatement for the structure beside us. I was expecting some small basin on a pedestal, like I kept in my own backyard. This thing was enormous. The basin had to have at least a four-foot circumference. The pedestal was so thick I didn't think my arms would have fit around it. It had a second tier with a smaller basin on top. Intricately carved stone birds decorated the base.

Eric and I walked closer. The bath was taller than me. I reached it first and turned my back to it. Eric stopped just in front of me, sensing what I wanted to understand. I stood with my back to the basins. The second, highest one came just to the top of my shoulders.

I put one foot forward. Eric put his hands on my upper arms.

"If she fell," he said, "I see how she could have struck her head on that thing."

He carefully tipped me back. I gripped his arms. He was right. A backward fall and I could have easily struck my head on the edge of the second tier.

I turned and absently ran my fingers along the stone ridge. I don't know what I thought I might see. Bloodstains? Surely not after all this time. Plus, I hadn't seen anything like that in the crime scene photos.

"It would have been almost impossible to see anyone back here from the patio," Eric said. I followed his finger as he pointed toward the garden. He was right. The trees would have easily shielded the majority of this area from view. You might be able to see two people back here. Appreciate that they were arguing. But positioned a certain way and the trees would have completely blocked them from view.

"And it was dark," I said. "I don't suppose the floodlights on the patio would cast this far."

"No," he said. "Plus the deputies took pictures of this area in the dark. There was nothing but shadows this far out."

"Unless anyone else was on that footpath leading up to the main patio."

"You have no testimony or statements from any witness to support that," he said.

"I don't have anything. Eric, don't you think it's unconscionable that Andrew's lawyer didn't come out here himself? The patio is a pretty good distance away. The people up at the house were drinking. They might have seen Andrew and Daria walk out this way, but I don't see how anyone could credibly testify to much more than that. But Nadler never hammered that home. He just let the jury take the witnesses at face value."

Eric grumbled, but didn't answer.

"Where's the pond?" I asked.

Eric looked around. "I'm assuming that way." He pointed toward a small clearing to the north of the birdbath. He was right. It was the only logical way someone could have dragged a body out. The rest of the area was too thick with brush. Plus, Daria's trail of blood went right through that opening.

"Come on," I said. I stepped past Eric and walked down the path. We went fifty yards through the woods until we came to the edge of the pond.

It stunk back here. Fetid water and wood rot. Plus the pungent scent of decaying fish. A bullfrog called out, protesting our presence. Two sand cranes flew out of the bush; we'd clearly disrupted their peace.

"Watch your step," he said. "Christ, it's pure muck through here."

I'd worn jeans and a pair of hiking boots, knowing we'd be trudging through the woods. Eric, too, had on a pair of work boots with the hem of his jeans over them. He quickly pegged his pants and tucked them into the boots. I did the same. But within five seconds, we sank about an inch into the soft earth.

"They didn't find any mud on Andrew's shoes," I said.

"You're sure?" Eric asked.

"I didn't see anything about that in the report."

"Hmm." Eric let out that same grumble. Then he took my hand as I stepped closer to the edge of the pond.

"It's a mosquito breeding ground," he said. It was. The pond water was stagnant here. It smelled terrible. An almost neon-green layer of slime and algae rested on the top.

"God," Eric said. "I think it would have been better if someone had just thrown her body in a dumpster." He covered his mouth. On the shore, I spotted three bloated dead carp resting belly up. Flies buzzed everywhere.

"Why doesn't she have this cleaned up?" I asked.

"These are probably protected wetlands," he said. "There's a limit to what EGLE will let you do. It's pretty from a distance, I suppose." Michigan's Department of Environment, Great Lakes and Energy did indeed have strict rules about what could and couldn't be done around natural sources of water. I'd fought with them recently myself when trying to install a drainage system near the barn.

I turned and looked back the way we'd come through. "It would have taken some muscle to drag a body through there, don't you think? I can barely imagine it."

"Well, Daria was covered with muck and slime. The drag marks were easy enough to find. Ugh. To leave her in this. She was somebody's kid."

"That's what Grace Doyle said. That it would have been one thing for Andrew to have accidentally killed Daria. But she swears he wouldn't have had it in him to just dump her body out here."

"She's not impartial," he said. "What else would you have expected her to say?" He was frowning. He had been since we sat down with Vivian Lanski.

"What are you thinking?" I asked.

"It's just ... it bothers me. It bothers me a lot. They found footprints. Nobody took moldings. It should have been pretty easy to figure out which direction the killer came and went from. And it really bothers me how little effort went into tracking down more witnesses."

"That's been one of my biggest beefs since the beginning. And that Nadler never came out here himself. It took us what, two seconds to realize the visibility issues from the patio to the birdbath?"

"So what's your theory, Detective Leary?"

He smiled, pleased with himself for the rhyme. Also, he was testing me. I knew he was in pure detective mode now. He wanted to see how much had rubbed off on me.

"The menus," I said. "Vivian Lanski pretty much gift-wrapped the next investigative step. I didn't see anything in the police report about anyone calling the owners of that service, MealHopper. Wouldn't they potentially have records of who made the delivery orders to the property that night?"

"You'd think," he said. "Though I would have serious doubts they'd have kept those records this long."

"It's at least worth an ask. One that Nadler should have made."

"Yeah," Eric said, his scowl back in place. "And definitely one the lead detective on this case should have asked. It all just feels ... I don't know."

We started walking out of the muck and back up the trail to the birdbath. Eric had to help me when my boot got stuck in the muck and came clean off. We were filthy by the time we made it back to the trail. The bottom of my pants were ruined. I had dots of mud all the way up to my waist and down one arm. So did Eric.

As we got to the garden patio, we left muddy footprints across the pavers. Eric stopped. He looked down, turned, and looked back the way we came.

"What is it?" I asked.

"I don't know. Something doesn't make sense. Did you see muddy footprints in any of the crime scene photos?"

"No," I said. "Just the ones near the bog. The ones you're mad nobody made impressions of."

"Hmm. They never found muddy shoes or clothes belonging to any of the boys?"

"No."

"How long was it between her disappearance and when her body was found?"

"A day and a half. What are you thinking?" I asked.

"It was late at night. All three of those boys admitted to drinking that night. From those crime scene photos, the ground was pretty much like it is now. There should have been a mud trail somewhere. If it was Andrew, his shoes and pants would have been caked, just like mine are. He had plenty of time to clean up. Sure. But nobody's that good. They should have left tracks. There should have been traces of this stuff somewhere in the house. In the washing machine. The grass. The floor. Somewhere."

"There wasn't though. Like you said. We saw the crime scene photos."

"I don't know. It just feels ..."

"It feels rigged," I said, completing his sentence.

He turned to me. "Maybe. Yeah. I mean ... I get why this case is under your skin the way it is. Regardless of whether Andrew Doyle killed that girl or not. There's been something else going on along with it. You can feel it."

I couldn't tell him my suspicions about Marcus Savitch. But everything about this case seemed to reek of him. Just as bad as the stench out by that pond.

Chapter 17

THERE'S ALWAYS a risk when you hire family to work for you. An awkwardness to telling them what to do and having to critique the job they've done. You don't want to be too lenient or too harsh. But with my niece Emma, she'd proven within the first week how valuable she was.

By ten a.m. the next morning, she had Christopher Tindall, the current owner and creator of the MealHopper app, on the phone. Better yet, the man kept detailed records.

Emma waved me into her office and put her phone on speaker.

"Can you say that again, Chris?" she asked. "I've got my boss in front of me."

"Oh," a young-sounding male voice answered. "I was just saying I can give you log records for the timeframe you asked for. I keep everything in my scheduling software. I use it to track trends and the effectiveness of whatever promotions or advertising I'm running. Every entry is linked to where the order originated from. Like it's tagged if the customer linked through from an online ad. Or I have my drivers manually enter that data if the customer tells them. It also helps me track retention. How many repeat customers I get."

"That's all very organized," I said. "This is Cass Leary. I really appreciate you taking the time to talk to us."

"No problem. Happy to do it. It's been a shame Vivian's not able to rent her place for very much anymore. She sent a lot of business my dad's way before I took everything over last year."

"So," Emma interjected. "We're looking at the night of Sunday, July 24, two summers ago. Whatever entries you have about deliveries out to the Colby House. Can you look at the twelve-hour period between eight p.m. and eight a.m.?"

Emma caught my eye with an unspoken question. I gave her a thumbs up in answer. That inquiry fell squarely within the window of time Daria likely died.

"Sure," Chris answered. "Spreadsheet form okay? I can email it in about ten seconds."

"That's perfect," I said.

"You bet."

"Could you also give us contact information for any of the delivery drivers who fulfilled those orders?"

"It'd just be the one," Chris said. "I'm only showing Nate Zender working that night. He went back and forth multiple times. Looks like three different restaurants."

"Do you know how to get a hold of Nate?" I asked.

"Sure. He doesn't work for me anymore, but he's my sister's nephew. Good kid. He just graduated from MSU. He's gonna be a large animal vet, I think my sister told me."

Emma had her laptop open. I heard the ping from her inbox. A second later, I heard the printer out by Miranda's desk start running.

"That's great," Emma said. "Is it okay if I call you back if I have more questions?"

"Sure."

"Chris," I said. "I just have one more. Have you ever provided this information to anyone else connected to this case? The police? The prosecutor? Another defense attorney, maybe?"

"Nobody ever asked," he said. "At least as far as I remember. I can ask my dad if he remembers. But there's no way he wouldn't have had me involved if the police showed up. It would have freaked him out."

I found that incredible. Absolutely incredible. Emma thanked Chris again, then clicked off the call. As we walked out of Emma's office, Miranda had already made a duplicate copy of the four-page printout. She handed one to each of us.

"Thanks," I said. "We'll be up in the conference room if anybody needs us."

She promised to do just that. When we got up there, Jeanie was already waiting. She just hung up a call of her own.

"That was a records clerk at Henry Ford Health," she said. "They've accepted Jacqueline Moreau's waiver. She's gonna give me a call back to let me know when to expect Daria's medical records."

"Perfect," I said. I sat down and started thumbing through Chris Tindall's delivery log.

"Six deliveries," Emma said, as she reviewed the same records I did.

Jeanie slid next to me and read over my shoulder. "Andrew ordered the first one," I said. "Six large pepperoni pizzas at 7:18 p.m. Delivery came at eight on the dot."

"He paid cash," Emma said.

"Somebody liked Charlie's wings," Jeanie said. "You've got three separate deliveries. One at eight thirty, another at eleven thirty. One more just past one a.m."

"They're an East Lansing staple," Emma said. "I had a friend at MSU when we were both in college. I visited her a couple of times at her apartment. We ordered from there. They're amazing. Especially the garlic Parmesan flavored."

"Still," Jeanie said. "That's a lot of wings."

Emma smiled. "They're, uh, especially popular for the munchie crowd." Emma squeezed her thumb and forefinger together, brought them to her lips and sharply inhaled, mimicking someone smoking a joint.

"I'm sure there was plenty of that going on too," I said. I looked back at the log. "That one a.m. entry was the last delivery of the night. Daria could have already been dead by then."

"Jason Lin ordered the bucket of wings at eleven thirty," Jeanie said. "That's consistent with his testimony. He said his wings had just arrived and he was just starting to dig into them when he saw Marcus arguing with Daria about halfway down the path to the birdbath."

"I'd like to talk to him again anyway," I said. "Emma, do you think you could get me a current number?"

"No problem."

I grabbed a highlighter out of the cup in the center of the table. I ran it over the last food delivery entry. It was placed by a Laneesha Dey. Also delivered by Nate Zender at 1:13 a.m.

"Nobody ever talked to Dey?" Jeanie said. She had her binder in front of her. She flipped through to the police report tab. She ran her finger down the indexed witness statements. No Laneesha Dey appeared.

"It doesn't surprise me," I said. "Chris Tindall said nobody but me has ever asked for this delivery log."

"I don't get why," Emma said. "It took me no more than a ten-minute phone call."

"They had what they needed," Jeanie said. "The other witness, Henry Barber, confirmed he saw Andrew and Daria arguing together at 12:45 a.m. He pinpointed it exactly because it coincided with when his girlfriend called him. The cops stopped right there."

"Yeah," I said. "But the fact nobody asked for these records, that alone won't be enough to get Andrew a new trial."

"It's part of Russ Nadler's pattern of incompetence," Jeanie said. "It doesn't have to be a single thing. Tori's working on the brief. That's the angle she's taking. It's a good one."

I hoped so.

"I'll find Laneesha Dey too," Emma promised. She reached for the bar journal, flipping to the member directory.

"Ha," she said. "What did that take me, thirty seconds? Laneesha Dey was also there for the bar exam. Says here she was admitted to practice also in November of 2022. It's enough to go on. That's not a super common name."

"Great," I said. "That'll help a lot. Jeanie, what time did you say you expected those medical records?"

"Gal on the phone said she'd let me know just as soon as she does."

"Perfect," I said. "Shoot me a text when you have them. In the meantime, I'm going to head over to Riley's Farm Store. Eric says we need more chick starter feed."

Jeanie smiled and shook her head as she closed up her binder and reorganized the documents in front of her.

"Oh!" Emma said. "You'll pass by my dad's house. Can you drop off a package for me? Let me go down and grab it." She gave Jeanie a strange look. The second Emma disappeared, I turned to Jeanie.

Before I could even ask the question, she put her hands up. "Relax. It's nothing ominous. Emma finally got Joe to update all of his advanced directives for health care. He's naming her as his patient advocate and giving her his durable power of attorney."

I stopped myself from protesting that she's just a kid. She wasn't. She was twenty-three years old and living on her own.

Emma reappeared in the doorway. She handed me a thick manila envelope. It struck me suddenly. But for a second, I had to stop myself from getting teary-eyed. Two minutes ago, this gorgeous human had been a baby.

I DIDN'T EXPECT my brother to be home. Six months ago, he'd finally moved out of my barn annex and into his own place. He usually worked on Tuesdays. But an unexpected thunderstorm kicked up, making it unsafe to do any work outside. For the last month, Joe had taken side work with a crew reroofing one of the big mega churches off US 23.

I snapped my umbrella open and clutched Emma's envelope to my chest. I punched in Joe's garage door code, our mother's birthday. Shaking off the water, I propped my umbrella next to his service door and headed in.

The house was quiet, but Joe's car was in the garage.

"Joe?" I yelled out. "I've got your forms from Emma. You wanna grab some lunch or something? I've got some free time."

I liked his new little house. When he and Katie divorced, he gave her the house they'd shared together. He bought a Craftsman-style three-bedroom, one-bath on Beecham Street, putting him just a mile down the road from me.

He'd remodeled the kitchen just last month. Emma helped him pick out the tile and he installed a repurposed hardwood floor throughout.

"Joe!" I shouted. I heard a thump coming from the back bedroom.

"I'll be right there!" Joe called back. There was something weird about his voice. An urgency. Not the easy, familiar tone we usually used with each other.

Thirty seconds later, the reason why walked down the hallway toward me, with unmistakable sex hair and a bona fide hickey on her neck.

"Katie," I said through gritted teeth.

She made a desperate attempt to smooth her hair into a presentable shape. Joe came up behind her wearing jeans he'd clearly just pulled on, bare feet, and his tee shirt on backwards.

"You've got to be kidding me," I said.

"Don't start," Joe said. He went to the fridge and took out a half gallon of milk and drank it straight from the carton.

"I need to go," Katie said. "It was nice seeing you, Cass."

"Can't say the same, Katie," I answered.

"Cass!" Joe said. "I said don't start."

"Me? You think I'm the one starting? Christ, Joe. She's married. You're *married*, Katie. Last time I checked, not to him." I jabbed a finger in my brother's stomach.

"I should go," she said. She fumbled for her keys, having grabbed her purse off the counter.

"You heading home?" I asked. "Because you'll maybe want to fix your damn blouse. Your buttons aren't lined up."

She looked down. There was a huge gap between her breasts where she'd put two buttons in the wrong holes. She started fixing it as she walked toward the back door.

I followed her line of sight. Joe lived on a corner lot. I could see Katie's brand-new red Audi TT parked in front of one of his neighbor's houses further down the street. Along with the car, her new husband had bought her vanity plates that said, "TOMSGRL."

"Walk of shame in broad daylight," I said. "Nice."

174

Katie went through the slider and rushed across the lawn.

"Knock it off, Cass."

I turned to him. "How exactly do you think this is gonna end, Joe? You think she's gonna leave her new hubby for you? Did she say she would?"

"No," he said, taking another sip of milk.

"So, what is this for you? Revenge sex?"

He didn't answer. I admittedly said it to be mean. But his lack of response spoke volumes.

"Just great."

"I know what I'm doing," he said. "I'm a grown man. She's a grown woman."

"With a ring on her finger that doesn't belong to you. What about Emma? She's a grown woman too, much as it makes me feel old to admit it. How do you think all this will make her feel?"

"Katie's not her mother."

"She might as well be. And a year ago, when you were a basket case dealing with the divorce, you made the same argument to me. You married her when Emma was three years old. She barely remembers her biological mother."

"She does. And they've reconnected."

"That might be even worse for her than finding out about all of this. Josie's not exactly been a stable force in her life. Is she clean now at least?"

"Cass, stop. You don't have a right to tell me how to live my life."

I couldn't help it. That got a laugh out of me. "We've been telling each other how to live our lives since we were old enough to talk, Joe. It's part of the job description. I just don't want to see you get hurt. And if Katie's just using you and has no plans to leave Tom Loomis, that's just another reason for me to hate her. This is bad news. And I know I'm not telling you anything you don't already know."

He put the milk back in the fridge. When he turned to face me, I saw pain in my brother's eyes.

"I can handle it, okay? Truth is, I don't know what this is. I don't have some big master plan for the future. Katie came to me. I think it finally dawned on her what she's done. She was trying to make things right between us."

"With her vagina?"

Joe barked out a laugh, then quickly recovered. "Not exactly, I mean, sort of. Ugh. Just ... I don't know. Okay?"

"How long has this been going on?"

"Come on. I know you know."

"Yeah. I do. But not from you directly, which is how I should have found out. Joe, I'm worried about you. You've been different since Katie left you. Reckless. Kinda hostile. But you were finally starting to get to the other side of it. This place? It was part of it. You were moving on. Now you're gonna be right back in that dark hole when Katie decides she's done with you. And she *will* decide she's done with you. Trust me."

"I said I can handle it."

"You always say that. How many times did you take Josie back in the beginning?"

"This isn't the same," he said.

"Except it is. Joe, I love you. But you tend to stick with one woman no matter what. Which normally I'd think is admirable. But in your case, you keep picking the wrong women."

I could keep going. I had a million other things to say on the subject. But I could see in my brother's face he wasn't going to listen. On the subject of women, he never did. To be fair, he accused me (mostly correctly) of the exact same thing. Eric had been the rare exception. Thank God for him.

I walked up to him and slid my arms up around his neck. I kissed my brother on the cheek. He hugged me back and we stood there for a moment.

"Anyway," I said. "There's your paperwork. It's all signed. Keep it somewhere safe. Load a copy into your MyChart. And for the love of God, don't give Katie any more money."

His eyes twinkled as he smiled. I knew I had no choice but to walk away. It shouldn't be any of my business. But what I said was true. Things with Joe and me didn't work that way.

As I climbed back into my car, Jeanie's text came through. Daria Moreau's medical records would hit her inbox first thing in the morning. She'd have Miranda leave a copy for me on my desk.

Chapter 18

"How far do these go back?" I asked. By eight o'clock the next morning, Miranda had printed out Daria Moreau's full medical records and made three copies of everything. The stack in front of me had to be at least one hundred pages.

"Ten years," Jeanie said. She walked in carrying her giant mug of coffee. It held twenty-four ounces. Miranda usually teased her that she should just put a straw in the damn pot.

"Since she was what, fourteen, fifteen?" I asked.

"You wanted the whole ball of wax," Jeanie said. "That's why this took so long. We've got every note from every doctor's visit, routine checkup, pelvic exam, procedures, surgeries. There's a lot. She was under the care of an orthopod since she was twelve years old. And then there was a team doctor at the University of Florida. My first reaction, this girl received more medical care, by a mile, than the average twenty-four-year-old woman."

"They didn't do us any favors organizing it," I said as I began to flip through the first few pages.

"They're oldest to newest," Miranda said. "The zip file contained about thirty subfolders. I did my best to put everything in order by date. I could have done it by doctor, but I was starting to drive myself crazy."

"It's fine," I said. "What I really want to know is when she was put on antidepressants and whether she ever saw a therapist."

Emma walked in. She had her copy of the medical records under her arm. I felt a little uncomfortable around her. It wasn't my place to spill the beans about her father and former stepmother. But it was this giant elephant in the room. One more reason to want to strangle Joe.

"I think my grandma had a bigger medical file than this, and she had MS," Emma said. She was referring to Katie's mother. She passed away, maybe ten years ago.

After a few minutes, I finally landed on the visit with her primary care physician where the Prozac was prescribed.

"The aftercare summary doesn't say too much," I said. "Page fifty-seven."

Jeanie and Emma flipped to that page.

"She reports feeling tired, overwhelmed, having trouble getting out of bed in the morning," Emma read out loud.

"No indication of any thoughts of self-harm," I said.

"This was six years ago," Jeanie said. "She was still on her parents' insurance but she was over eighteen. Do we even know if her mom and dad knew she was taking it?"

"I didn't ask that," I said. "Jacqueline Moreau was in a pretty dark place. She said she wished Daria had never been born."

"That's awful," Emma said.

"Honestly, I understood what she meant. It was more that if she could have spared Daria her manner of death, she'd have done that even if it meant she'd never had her in her life. But yeah. That's what I mean. Dark."

"I don't see any referrals to psychiatry or a counselor," Jeanie said. She pulled out a separate stack.

"From eighteen to twenty-one, she was in Florida," Jeanie said. "She saw a doctor at the health clinic associated with the university. Looks like that's the one who kept writing the prescription from then on. There's a generic note on the aftercare summary about seeking help if she had thoughts of self-harm. But I see nothing about a referral or her actually going to a therapist."

"So they basically pushed Prozac on her without any professional mental health care follow-up," I said.

"It's not malpractice," Emma said. "I'd assume PCPs have been prescribing that particular drug for decades. And she's not reporting any negative side effects. She's on the same dose for six years, up until she died."

"Most of this stuff relates to her ACL and meniscus problems," Jeanie said. "Twenty pages is just about her knee surgery alone. Notes from her physical therapist when she rehabbed it. I mean, other than the problems associated with her being a top-tier athlete, I don't see anything all that interesting in here."

For the next few minutes, the three of us quietly read independently. A picture emerged for me. In the years Daria was a competitive gymnast, she struggled with her weight. Note after note recorded her BMI as 17. Underweight for her height.

"She was starving herself," Jeanie said, as if we were mind-melded.

"That can't have been good with her knee trouble," Emma said.

"She's anemic a lot," Jeanie said. "She's on half a dozen vitamin supplements."

"She was driven," I said. "That's what Jacqueline described. The kind of kid who set her mind to something and reached her goals, no matter the toll it took. Moral. Rigid almost."

"Exactly the kind of person who would have felt compelled to report someone she found out was about to cheat on the bar exam," Emma said. "I gotta be honest. I'm taking it next year. If I found out one of the people in my core study group was planning the same thing, I'd have a hard time not blowing the whistle. I mean, it's like a slap in the face. You know? If the rest of us were doing the work, putting in the time, I'd be furious."

"Any luck getting a hold of the imposter test-taker?" Jeanie asked.

"Not so far. Cannon found the fake driver's license used in the FBI sting operation, but he's still trying to match it with an individual. It might be a needle-in-a-haystack situation."

The conversation died down and I immersed myself back in Daria's records. When she started law school, her trips to the doctor became a lot less frequent. Toward the bottom of the stack, I found a single visit to a physician's assistant at the University Health Service where they refilled all her meds.

Then I turned the page.

It took me a moment to register what I was looking at. The words were unfamiliar for a second. I had to go back and reread them to be sure. I pulled the page out of the stack and slowly rose to my feet.

"Aunt Cass," Emma said. She had just pulled a single page out of her stack as well. She went to her feet right along with me.

"December," she said. "Seven months before she was murdered."

"What's the matter, you guys?" Jeanie asked.

I gave her the page I was holding. Jeanie squinted at it, then pushed her readers further up her nose.

"She had an abortion," I said. "Right before Christmas. Her last Christmas."

Emma sat down hard and started furiously flipping through the rest of the pages in her stack.

Jeanie handed the page back and thumbed through until she found her own copy.

"Thirteen weeks gestation," I read. "They performed a vacuum aspiration. Gosh, that's right on the bubble of when they have to switch to something more invasive. I have to think Daria was the type of woman to be fully in tune with her body. She'd have to be. I mean, right?"

"I would think so," Emma said. "We've all been there, right? We've all had this same scare, haven't we?"

I pushed aside the fourteen questions that popped into my head more related to being Emma's aunt. But she was right. I could count about four times in my own life, all in my twenties, where I came close to facing the same question.

"I mean … thirteen weeks is a really long time," Emma said. "She probably would have missed three periods if she were regular."

I found the clinical notes from the procedure. God bless the person who prepared them at Planned Parenthood. She'd given us every scrap of paper generated that visit. Including who accompanied her to the visit.

"Kade Barclay," Emma read. "Holy crap. Kade Barclay drove her to and from the visit. He signed her out. He was her person. Cass, I don't want to make too big a leap here, but it feels pretty likely that Kade was the father."

Jeanie grabbed the trial transcript folder. "Was he ever asked about it?" she said. "I don't remember reading anything about it."

"He wasn't asked," I said. "Not by the cops, not by the prosecutor, not by Andrew's defense lawyer. And he certainly didn't volunteer it."

"Man, that was risky," Emma said. "They knew he was dating her the prior year."

"He testified they broke up just before Thanksgiving the year before she died," Jeanie said, reading from the transcript.

"She would have already been pregnant," Emma said. "It might have had something to do with why they ended it. Maybe he wanted her to have it and she didn't. Or the other way around. Or it made something he said was supposed to be casual into something totally different."

"That little weasel," Jeanie said. "He knew what he was doing. He knew full well he had no legal obligation to reveal that detail. Not unless somebody asked him point-blank. I guarantee you that's what he's going to say."

"It's still obstruction, isn't it?" Emma said.

"Maybe," I said. The facts pounded in my head in time with my pulse.

Kade Barclay probably got Daria Moreau pregnant. She had an abortion just seven months before she was murdered. Kade never told anyone about it. He just got lucky that no one bothered to pull Daria's full medical records but me. Kade Barclay was allegedly the first to notice Daria went missing. He didn't call the cops. Not until almost eight hours after he claims he realized she was gone.

"What is going on?" Jeanie said. "They're lying. All three of them. They're all liars."

I picked up the conference phone and buzzed down to Miranda.

"Yo!" she said when she picked up.

"I need to talk to Kade Barclay again. Can you make an appointment? Tell his office I'm a new client. Tell them anything. I need help with a property dispute. Whatever. Get me his next available."

"You got it," she said. "Give me one second."

I hung up. "He's just going to lie to you again," Emma said. "Is this enough? I mean, for the motion?"

"No. Maybe. I don't know," I said.

"Do you think Andrew knows about this?" Jeanie asked. "Or Marcus?"

"If they do, they've never told anyone either," I said.

"But why? I mean, if Andrew knew Daria aborted Kade's baby just seven months before she was murdered. He's been protesting his innocence for almost three years. You'd think he'd be shouting that little fact from the rooftops."

"None of this makes any damn sense," Jeanie said.

Miranda came through on the intercom. "You have your meeting," she said. "Tomorrow at two. He thinks you're coming about a boundary dispute with your neighbor. It's a free consultation. Lucky you. You're on his books as Lori Castle. Have fun."

"Thanks, Miranda."

That would at least get me past his front desk, I thought. But after that, there was every chance Kade Barclay would slam his office door in my face.

Chapter 19

My ruse worked. Kade Barclay's receptionist set me up in his office. His paralegal waited for me, sitting in one chair in front of Barclay's ergonomic desk.

"Kade's running a minute or two late; I'm Conan," he said. He pronounced it like O'Brien, not the Barbarian. "Do you mind if I go over a few intake questions with you before Kade gets here?"

"Actually, I do," I said. "I can wait. And I'm not trying to be rude, but I can pretty much guarantee you your boss won't want you in this meeting."

The kid's face fell. His smile turned into a scowl but he didn't argue with me. He abruptly stood, grabbed his tablet off the desk, and left without a word. I heard muffled voices in the hall. Conan, no doubt, was filling Kade in on the bitchy new client he had in store. Fine. It was an accurate description for the moment.

The door opened. Kade walked in, smoothing his tie. He had his hand on the knob as he realized he'd been duped. But as I suspected he would, he quickly closed the door behind him so nobody else could see me or hear what I had to say.

"What the hell is this? I told you I was done talking to you. And if I did, you damn well know I wouldn't want to do it here."

I stood and faced him. "I don't really care. You're lucky I didn't show up with a subpoena. That'll probably be next."

His face went a little white. He came around his desk and sat down. I pulled the file I'd brought out of my bag and tossed it at him. The papers flew out of it. The breeze my throw made lifted his hair. I sat back down.

"You're a liar," I said. "You lied to the cops and you lied on the witness stand."

He picked up the papers and quickly scanned the top. As I suspected, he didn't need to read all of it to understand what this was about.

"Daria Moreau was pregnant with your baby," I said. "A baby you took her to be aborted. And you didn't see fit to mention that to anyone."

He regained his composure and switched over to anger. I'd anticipated that too. "You're right. Because it was nobody's business. And I'd advise you not to call me a liar again."

"Start splitting hairs. You gonna tell me it depends on what the definition of *is* is?"

He narrowed his eyes in confusion. If Conan hadn't made me feel ancient, Kade sure did. He didn't get the Clinton deposition reference.

"Nobody asked," he said. I expected that too.

"So it wasn't technically perjury," I said. "Sure, Kade. You can weasel your way out of it claiming omission isn't the same thing as a lie. And you might even be right, legally. But you know you're wrong morally. And you know your bullshit impeded the investigation into the murder of the woman you claimed to care about. Not to mention the fact you concealed a possible motive for killing her yourself."

"I think I want my own lawyer here."

"I'm not the cops," I said.

"I didn't kill Daria. And I'm done defending myself. Think what you want. I did everything I could to try to help with that investigation."

"Except not calling the police for almost a day after she went missing. Except not being candid about your relationship with her."

"Because it wasn't relevant!"

"And you know that's not your call to make. Just stop it. You know what you did. So what I want to know is why you did it?"

"You think I killed her?" he asked, his voice hitting a fever pitch.

"I think you were worried enough people would think you did. So much so that you lied. And if you come at me with your crap about never being asked I think I'm gonna walk right out into that reception area and scream out why I'm here."

"Lower your voice," he said. "This doesn't have to be like that."

"How should it be?"

"I'm telling you. Every substantial thing I could tell the cops, or the jury, I did. And I didn't kill Daria."

"Doesn't mean you're innocent. Doesn't mean you haven't been trying to cover your own tracks. And it doesn't give me a reason not to go to the cops now. I'm going to be filing a motion, Kade. Consider my visit a courtesy. You're going to be mentioned in it. Those medical records will be attached as exhibits to the brief."

"Are you interested in my side at all?"

"Yes. I was. That's why I wanted to meet with you a month ago, Kade. Now, how am I supposed to trust anything you say?"

He picked up the excerpt from Daria's medical file. "How did you even get this? These weren't part of the evidence produced at trial."

"Wow," I said. "You really have put some thought into this. That was a hell of a risk you took. That the cops or Andrew's lawyer weren't going to request them. If you're a halfway decent lawyer, you would have. Right? It was one of the first things I did when I agreed to look into this case."

"How? You'd have to get consent."

I didn't answer. I let the truth roll its way through Kade Barclay's brain.

"Jacqueline?" he asked. "Christ. What did you say to her? Does she know about this?"

"Not from me. Not yet."

"You wanna know why I didn't say anything? It's not for the reason you think it is. So you've met her? Jacqueline?"

"Yes."

He closed his eyes. When he opened them, a new calm settled into his face. "Then maybe you already have a sense of it. She's a pretty intractable woman. She had high expectations of Daria. Put a lot of pressure on her. But she loved her. Daria was her world. Her father's too. Was he with her? Did you meet Michael?"

"No," I said, starting to become intrigued by whatever story he was about to spin. "He changed his mind about meeting me at the last minute. But Jacqueline believes what I believe. She's long suspected there's more to the story about what happened that weekend." I stopped short of mentioning that Daria's mother thought both Kade and Marcus had something more to do with it.

"I'm not surprised," he said. "About Michael, I mean. He's been in denial about a lot of things. But they're the reason I didn't say anything about Daria's abortion. It has nothing to do with trying to save my own skin."

"What are you talking about?"

"You didn't notice the crucifix Jacqueline wears on a chain? She never takes it off. Daria said not even in the shower. She and Michael are staunch Catholics. The old-school kind. One of her great sorrows is that she wasn't able to have more kids with Michael. They would not have approved of Daria having an abortion. It would have crushed them knowing she was having sex before marriage. Daria had to keep a lot of aspects of her life secret from them."

"Tell me what happened," I asked.

He let out a hard breath. "I loved her. I did. It wasn't a soulmate kind of thing. We both knew that. But we were compatible. I could tell her things. She was a good listener. When we took it to a different level, I knew it wouldn't last forever. I told you that much before. But yeah. She got pregnant. It wasn't planned.

And she struggled for a really long time with what to do about it. I told her I'd support whatever decision she made. She was mad at me for that. Like she wanted me to make it for her or something."

"She was thirteen weeks pregnant," I said.

"Yeah. That appointment? That day? It was her third one. The first two, she chickened out. Then, I don't know. She just finally realized it's what she wanted. So I went with her. Like I'd gone with her all the other times. I held her hand through the procedure. Then I took her home. She didn't get out of bed for three days. I made sure she ate. Helped her take a shower. But it was over between us. It had been for a while. She was my friend. Okay? She mattered to me. And there was no way I wasn't going to be there with her through that."

"If you're telling the truth," I said. "Why didn't you tell that story to the police? It would have made you look far more sympathetic than the guy who didn't bother calling the cops or going out and looking for her as soon as you realized she wasn't where she was supposed to be."

"I hate myself for that! God. You don't think I've gone through that day a thousand times in my head? The what ifs are enough to kill a person. But Daria was starting to pull away from me. It had been going on for a few months. Ever since the ... procedure. I don't know. I felt like part of her blamed me for all of it. And it was fair if she did. I'm responsible. It was my baby."

"So why didn't you call the cops sooner?" I asked.

"She was tired of me checking up on her all the time. Tired of the look of concern in my eyes. She said that. She resented it. I knew the second we were done that week, she was going to float out of my life forever."

"You understand what that sounds like?" I asked.

"I don't care what it sounds like. I didn't hurt her. I would never hurt her. She knew that. And the fact is, she also knew she could count on me. That I'd always show up for her. I was trying to respect her. Give her the space she asked for, that's all."

"And after?"

He tore a hand through his hair. "After, I had to take that phone call from her mother and explain to her what I knew about what happened. That her daughter had died under my watch. That she'd asked me to intervene, to get Andrew to back off. Instead, he hurt her. I don't know if he meant to. Nobody will ever know. But you understand that news destroyed that woman's life. If you met her. If you spent more than two minutes with her, you know how much."

Everything he said about Jacqueline was true. He was good. Convincing. And yet he was still a liar.

"I didn't say anything," he went on, "because then, in addition to having to bury Daria, and knowing she died by violent means, Jacqueline would have believed her daughter was burning in hell. Abortion is a mortal sin in her eyes. Premarital sex is a mortal sin. I thought the very least I could do was spare her that. Let her believe Daria was the person she thought she was. She's dead. Forever. I knew I could bring that one small measure of peace to Daria's parents. So I did. No matter the risk to me. And I knew in my heart it's what Daria would have asked of me. So yes. When it became clear nobody was going to find out about the abortion, I kept my mouth shut. Because it doesn't matter. It doesn't. I didn't kill her. I had nothing to do with a cover-up."

When he finished, I let the air settle between us. I let him sit in silence for a moment. To collect himself.

"Except you did," I said. "Tell me the truth."

"What are you talking about?"

"I'm talking about Marcus. Andrew says Marcus pulled the both of you aside and told you to back each other up. Provide mutual alibis. Tell the cops you were all with each other that night."

He blanched. "Andrew said that? He told you that?"

"That's not exactly a denial. Kade. Please. If you cared about that girl as much as you say you do, be honest now. Did Marcus have something to do with this? Even if it was only after the fact?"

"He was worried. Yeah. He said something like that. But not directly. He said we all knew where we were that night. So sure, it was implied."

"He wanted all of you to have your stories straight?"

"Yeah. But that was just Marcus being Marcus. He liked the illusion of being some kind of group leader. But I didn't lie to the cops. You've read my statement. You've read my trial testimony. I told the truth. I went to bed. I didn't see Marcus. I didn't see Andrew. And I didn't see Daria after about ten o'clock. I didn't tell Andrew to lie. I didn't say I saw him or Marcus when I didn't. I'm not responsible for whatever either of them told the police. So if Andrew said he was with me after ten, then he's lying. And it has nothing to do with me. I've said all I'm going to say. I need you to leave. If you have to serve me with a subpoena, I can't stop you. Please think about it long and hard. I won't lie to the cops now, either. Me telling the world about Daria's abortion won't help. It will only hurt. She wouldn't want that. It's not justice. It's just cruel."

He showed me to the door. As I walked back to my car, he'd given me a lot to think about. I wasn't sure I believed his story about why he omitted the truth. But he was right. If it got out, it would put Michael and Jacqueline Moreau through a different kind of hell. One they didn't deserve.

Chapter 20

HEAVEN IS STRETCHED out on the back of the pontoon on a sunny day with just the slightest breeze. Two swans flew overhead as Eric dropped anchor a few yards from the sandbar. It was warm enough to lie in the sun, but the water was still too chilly to swim in for my tastes. A couple of teenagers anchored to the north end of the lake didn't agree. Their laughter carried across the whole lake.

It was just the two of us today. Joe was still miffed at me from the other day. As if it were my fault he couldn't help himself around his toxic ex-wife. Matty, Tori, Vangie, and her off-and-on boyfriend, Deputy Jeff Steuben, took a four-day weekend up to Petoskey.

I should have felt tranquil. It had been a while since Eric and I could enjoy a weekend of quiet. Besides the ever-growing chickens, we were chaos free. And yet, I didn't feel peaceful. My mind raced. Daria Moreau's murder had taken over every bit of brain space I had. If I wasn't talking about it, I was thinking of every angle. Turning the problem over in my mind looking for what else I could exploit.

The boat rocked as Eric walked up from the captain's seat and sat on the bench seat beside me.

"Is it a private party or can anyone join?" he asked. Actually, he asked it twice before I realized he was talking to me.

"What?"

He tapped his temple. "In there," he said. "You wanna talk about it?"

"I'm sorry," I said. "I promised you a work-free weekend."

He laughed. Then his face grew serious.

"What is it?" I sat up.

"It's nothing ... it's just ... I used to say that all the time. To Wendy. She used to get so angry with me whenever I was working a homicide. It would take over my every waking thought. Just like this one is with you. I'm sorry to bring it up."

I put a hand on his knee. Wendy Wray had been Eric's wife of more than fifteen years. They had a complicated relationship. One that brought him tremendous grief. And it ended tragically. We rarely talked about her anymore.

"I don't mind," I said. "Wendy was part of your life. Part of why you are who you are."

"She never wanted me to be a cop. She worried. And it wasn't like I didn't give her cause. More than once she got a knock on the door in the middle of the night because I got hurt. But that was when I was pretty young and stupid. I was a hothead, if you can believe that."

I laughed. "You? Never."

"Do you want to talk about it? I never talked about it with Wendy. But she wasn't ... like you."

"You're already involved with this," I said. "Our plan to keep you siloed off from my cases didn't really work out, did it? I'm sorry for that. Turns out I need you. I need your brain."

He got that wicked smirk on his face and swung my legs over his lap. "Just my brain."

The ragged tone of his breath warmed me all the way to my toes. When he started rubbing my feet, I nearly gave way to ecstasy.

"Oooh," I said. "Ever thought about another career change as a masseuse?"

He smiled, but a shadow crossed his face. He quickly recovered. "I don't mind talking about it," he said. "You aren't going to be able to stop thinking about it."

"Eric ..."

"It's okay. I'm trying to tell you I get it. That I'm not Wendy in this scenario."

I drew my legs up and faced him. "I just don't know if it's enough." He already knew what I'd learned from Daria Moreau's medical records. I also told him what I learned about Kade and Marcus. Whether we made it official with a paycheck or not, Eric had been working on this case with me.

"You're as good at reading people as I am," he said. "You know when they're lying. I've seen you in action when you're cross-examining someone. Do you think Kade knows more about Daria's murder than he's letting on?"

"I don't know. My gut says no. As angry as I am that he withheld information from the cops, his explanation for it makes a certain kind of sense. He's right. Knowing their daughter aborted a baby would have added another layer of pain to Michael and Jacqueline Moreau's grief."

Eric let out a huff. "You think he did it to be noble? It's a pretty convenient story."

"I know. And it really is unforgivable. Had I defended Andrew at trial, I would have skewered Kade with it."

"You think it would have been enough to raise reasonable doubt?"

"Maybe. That, and if I'd been able to cross-examine Marcus about his fraud against the state bar, maybe. At the very least, it raises serious questions about Marcus and Kade's credibility that the jury should have considered in their deliberations."

"Is it enough for appealable error?" he asked.

"I don't know."

"Cass," he said. "There's a big fat problem. One you can't keep overlooking."

"What do you mean?"

"Kade Barclay and Marcus Savitch weren't the friends they said they were to Daria. They both let her down. Maybe one of them killed her. Maybe not. But the fact remains there was no physical evidence tying them to Daria's murder. But there was for Andrew."

"You think he's guilty?"

He pursed his lips. "I think he's the one I would have arrested. Yeah. I agree with you that the detective in this case left a lot of loose ends. I'll even agree he rushed to judgment. Had blinders on when it came to Andrew Doyle. But it doesn't mean he was wrong. You need more. And your client's not cooperating. He's his own worst enemy. Sometimes you just have to accept that and move on. You may finally have an unwinnable case."

He looked over my head. Squinting against the sun, he rose.

"What is it?" I turned.

"Emma's on the dock. She's waving her arms above her head."

"Where's my phone?" I asked.

"You didn't bring it." He went to the front of the boat and started pulling up the anchor. I got behind the wheel. As soon as he had the anchor up, I turned the ignition and swung the boat around. It took us just two minutes to reach the dock.

Emma grabbed the side of the pontoon, guided it forward, then tied it off on one side.

"I'll get the rest of the ropes," Eric said. He saw the same alarm on Emma's face as I did. I braced myself, hoping it wasn't more drama with her father.

"I'm sorry," she said. "I tried to call. I didn't want to mess up your day, but I knew you'd want to know what I know as soon as I knew it."

I looked back at Eric. He waved me off, having the boat well in hand. Emma and I walked up to the house. I grabbed my cover-up and threw it over my head. We sat on the porch in the shade.

"What'd you find out?" I asked.

"You asked me to look into Bill and Jenny Doyle. If there was any kind of dirt on them Marcus Savitch might have exploited. I think I found something."

Eric started up the dock. Emma gave me a look. "It's okay," I said. "He knows everything anyway."

Emma's briefcase was on the side of the porch. She picked it up and pulled out a file.

"So I did some checking," she said. "They've been running their little farm and feed for about ten years. Not successfully. I pulled up the tax records, their real estate transaction when they purchased the store. And I went down to Walkerton and asked some questions."

"Do they know?" I asked. "Were you discreet?"

"Of course. But I didn't really have to be. The whole town knows they're trying to get Andrew exonerated. There are flyers all over town asking for contributions to his legal fund. He's got a lot of supporters down there. To be honest, I didn't run into a single person who doesn't hope your efforts are successful in getting him out."

"That's incredible," I said.

"Bill and Jenny Doyle must be pretty well liked," Eric said.

"They are. The word I heard used a lot was beloved."

"Okay," I said. "So, what's the other side of that story?"

"They've barely been making ends meet. Bill mortgaged his house twice to keep the store running. He's sold off all his tillable land. They just own the house they're living in and about ten acres around it. And until about a year ago, they were headed for foreclosure."

I sat back hard against the wooden porch chair. "What happened?"

"So, a year ago, things took a turn. Before that, Bill had put some feelers out trying to see if he could find a buyer for the store. I found that out from one of the business owners across the street from him. The local barbershop owner. He painted a pretty different picture of Bill Doyle. And it took some doing to get it out of him. But Bill Doyle wrote some bad checks to his suppliers."

I knew where this was going. I felt a little sick as Emma continued.

"The barber said it was really bad. Bill got into a physical altercation with another guy in town Bill bought seed from. The barber said he'd heard Bill ask for a loan from the seed guy. When the guy came to collect, Bill didn't have it. So he wasn't about to ruin his own business. He was about to take someone else down with him."

"What happened?" I said, though I could already guess the answer.

"A little over a year ago, right before Andrew's trial started, things changed."

"Christ," Eric said. "Let me guess. All of a sudden, Bill Doyle was flush with cash. He paid off all his creditors and this seed guy."

"Pretty much," Emma said. "I tried to follow the money trail. The Doyles tried to take out loans to cover their debts from the local credit union but got turned down. The credit union owned the mortgage to both Bill's house and his store. But in May last year, he all of a sudden got approved for a pretty big small-business loan. He's still paying off loans he's taken out for operating costs, but he's been making steady payments on those for eight months. And hasn't missed a single month. Plus, he paid off the mortgages on both the house and store with the loan money. It was almost a million dollars."

"How the hell did you find all that out without a subpoena?" Eric asked. I had the same question.

Emma gave us a sly smile. "Turns out the barber's wife is a teller at the credit union. Let's just say she's not very bright."

"Is it gonna get back to the Doyles that you were asking?" Eric asked.

"I don't think so. This barber, he's also one of the people Bill pissed off. He was giving him free cuts for years because he knew how much the Doyles were struggling. The barber's wife never liked that. When Bill started flashing money around town, he never came in and paid the barber. They're no longer on speaking terms."

"Well, there's some juicy small-town drama for you," Eric said. "You'd make a pretty good detective yourself, Emma."

"The Savitches," I said. "They're the only people I can think of who would have that kind of liquidity. That could either cosign or put up collateral for a loan like that."

"A million bucks is probably pocket change to them," Eric said.

"He paid them off," I said. "Marcus paid down Andrew's family debt. In exchange for keeping the family secrets."

"We don't know that for sure," Emma said. "But the timing is certainly curious."

"You have documentation on all this?" I asked Emma, but I already knew the answer.

"Of course," she said. "Most of it's public record. I've got all the payments made to the township assessor, the mortgage payoffs that were recorded with the register of deeds. All of it happened in the same week."

"He wasn't even smart enough to cover his tracks," Eric said.

"Maybe he didn't know," I said. "Maybe Bill Doyle just didn't look a gift horse in the mouth."

"More like a Trojan horse," Eric said. "Dammit. Good work, Emma."

"Great work."

She blushed. She looked enough like her father that I could read her in much the same way.

"What?" I said. "What else do you have?"

"Laneesha Dey," she said. "I found her. She's no longer in Michigan. In addition to taking that July 2022 Michigan exam, she passed the Florida bar the preceding July. She works for an estate planning firm in St. Petersburg. I emailed her. She responded pretty quickly. She said she remembers that party. She was there. And she said she's willing to talk to me. I've set up a Zoom call with her for Monday morning."

"That's fantastic. Wow. Emma. Just … wow."

Eric walked over and kissed me on the forehead. Then he did the same to Emma. "You two are damn good at this. As good as any detectives I've ever worked with. Better than many. You might want to switch your specialty to private investigations."

"No," I said. "No way. After this, I'd rather be in a courtroom. Andrew Doyle might just be the death of me yet."

Eric's face went dark like it had on the boat.

"I'm kidding," I said.

He nodded, but his smile didn't reach his eyes. He was worried about me. Just like Wendy had worried about him. But for the first time since I agreed to take this case, I felt like there might be a light at the end of this tunnel of hell.

Chapter 21

"SHE'S RUNNING LATE," Emma said. She set up the big forty-three-inch monitor at the end of the conference room table, angling it so the camera had both of us in frame.

"I hate this stuff," I said. "I like face-to-face meetings."

"Whatever, boomer," she said, smiling.

"I'm barely Gen X, you turd," I said.

"Well, you're still old," she kept teasing. "Ancient. I saw two new gray hairs near your face just yesterday."

My hand flew to my part. I leaned forward, making myself bigger in the camera.

"You did not," I said.

"Relax, Grandma. You're still cute."

Before I could zing her with any kind of comeback, the screen in front of us flared to life as Laneesha Dey joined the meeting. Her hand covered her camera as she adjusted it. She was home. Her Dalmatian slept on the couch behind her.

"Hello," I said, waving at the camera. "Thanks so much for doing this. I'm Cass Leary."

Laneesha had a large bookshelf behind her. Her law school diploma sat angled on the top shelf.

"Oh, I don't mind," she said. "I get to sit in dry depositions all afternoon."

"I don't envy you," I said. "But I'll try to make this as brief as I can. I know my associate here, Emma, filled you in on what I wanted to talk to you about."

Emma waved. Laneesha waved back.

"A little, yes," Laneesha said. "You wanted to talk about the week we took the Michigan bar exam."

"I understand you have some clear memories about the party you attended in Williamston the weekend before? That's primarily what I wanted to talk to you about. We tracked you down based on a food delivery order you made at that party."

"Sure," she said. "I remember it. I remember most of what happened that week. Though I wish I didn't."

"Why's that?"

She smiled. "I barely passed that thing."

"I'm curious. Why did you take it?" Emma asked. "Your degree behind you is from UF Levin."

"I work for an estate planning firm," she said. "St. Petersburg has a lot of snowbirds here. Are you familiar with the term?"

I laughed. I hadn't heard it in a while, but I knew what she meant. "Mostly retired Michiganders who flock to Florida to avoid the harsh winters."

"Right," she said. "My firm wanted someone with a dual license. I was the sacrificial goat that year. In my defense, I didn't have a lot of time to prepare and it had been a year since I passed the Florida bar. I was rusty on some of that stuff."

"How did you hear about the party at the Colby House?" I asked.

"I was online friends with a guy who'd just graduated from U of M. He was taking the bar too and I stayed at his place that week. I think he heard about it. I really didn't want to go. But he talked me into it."

That tracked with everything we already knew about how Marcus's party snowballed into the big bash it became.

"Laneesha," Emma said. "Did you know about what ended up happening that night?"

Laneesha's expression grew serious. "I'm sorry. I didn't. I've lived in St. Petersburg my whole life. That was actually the first time I'd ever been to Michigan. Ever been anywhere that far north? I was pretty much in an exam cram bubble the rest of that week. I don't really watch local news. I mean, why would I? After that Sunday, I turned off my phone except for two times when I called my parents just to check in. As soon as the exam was done, I got on a plane and went home. I mean, my suitcase was in my friend's trunk that second day. He drove me straight to the airport after we finished."

"That makes sense," I said.

"Emma, when you called me, I was really shocked. I had no idea somebody got hurt at that party, let alone killed. I had no idea they were putting out Crime Stopper alerts up there about it."

"Don't beat yourself up over any of that," I said. "I'm just glad you're talking to us now. But do you recognize Daria Moreau? I know Emma's since shown you her picture?"

"Yes," she said. "Absolutely. She was kind of hard to miss. She was this tiny, gorgeous blonde. Everybody noticed her. At least everybody I was with. And I talked to her for a few minutes."

"What about?" I asked.

"Just small talk, really. I spent most of that evening out on the patio. My friend, A.J., the one who invited me to come, they had these little bistro tables set up out there near the garden. We claimed one and parked there most of the night. Anyway, I remember this big stone barbecue and pizza oven thing. That's where people started putting food out. Plus, there was a keg, some soft drinks, and liquor people brought. The patio turned into a sort of hub. When I went to get a drink, I got in line behind Daria. We talked a little. Basic stuff. Where we were from. Future plans. She was interested in me because I was already a practicing lawyer. I don't think anybody else at that party was."

"How did she seem to you?" I asked.

"Just polite. A little aloof. But she also seemed a little uncomfortable. During our conversation, she must have mentioned she was one of the ones renting the house. I think I thanked her. Said something about how generous I thought it was that they put this party together. People were having fun. It was a pressure release. Anyway, I got the impression she wasn't happy about it. She said something like it wasn't her idea. You know, in a pretty negative way. And that was it. She got her drink. I got mine. I went back to my little table."

"Do you, by chance, remember what time that was?" Emma asked.

"I can't say for sure. But A.J. and I didn't get there until pretty late. Like ten o'clock. We were actually at this bar not far from there when A.J. got a text from someone inviting us over."

"How long did you stay?" I asked.

"Late. Way later than I wanted to. A.J. got pretty drunk. I was mad at him about that. He was my ride. To be honest, that night was pretty much the end of our relationship. We weren't serious or anything. We'd just been talking. But he drank a *lot* of alcohol that night. I just had that one drink. I made a screwdriver. A.J. got sloppy drunk and started flirting with some other girl. I wasn't into it. So around two o'clock, I wanna say, I finally called an Uber and got the hell out."

"So you saw Daria Moreau sometime between ten and two?" I asked.

"I talked to her not long after we got there. Again, I can't give you an exact time. But I'd say it was within the first hour of my arrival. So say between ten thirty and eleven."

Emma had the timeline in front of her. Jason Lin testified to seeing Daria arguing with Marcus at eleven thirty.

"Did you see her again?" I asked. "Anytime after standing in the drink line? The records from the food delivery app you used have you ordering wings at 12:52 a.m. They were delivered at 1:13 a.m."

"Yes," she said. "That sounds about right. Also yes. I saw her again. But I didn't talk to her. She walked off with the guy everybody said was paying for the party. I thought he was her boyfriend or something."

I had a photo of Andrew. I held it up. "You saw her with him?"

Laneesha squinted at the camera. "No. Though he looks familiar. He might have been there too. But no. I ordered those wings because somebody put them out and they were damn delicious. I asked A.J. where they came from and he told me. So I ordered another batch after the first one ran out."

That was also consistent with Jason Lin's testimony. He'd seen Daria and Marcus arguing right around the time his batch of wings was delivered at eleven thirty.

"What about this guy?" Emma said, holding up a photo of Marcus Savitch.

"Yes," she said. "That's who I saw Daria with. See, there was this path right behind the barbecue. The delivery kid would use it to come around the house. Same guy. I bet he had to have been there like four or five times. We were joking about it. After about the third time, when we saw him, everybody would yell 'Food Guy!'. And he'd get a round of applause. There was this little path further away from that. Like deeper in the woods. You could see some kind of clearing out there with statues maybe? Might have been a birdbath or something. Anyway, when Food Guy brought my order, I went to give him a tip. That's when I saw Daria talking to that guy."

Emma was still holding Marcus's picture. I looked back down at the timeline I'd drafted from the MealHopper delivery records. 1:13 a.m. That's when Laneesha's order came.

"Wait a minute," I said. "You're saying you saw Daria with Marcus out by that birdbath at one thirteen?"

"If that's when my food came, yes."

"What did you see?" Emma asked. She drew a big red circle around the one thirteen time.

"She was mad. I couldn't hear what they were saying. But like I said, mad. Waving her arms. She pointed her finger in his face. His posture was pretty casual. It irritated me."

"Why?" I asked.

"Just cuz he kind of looked like a dick. Just arrogant. And that's the vibe he was putting off all night. Like she was all upset and he wasn't taking her seriously. Like I said, I couldn't hear anything, but I'd bet money he called her hysterical or something. I wasn't the only one who noticed. The kid who ordered the first batch of wings was standing right next to me. The two of them, Daria and the other guy, caught our attention at the same time. I got a bit of an ovation when Food Guy brought me that big bucket."

"At one thirteen," Emma repeated. "You're absolutely sure?"

"Yeah," she said. "I gave Food Guy his tip. I turned to walk back to the patio. That's when that little grotto or whatever was in my line of sight. I saw them arguing. Figured it was none of my business. And I walked back around to put my food down. People were kind of clamoring for those wings. I mean, they were that good."

"One thirteen," Emma whispered.

"Wait a second," I said. "You said you were standing next to the guy who bought the first order of Charlie's wings? You're sure?"

"Yeah."

"How?"

"Because I asked him. We were getting the munchies again and I wanted to know where the wings were from. He was out on the patio; I walked up and asked him right before I put my order in. Then, when they were delivered, he was standing right next to me. I wanna say his name was Jason."

"How do you remember that?" Emma asked.

"I'm good with names. And he was wearing this tee shirt with my favorite indie band on it. Gulf Theory. They're from St. Petersburg. It caught my eye. It was so random. We talked about that too."

Emma had put photos she found on social media of every witness who testified. I tore Jason Lin's off the board.

"Do you recognize him?" I asked, showing Laneesha the photo.

"That's him," she said. "That's Jason."

Laneesha's dog woke up and started barking loudly at something out the window.

"I'm sorry," Laneesha said. "He needs to be walked. That really is all I remember. It wasn't very long after that; I decided I'd had enough. A.J. was so drunk he was staggering. I asked him to give me his keys. He made fun of me. Just being a mean drunk. He dangled his keys, then snatched them away when I tried to take them. Twice. I just turned my back on him, called for an Uber, then walked up to the front of the house and waited for it. I got back to A.J.'s apartment before he did. His roommate let me in. A.J. showed up maybe a half an hour later. He'd given some other girl his keys and she drove him home. I mean, that's how much of a jerk he was that night."

"Laneesha," I said. "If I had to call you to testify or give an affidavit, could you swear that you saw Marcus Savitch and Daria Moreau arguing at 1:13 a.m.?"

"Sure," she said. "It's true. Do you think he's the one who killed her? She was mad. She looked mad. I certainly didn't get the vibe that he was about to hurt her. But if you're telling me I witnessed something material ... God. Are you saying I could have helped the cops or something?"

"Maybe," I said. There was no point in upsetting her now.

"You're sure nobody's ever asked you about this before?" Emma asked.

"No. Not until you called me out of the blue. I called A.J. after I talked to you. I hadn't talked to him much at all since that week. I was just shocked to learn something so awful happened that night and I didn't know anything about it. I asked A.J. if he did. He said he did. But he doesn't remember very much about that night at all. He passed out about ten seconds after he got dropped off at home."

Laneesha's phone rang. She looked at it. "I'm really sorry. I have to take this. I've got to get back to work. But yes. I'm happy to help. I'll swear to everything I saw. Do you want me to write up an affidavit?"

"That would be fantastic," I said. "We'll be in touch."

"I'll have it for you by the end of the week," she said. She already had her phone to her ear and clicked out of the meeting.

Emma's jaw was on the floor beside me. "Aunt Cass," she started.

I stared at my timeline. "Jason Lin swore he saw Marcus and Daria arguing right around eleven thirty. Marcus admitted to arguing with her. He backed up Jason Lin's timeline. Then he swore he went inside and never saw Daria again."

"Maybe he did," she said. "Maybe they argued twice?"

"No," I said. "Something's wrong. Either Marcus is mistaken about the timeline or Jason Lin is. The prosecution's other eyewitness, Henry Barber, said he saw Andrew with Daria around twelve forty-five. Remember? He was so specific because that's the time on his phone when his girlfriend called and pulled his attention away. The prosecution relied on Lin's faulty memory. They used Lin's credit card receipt, not the MealHopper delivery records. Lin's misremembering if Laneesha is accurate. Lin didn't see Marcus with Daria at eleven thirty when his wings were delivered. He saw them at one thirteen when Laneesha's order was delivered."

"Their whole timeline is wrong," Emma said, getting to the conclusion I'd already made. "There were *two* deliveries of the same wings from the same restaurant. Jason's was at eleven thirty. But Laneesha's was at one thirteen. Andrew wasn't the last one seen arguing with Daria."

"Marcus was," I said. "A half an hour after the last time anyone saw Andrew with her."

"Andrew's defense lawyer never tried to track her down," Emma said. "Nobody did. Aunt Cass, this is reasonable doubt. Is it enough? With everything else we now know about Nadler's trial mistakes and Kade's and Marcus's lies?"

"Maybe," I said. "Probably. At least enough to get a new trial. Laneesha's credible. The delivery records don't lie."

"Marcus was the last person seen with Daria," Emma said. "Not Andrew."

I picked up the conference phone. "Miranda," I said. "Can you coordinate a meeting for me with Andrew Doyle? As soon as you can. Today if possible."

Chapter 22

HE TRIED TO HIDE IT, but it was no good. Andrew Doyle had been beaten. His cuts had crusted over under his right eye. He had yellow bruising up his left forearm. The knuckles on both of his hands were scabbed over as well. So at least whoever did this to him had to work for it.

"I suppose I'm wasting my breath asking you what happened," I said.

He kept his chin down. "There's nothing you can do about it anyway."

"I can try," I said. "If you're not safe, you need to let me help you."

"It's handled," he said. He made two fists, making sure I could see the healing cuts on his hands.

It struck me how different Andrew's life had turned out. I'd known a dozen guys like him in law school and almost twenty years of practice. Small-town boys, the smartest in their class, probably with well-meaning teachers that might not have known what to do with them. Like me, he might have truly found himself in law school, surrounded by other serious people. But he was here, on the other side of that table in a faded jumpsuit looking at a bleak future.

"I have some news," I said. I'd brought a copy of the affidavit Laneesha Dey sent over. A single page from Daria's medical records. I had another stack of papers in my bag that I hoped I wouldn't have to show him.

I laid the affidavit and medical record in front of him. He kept his hands folded in his lap, but leaned over to skim them. I'd highlighted the biggest bombshell facts from Laneesha's statement. As Andrew read it, his face stayed blank. When he read Daria's medical information, he furrowed his brow.

"I don't understand," he said.

"Kade was lying, too. Seven months before she died, Daria had an abortion. The baby was Kade's. Did you have any idea?"

Andrew's face went whiter. "No. I had no idea. I knew they hooked up earlier that year. I already told you that. How did you get this?"

"Jacqueline Moreau wants to know what really happened that weekend. She suspected Marcus and Kade knew more than they were telling. She was right."

"Does she know about this?" he asked.

"What do you think?"

"I can't ... God ... they would have killed her." The moment he said it, he seemed to realize how unsettling a statement that was.

"They're religious," he said. "Daria was always covering when they'd call. She didn't want them knowing she was renting a house with us that last weekend. Marcus teased her about that a little. She was twenty-four years old. She hadn't lived under their roof in seven years."

"That's pretty much what Kade said."

"He lied?"

"He'll tell you he wasn't lying because nobody ever asked."

"She never said anything," Andrew whispered. He seemed more shocked about the pregnancy than the fact Kade hid the facts and the impact that could have on his case.

"It must have devastated her," he continued. "I wish I would have known."

"What would you have done if you did?"

"I ... I don't know. Be her friend. Take her to the appointment if she wanted me to."

"Kade did that," I said. "That's one of the ways I put it together. He was the father."

"Is it enough to get me a new trial?"

"No," I said bluntly. "But this might be."

I tapped my finger on the highlighted portions of Laneesha's statement. "Jason Lin's testimony was wrong, Andrew. Laneesha was very clear and very credible. She positively IDd Jason Lin as well. He was standing near her when she saw Marcus and Daria arguing not far from where you had your confrontation with her. But thirty minutes later. The prosecution's timeline is completely off. You weren't the last one seen with Daria. Marcus was."

He ran a hand over his mouth.

"Neither the cops, the prosecutor nor Russ Nadler tried very hard to find other witnesses from that party. All I had to do was talk to Vivian Lanski, the woman Marcus rented the house from. She put me in touch with the owner of MealHopper, the local food delivery service. They came out there at least five times. Same driver. There was a log. It creates a reliable timeline. Both Jason Lin and Laneesha Dey ordered food at different times. The same thing. Wings from Charlie's. Jason assumed he saw Marcus and Daria right when his delivery came at eleven thirty. He was wrong though. It was at one thirteen when Laneesha's identical order came."

"Did he lie?" Andrew said.

"Don't know. I haven't talked to him yet. It's next on my list. I'm hoping he'll recant when he sees what Laneesha had to say. Then I'll have two eyewitnesses who can put Marcus and Daria together near the crime scene. Thirty minutes after you say you last spoke to her. That should be enough to get you a new trial. It might even be enough to get your conviction overturned, though that's a much longer shot. But it's reasonable doubt, Andrew. I know you can see that."

"You want to say Marcus killed Daria." It wasn't a question.

"I want to say it was a credible theory that the cops, the prosecutor, and your own lawyer should have pursued. He had a motive, Andrew. You've all said versions of the same thing about Daria. She was the moral compass of your group. The most serious. The most studious. If she somehow found out Marcus was about to cheat on that exam, it would have absolutely upset her. I think she would have tried to talk Marcus out of it. Failing that, you tell me. Was it in her character to threaten to report him?"

He shook his head.

"Answer me."

"I can't. I don't know. I can't."

"Can't what?"

"You want me to let you make people think Marcus killed her?"

"I want you to let me help *you*! I think Marcus Savitch knows full well how to take care of himself. Kade Barclay as much as admitted it was Marcus who tried to manipulate you into giving mutual false alibis. The very thing that first put you under suspicion with the cops. I think Marcus knew that. Whether he was trying to cover his ass for killing Daria, or just the fraud he was about to commit against the state bar. I don't know. And I don't really care."

"I have to care," he said, pounding his fist on the table.

"Marcus Savitch will have access to the best lawyers. I don't know if the Ingham County prosecutor would even pursue a case against him. The Attorney Grievance Commission will. But that's not your problem."

"You don't understand," he said.

"So explain it to me. Explain to me why you feel it's your responsibility to protect Marcus Savitch or cover up his lies."

He just kept shaking his head.

"The way I see it," I continued, "it's one of two things. Either you really did kill Daria and Marcus knows it. But he's involved. Maybe he helped you drag her body to that pond. Or maybe it's the other way around. He killed her but you're helping him cover it up."

"No," he said. "No!"

"Or," I said. "He's using you. You're his patsy. Because he has something on you or over you. Something big enough you're willing to risk spending the rest of your life in this place. And the only thing I can think of that would compel *me* to do something like that is if I were trying to protect somebody I loved. Somebody whose freedom and safety meant more to me than my own."

I pulled out the last stack of papers from my bag. Emma had put together a summary of Bill Doyle's financial picture. The foreclosure notices. A money judgment one of his suppliers managed to get. Then the mortgage payoff and large orders for supplies right after it. All paid for with cash.

Andrew turned gray. Beads of sweat broke out on his brow.

"What is this? What the hell does my father's business have to do with anything? What are you trying to do?"

"I'm trying to save you. This is it, isn't it? This is what Marcus threatened you with. He was in a position to ruin your family or save them. Your father was up to his chin in bad debt. He was going to lose everything. His business, the farm, all of it. I'm going to take a wild guess there were threats of lawsuits and maybe even fraud charges. The criminal stuff might have even been drummed up just for the occasion."

"You don't know what you're talking about."

"I think I do. I think Marcus Savitch knew exactly how to play you. He knew your weak spots. The two of you had been close friends for three years. He knew about you. Knew about your family. Knew exactly what pressure points to exploit to get what he needed."

"I don't have anything to say about that," he said.

"Fine. Just keep listening. Do you really think your parents would want this for you? Andrew, they came to me. They reached out to your community to raise the funds to pay my bill. I'm not saying your dad knows what you did for him. He probably doesn't. All he knows is that a loan he applied for all of a sudden came through. Maybe he didn't question it. Maybe the Savitches knew exactly how to set it all up so he wouldn't be suspicious. Maybe I wouldn't have been. Except for the timing. And except for the fact that you have tried to push me off Marcus's trail since day one."

"Stop it," Andrew shouted. "You have to stop this. This isn't about Marcus. I swear it."

"Swear it to whom? To me? To God? On your life?"

"I won't allow it. I will not bargain for my freedom like this. You do not have my authorization to drag Marcus or anybody else into this."

"Did he kill her?" I asked. "The truth, Andrew. What do you know? What did you see that night?"

"Nothing. I haven't lied about what happened that night. Not to anybody. I didn't kill Daria."

"But you know who did."

He flicked his eyes downward. He wouldn't look at me.

"Dammit, Andrew, you're out of options here. You asked me to help prove your innocence. I think I have. Or at least I've proven you weren't alone in this. Kade lied. Marcus lied. The prosecution's star eyewitness was wrong about what he saw and when he saw it."

"I didn't ask for that!" he shouted. "I asked you to look into Russ Nadler's performance during the trial, not try to dig up damaging facts about my friends."

"Those aren't separate things."

"And I didn't really ask you at all," he said. "My parents came to you. Not me. I did this for them. Because they've suffered enough. But we aren't doing this. I'm not throwing Marcus and Kade under the bus. I won't do it. Not this way."

For an instant, I wanted to reach across the table and strangle him myself. Jacqueline Moreau had been right about everything. Kade, Marcus, Andrew. They were not good men. They were not protecting her daughter. They were not her friends. But then, as Andrew stared at me, tears running down his cheeks, I had a different moment of clarity. I knew there was only one thing left to do.

"Fine," I said, gathering the papers and stuffing them back into my bag. "I quit."

Chapter 23

"You CAN'T," Emma said. I stood in the doorway of her office. I got in late this morning, suffering from a pounding migraine after I left Bellamy State Prison.

"We can't!" Emma pleaded. "Laneesha Dey is all set to testify at an evidentiary hearing. We'll get one. This isn't just harmless error, Aunt Cass."

Miranda came up behind me and handed me a cup of coffee. She'd known me long enough to recognize my post-migraine hangover face.

"Bless you," I mouthed to her.

"Emma, I didn't have a choice. Andrew refuses to cooperate. If I were a medical doctor and he refused treatment, I would have discharged him AMA by now."

"No," she said, pushing herself out of her chair. "No way. He didn't do this. Or at least he didn't do it alone. Marcus Savitch was involved. Maybe Kade Barclay too. But we both know

Andrew's got to be protecting Marcus. Marcus blackmailed him into taking the fall. Andrew's parents have to be told."

"We don't even know if they're in the dark about it, Emma. For all I know, Bill Doyle is allowing his son to sacrifice himself for this."

"And how many fathers do you know who would do that?" she said. "I know mine wouldn't."

I let out a sarcastic huff. "Actually, mine would."

"Aunt Cass!" Her voice bounced off the walls of the small space. I put a hand to my head and backed out into the reception area. Miranda gave me a cool eye but didn't interject.

"I need to put my schedule back together," I said to Emma. "I've been back-burnering this entire practice since the Doyles walked through that door."

I hoped she'd cool off. But Emma had Leary DNA. The same hot-tempered strain that ran through Vangie's veins. It came from my dad. Matty, Joe, and I had temperaments more like our mom. Calmer. More level.

Emma was on my heels as I walked into the conference room. Miranda had already begun the process of boxing up Andrew Doyle's case file.

"This isn't right," she said. "The Doyles paid us a lot of money to dig into this. The job's not done."

"And we'll return every portion of their retainer that hasn't been used. Plus, it doesn't matter who pays our bill. Andrew's the client."

"So we're just going to let them get away with it?"

"Emma ..."

"No! This is wrong. I know you know that. Daria Moreau deserves better."

She wasn't wrong. Except for one critical fact. "I don't represent the Moreaus," I said. "They're not who hired us. There's nothing I can do if Andrew refuses to act in his own best interests."

"Then we have to tell someone. This is evidence of a murder, Aunt Cass. Why can't we call the prosecutor? Or the detective who investigated it in the first place? They got it wrong. They didn't dig deep enough."

I understood every bit of her frustration. I shared it. But it didn't matter. "Emma, this is the job. I don't like it any more than you do. But I am bound by attorney-client privilege. By silence. By Andrew Doyle's bloody secrets."

"Well, I'm not," she said. "I'm not an attorney. Let me report this somehow?"

"Emma, you work for me."

"I understand you could be disbarred. But I can't. I'm not a member of the bar yet."

"Yet," I said. "If you leak this, Andrew Doyle could report me to the state bar. I would face disciplinary action as your supervisor. In the not-too-distant future, you're going to have to go before a character and fitness board before you're sworn in. They'll know about it. So it *will* impact you. It could destroy your career before it even starts."

"Maybe I don't care," she said. "Maybe it's too much. If we have to keep these kinds of secrets, maybe I'm not cut out for it. Daria Moreau deserves better."

"You're right. She does. But I took an oath. I can't work for Andrew Doyle anymore, but the privilege survives the termination of our relationship. I don't see a way out of this yet."

"What about Savitch? He's out there engaging in the unauthorized practice of law. Don't you have a duty to report that? He's committing a crime every day."

It was a good question. One I'd grappled with since putting that particular piece of the puzzle together.

"I'm not sure what to do about that yet. If I can figure out a way to report him without violating my oath to my former client, I will."

"What if it's what Daria died for?" she asked. "What if Savitch actually killed her to keep her silent about what he'd done? I don't know if I can live with myself knowing that."

"I know," I said. "I just need some time to figure out what I can ethically do."

"I know we don't represent Daria's family, Aunt Cass. But maybe we should."

"You know we can't do that either. It would be a clear conflict of interest. Even though I don't represent Andrew anymore."

"We should call Grace Doyle," Emma said. "She's begged you more than once to keep helping him. She may not even know what's happened yet. I bet Andrew hasn't even told her. Surely that can't be violating privilege. We've been sending the bills to Andrew's parents. The minute they get their final one, they'll know what's going on. Maybe his family can talk some sense into him."

"It's a good thought," I said. "Only I'm not sure I want anything to do with Andrew Doyle anymore."

My head started pounding again. I sank into a chair. Emma stood over me. I looked up at her.

"Yes, you do," she said. "You're just frustrated. He's pushed you to your limit. But tell me you think he's guilty."

"What?"

"He didn't kill Daria. That's what I believe. She was alive and well after they had their confrontation. Marcus was the last one seen with her. And everything he's done in the wake of her murder makes him look guilty. He's taken a lot of risks and paid a lot of money to keep Andrew right where he is. Enough to make Andrew keep protecting him."

"I don't know what I believe anymore," I said. There was truth to it. "Nothing Andrew says or does makes sense to me now. I confronted him with what we know about his family. He didn't exactly deny Marcus's involvement in that. He claims he didn't know about Daria's abortion and Kade withholding the truth. He even claims he didn't know about Marcus's fraud. He's got a wife and a baby who will grow up not really knowing who he is."

"There has to be something else," Emma said. "Something bigger than just Marcus bailing his family out of debt. If Marcus killed once, maybe Andrew believes he's capable of doing it again."

I wanted to scream. Nothing Emma said was wrong. She had good instincts. And she reminded me a lot of myself when I was her age and just starting out in this profession. I wanted to save the world. I was arrogant enough to think I could.

"Let's regroup," I said. "You should take the rest of the day off. Actually, that's good advice for both of us."

"Will you reconsider?" she said hopefully. "We can go forward with filing the motion."

"Emma, I'm not the one who has to be convinced about that. Andrew told me point blank yesterday that he won't allow it. That is the problem."

"Fine. So maybe a day or two of him cooling off will make him come around. And I still want to talk to his wife. She's on our side. She can persuade him to do the right thing."

"We'll see," I said. "But I mean it. Go home. Binge-watch garbage TV for a day. We'll come back to it tomorrow."

She put her arms around me. "I'm sorry I yelled. You're not the one I'm mad at. I just want to strangle Andrew Doyle."

"So do I."

We walked out of the building together. I hoped she took my advice and cleared her head. Hell, I hoped I could take my own advice, too.

———

ERIC WAS JUST as good at reading my face as Miranda was. He'd been asleep when I woke up the next morning. In the middle of the night, I'd come down to sleep on the couch, not wanting to disturb him with my tossing and turning.

"You look like crap," he said.

"Thanks."

"Are you calling in sick?"

"I'm calling in defeated," I said. I gave him the rundown on my meeting with Andrew yesterday along with the argument I just had with Emma.

Eric didn't respond. He just took the information in. But when I plopped down on the couch, he grabbed my feet and rested them on his lap. His foot rubs were once again orgasmic and exactly what I needed.

"I can stay home today too," he said. "It's time to move the chickens into the coop."

"Good," I said. "It'll be nice to have the barn back. There are pine shavings everywhere."

"I'm switching to hemp bedding. It's supposed to be less dusty."

"Mmm. Can we smoke it?"

He laughed. "There's actually a label on the bag warning there's no THC in it. You know that's cuz some dipshit tried to do exactly that."

I snorted. He had to be right. "Well, good," I said. "About moving the chickens. I'll help you. It'll be a good distraction. When are they going to stop being freeloaders anyway?"

"It'll be a while. Probably three months at least."

"They'll be the most spoiled chickens in Michigan. I see they have a lake view from their coop window."

"I was thinking about getting some ducks next," he said. "Only I'm afraid I'd feel bad for them."

"Why?"

"Because of the lake view. They'd have to look at it but not be allowed to swim in it. You can't have domestic ducks intermingling with the native population."

I smiled. "I love you. And I love that you think about some ducks' feelings."

He leaned in and kissed me. "I love you too."

There was something in his expression. A worry line deepened in his forehead.

"You love me too, but what?" I said.

"Nothing."

I pulled my feet out of his lap and sat up. "But what?"

"Don't get mad at me. But Emma's right."

"What?"

"She's right. You shouldn't walk away from this case."

"My client hasn't exactly given me a choice. He won't cooperate."

"Then find a way around him."

I tossed my hands up in defeat. "How?"

"I don't know. But it's the kind of thing you excel at. Cass Leary, the patron lawyer of lost causes."

I threw a pillow at him. He dodged it easily and laughed. "It's true," he said. "You've had bigger turkeys as far as cases than this one. Only this one isn't really a turkey. You may actually have an innocent client."

"Most of my clients are innocent," I said.

He winced. "Yeah, but the ones that weren't were pretty terrible."

"What do you want me to do, Eric?"

"I don't know. It's probably the detective in me. But I want to know who killed that girl. Don't you?"

"Of course! But I'm not a detective. My role in this is pretty clear. Find a legal hook to get my client a new trial. I did that. Only now he won't let me move forward with any of it. I can't file a motion without his consent."

"I know. It's just ..."

"Just what?"

"You know, I kind of regret ever asking you about this case. Because it's under my skin now. You might be able to walk away. I just don't know if I can."

"What are you proposing?"

"How about ... maybe ..." He went silent, trying to work something out in his head. Then he looked at me. "Let me reach out to the lead detective on Daria's murder case. Just poke around a little. Detective to detective. I can keep it off book. Trust me."

"I do," I said. "I just don't see what good that will do. Daria's case is closed. The only way to reopen it is if someone actually comes forward and credibly confesses, or if Andrew would let me do my damn job."

"It's worth a conversation," he said. "That's all I'm suggesting."

He was right about one huge thing. This case was so far under my skin it might as well be tattooed on my forehead. And I did want to know once and for all who killed Daria Moreau.

"Okay," I said. "But just a conversation. Like I told Emma, none of this matters if Andrew won't let me act on his behalf."

"Got it. Leave it to me. I'll make a call. I've actually met the guy once or twice. He's a good cop, Cass. It might bear fruit we didn't expect."

I squeezed Eric's hand. For the last year, I'd been begging him to come back and work with me. Maybe his idea had already borne fruit *he* didn't expect.

Chapter 24

It DIDN'T SURPRISE me that Detective Tim Messer willingly talked to Eric. What surprised me was that he agreed to let me in on the call.

Eric walked into my office with his phone against his ear. "I'm just walking in," he said. "Let me put you on speaker."

I gave Eric a questioning look. He shot me a quick nod and put his phone on my desk between us.

"Go ahead, Tim," Eric said. "Can you repeat what you just told me?"

There was a pause. Tim Messer had a gravelly voice. Eric had met him in passing over the years and the man was just a few months from retiring.

"I was just saying, I think you're wasting your time. But it's your time to waste."

Eric wrote something on the legal pad in front of me then turned it so I could see it. "Let me do all the talking."

"Of course," I mouthed back.

"Here's what I know," Eric said. "I have a witness with credible testimony that the timeline presented at trial was completely wrong."

"In what way?" Messer asked.

"Did you have a chance to review your file before my call?"

"A little, yeah. But it wasn't necessary. I still know the case pretty well. It's one of the ones that stick with you."

"I get that. It's kind of gotten under my skin too. Anyway, we found a witness who can prove Andrew Doyle wasn't the last person seen with the victim. That the altercation between Doyle and Daria Moreau happened well before her altercation with Marcus Savitch. There are some other things too I'm not at liberty to disclose. But it's enough I think Doyle might not have done this."

"Who cares?" Messer said.

Eric put a hand up, gesturing for me not to say anything.

"What I mean is," Messer continued. "I don't think it matters who was the last person seen arguing with that girl. ME gave an eight-hour window for her time of death. Midnight to eight a.m. Can you prove Doyle didn't go find her later that night after everyone left?"

"It's not our job to prove that," I whispered through gritted teeth. Again, Eric gestured for my silence.

"No," Eric said. "I can't prove that. But ..."

"But," Messer cut him off. "I'm not saying it wouldn't have given me pause if I had a new witness like that two years ago. But it wouldn't have changed the outcome. Doyle's skin and blood was under the victim's nails. There's a record of her having real concerns about being around him. Doyle texted her some pretty creepy messages the day before she died. Messages that alarmed her enough to reach out to her ex-boyfriend to try to put a stop to it. And Doyle lied to my face about where he was that night. I put the best case together I could with the evidence I had. The prosecutor charged on it and a jury unanimously convicted him. I did my job."

"I know you did," Eric said. "Honestly, I don't think I would have handled it any differently than you did. But the other thing I wanted to talk to you about ... what did your gut tell you?"

"That Andrew Doyle started to get obsessed with Daria Moreau. He had some grand idea that he was in her league and that she would feel the same way about him. He had a little liquid courage. She was too nice to him. When he made his move, she rejected him. Firmly, unequivocally, bluntly. He couldn't handle it. He got rough. She fought back. He pushed her hard enough to kill her."

"I know you ..." Eric tried to interject.

"That by itself I could almost understand." Messer talked over him. "Things got a little heated. Doyle got emotional. Got caught up in the moment. It got out of hand. I could even believe he didn't mean to kill her. If the jury had convicted on second degree, I would have been at peace with that. But it didn't end there. Doyle tried to hide the body. Cover his tracks. And if you're telling me you have credible proof that there was a second altercation with her later that night, that only makes me even more certain he's the bad guy, Wray."

"I know," Eric said. "I get it. What was your read on Savitch and Barclay?"

Messer let out an audible sigh. "That they're a couple of idiots at best, real assholes at worst. It bothered me a lot that they didn't report her missing right away. But she was a grown woman. It wasn't out of character for her to go off by herself when she was angry. Do I think they maybe had something to do with trying to cover their tracks after the fact? Maybe. But it was never anything I could prove. The physical evidence was solid. And it only ever pointed to Andrew Doyle. I'd like to say I'm sorry I can't help you. But I'm not. And look, I'd be the first guy to say I was wrong if there was the slightest chance we put the wrong guy in prison for this. Only I know I'm not."

I knew this was going to be a waste of time. Eric couldn't say it yet, but I also knew when we hung up, he would tell me he agreed with most of what Messer said. If nothing else, maybe it would make us both more confident in my choice to walk away. Then, on impulse, I asked Messer a question of my own.

"Detective, this is Cass. I know I'm probably the last person you want to talk to about anything. Much less a rehashing of one of your own cases. So I won't do that. But I do want to ask you about Russ Nadler."

"What about him?"

"How well do you know him?" I asked. Eric gave me a thumbs up and picked up my legal pad. He wrote some notes down while I still had Messer on the line.

"Pretty well, actually," Messer answered. "At least I did. Russ has been around as long as I have. He was a blowhard. A pain in my ass."

240

"Was?" Eric wrote that single word on the pad and showed it to me. I nodded.

"What about during this trial?" I asked. "I've reviewed the transcripts. I know hindsight is twenty-twenty and I sure wouldn't appreciate somebody critiquing my work after the fact. Things happen when you're in that courtroom that you can't predict. But I have to admit, the way it read to me, he missed quite a few things."

Silence on the other end of the phone. I was about to ask Messer if he was still there.

"Yeah," he said. His voice lowered an octave.

"Yeah what?" Eric asked.

"Russ backed himself into a corner. Not on this case. In life. But yeah. If I'm being honest, he was off his game during that trial. I don't for one second think it made a difference to the outcome. Nor do I think any of Russ's conduct should get him in trouble. But right after, he really unraveled."

"He was eventually disbarred," I said. "What do you know about that?"

"Yeah, I don't know," Messer said. "Russ went through a tough divorce about five years ago. It absolutely broke him. His wife took him for everything. Not that he didn't deserve it. He cheated on her more than once. April finally reached the end of her rope. The word is he racked up some gambling debts."

"He embezzled money from his clients," I said.

"I can't speak to that," Messer said.

"I'd like to talk to him," I said. "Are you still in communication with him? Nadler's pretty much gone off the grid as far as I can tell. I have a lot of questions. I don't quite understand why my new witness wasn't discovered two years ago. She wasn't that hard to find. I ..."

Eric slapped his hand against the table. "Stop," he mouthed. I clenched a fist, but understood his point. If I pushed Messer too hard and started accusing him, he'd likely end the call.

"I just want to talk to him," I repeated. "Do you know where I might find him? Or could you get a message to him?"

Eric wrote another note and turned the pad to me. "So are you back in this thing?"

I didn't respond. I waited for Messer to say something.

"I don't have his number," Messer said. "Off the grid is a pretty accurate description of what Russ did. And I don't know why I'm even telling you this."

"You're colleagues," I said. "I understand."

"We are most certainly not. And we're not friends. Not by a long shot. Some of those clients he embezzled from? A couple of them were friends of mine. Friends I should have warned to stay away from him. He was your typical scumbag defense attorney."

I flared my nostrils. It was a not-so-subtle shot at me.

"But you know where he is," I concluded.

"I know where he might be. Or where everyone assumes he is. Russ lost everything in the divorce. His house. Most of his bank account. His muscle car. Even his damn dog. But he kept one thing. He had a hunting cabin up in St. Johns. I've been there a few times. Not to his place. But one of my actual friends has a place really close to his. I can send you the address."

"I would really appreciate that," I said.

"That's good of you, Tim," Eric said.

"Look," Messer said. "Good luck. Doesn't mean you're not wasting your time. But maybe Russ will talk to you. I said he's not my favorite person. We've clashed more than once. But I don't wish him ill. That's not who I am."

A second later, Eric got a text. He turned his phone toward me. It was the address Messer promised.

"Thanks, Messer," Eric said. "We won't keep you anymore. I hope you won't hold the last twenty minutes against me."

Messer let out a hearty laugh. "Don't count on it, Wray. And aren't you supposed to be retired?"

"I'm working on it," Eric said.

"Work harder," Messer said. "The second I'm out the door, I'm not planning to look back."

Eric's expression went serious. "Yeah," he said. "Turns out that's harder than you think."

Messer clicked off. Eric forwarded Messer's directions to me.

"Good," I said. "I'll go tomorrow."

Eric smiled. "I thought you quit, Cass."

"It's just a conversation," I said. "Think of it as a final punctuation. Then I can walk away for good knowing I tried everything I possibly could."

"Fine," Eric said. "But I'm going with you."

I knew exactly what Eric meant, even as it unsettled me. Getting out is harder than we think.

Chapter 25

"For someone who fired her client, I'm still doing an awful lot of work for him," I said. I had the address Detective Messer gave us. We were fifteen minutes out.

"I can still turn around if you want," Eric said, but he had a sly grin on his face.

"You could not," I said. "You'd be driving out here without me. You have to know as much as I do. Even if I'm no longer getting paid for it."

"Why is that?"

"What do you mean?"

"I mean ... why this girl? Why this case? I've investigated hundreds of these. Maybe more. Sure, some stick with you, there's no getting around it. But this wasn't my case. I wasn't at the crime scene. I've never talked to the victim's family one-on-one. And yet ..."

"You can't get it out of your head." I finished his sentence for him.

"Yeah."

"I don't know," I said. "I wish the Moreaus had come to me first.
I wish I was doing this for the good guys. But I feel like Daria's
haunting me or something. Like she's got a hold of me from
beyond the grave and she's telling me Andrew didn't do this. I
know that sounds crazy."

"It does. Only that's how I feel, too. It's more than that though.
If we're right. If Marcus Savitch got his family to cover this up, it
worries me what else they might do. If he got away with murder
once, odds are he'll do it again."

"There," I said. We almost missed the road. It was unmarked,
but showed up on my GPS app as Sandhill Drive. It wasn't
much more than a muddy two-track and I was grateful Eric
talked me into letting him drive his truck. He slowly made the
turn. We drove uphill for a quarter of a mile before reaching
the small blue house with a wraparound porch. It sat
overlooking a kidney-shaped lake, probably no bigger than fifty
acres.

"Nice place," Eric said, exiting the truck. He slipped on a pair of
sunglasses. I got out and walked around to stand beside him.
There was no garage. Only a carport, but it was empty. Two
black and white cats darted out from under the porch and ran
into the woods.

Before we took another step, a woman came out of the house,
slamming the storm door behind her. She wore a purple
muumuu and her white hair was tied back in a ponytail.

"What's your business here?" she asked. Though it was a blunt
question, her voice wasn't unfriendly.

Eric pulled out a business card. It shocked me a little that he still had them on him. I had them made when he officially worked for me as a private investigator.

"I'm looking for Russ Nadler," he said. "I was told he lives up here."

She took the card, inspected it, then slipped it in her pocket. "Messer sent you," she said. "He told me someone like you might be stopping by. You're the other lawyer?"

"Sort of," I said.

"Sort of? Do I want to know what you mean by that?"

"Probably not," I said. "Is Nadler here?"

"He's here," she said. "But he's down at the shore fishing off the dock. He's been down there all morning. Once he goes, he stays. The stairs are hard on his knees."

"May I ask your name?" Eric said.

"Doreen," she answered. "Russ is my ... well ... he's just mine."

I looked more closely at her. Doreen. The Doyles gave me every correspondence Nadler sent to Andrew. A lot of them were signed by a Doreen Roselle on Nadler's behalf. His legal secretary, mostly likely.

"Then you know why I'm here," I said. "I was asked to look into Andrew Doyle's case. He's hoping to file an appeal or ask for a new trial."

"Which means you're planning on throwing Russ under the bus. You'd have to say Andrew had ineffective assistance of counsel."

I took a breath, thinking of some way to be diplomatic. But the cold eye she trained on me made me think the better of it.

247

"Probably," I said. "And I understand Russ has had some difficulties with the state bar after his work with Andrew."

"One doesn't directly have anything to do with the other," she said. "But you need to know, Russ is better now. Stepping away from his law practice was the best thing for him. It was a long road back, but he's happy here. At least he's learning to find reasons to get up every morning."

"And I don't mean to impede that progress," I said. "I just have a few questions for him. But I can't promise they won't upset him."

We heard thudding footsteps behind her. Then Russ Nadler himself walked around the side of the house holding a fishing pole and tackle box. He didn't exactly seem surprised to see us. He leaned the pole against the house and set down the tackle box.

"How long have they been here?" he asked Doreen.

"You didn't miss anything," she answered. "You gonna talk to them?"

Nadler regarded me. I knew he was barely past sixty. He looked older though. He had thick, gray stubble and hard lines in his face. He was maybe thirty pounds overweight and favored his right leg when he walked.

"Out here," he said. "I'm all right, Dor. You can go back inside."

She gave him a cautious glance, but did as he asked. Nadler pulled a cigarette and lighter out of his fishing vest and sat down on one of the porch chairs. He lit up and gestured toward two other empty chairs. I took one, but Eric stood on the porch steps, leaning against the railing.

"How's Andrew?" Nadler asked.

"Not great," I said. "He's got a lot of questions about how things went down."

Nadler blew a puff of smoke then waved it away from his face. "That's your first lie. You wanna keep going? Because I'd rather just go take a nap."

Eric took a step forward. I gestured to him to stand down.

"It was his family who hired me," I said.

Nadler laughed. "Right. Now that sounds true."

"I don't think Andrew's been an active participant in his own defense since before the trial started," I said. Nadler blew another puff of smoke. He said nothing, but he didn't deny it either.

"Do you know why that is?" Eric asked. "Your guy says he's innocent. But he rolled over anyway."

"He's not my guy," Nadler said. "I don't work for him anymore. Thank God."

"You know he didn't do it," I said. It wasn't a question. "You know he was nowhere near Daria Moreau when she was murdered. So what I want to know is why you didn't do your job."

No reaction. No righteous indignation of defensiveness. Just nothing.

I had loaded up another set of questions. Why hadn't he pursued other party witnesses? Why had he lay down on Savitch and Barclay's cross-examinations? But it hit me then.

Those were all the wrong questions. I was using the wrong playbook if what I suspected about Nadler was true.

The Savitch family paid him off, too. It would have been easy. Nadler was drowning in debt and soon to face disciplinary action. He would have made a deal with the strongest devil he could.

The strongest devil ...

I rose from my chair and walked over to him.

"Nadler," I said. "You know why I'm here. But I don't think you've truly thought through what that means."

He didn't look at me. From the corner of my eye, I saw Eric raise a brow. I hadn't planned to approach things this way. It was a risk. But I banked on the fact Russ Nadler was too far out of the loop to question what I was about to say.

"Have you looked at me?" I asked.

He snuffed his cigarette out on his chair arm. "I've googled you," he said. "You've got some game. Had some luck with some big murder cases."

"Luck? We make our own luck. But I'm not talking about my reputation as a defense lawyer. That's new. I mean ... do you really know who I am? Who I work for?"

Eric stifled a cough. He was catching on. It wasn't approval I saw in his expression. But he was at least shrewd enough to know this might work.

"You've heard of the Thorne Law Group," I said. "My former employers."

Finally, a reaction from Nadler. He wouldn't meet my eye.

"What interest would the Thorne family have in a two-year-old local murder case?"

"None," I said. "But they're interested in the Savitches." Nadler was right. I'd been telling lies since the second I stepped on this porch. I just hoped that was the end of his sophisticated guesses. He'd responded to threats before. I just had to convince him I was an even bigger one.

"Let's just say a man like Killian Thorne would appreciate your insight into that family."

"Cass," Eric said. I shot him a look. He clamped his mouth shut. Killian was a sore point between us. He recruited me to work for his family almost two decades ago. I spent the first part of my career as a mob lawyer. That was all finished. I'd broken ties. Got out with my life. But maybe Russ Nadler didn't know that. He'd spent thirty years as a defense attorney in Michigan. There's no way he didn't know who the Thornes were.

"You need to confirm something for me," I said.

Nadler was sweating. "I can't help you. I want no part of this."

"You're already part of it. You were part of it the second you took Savitch's money."

"You can't prove that!"

I laughed. "Not exactly a denial, Russ."

Silence.

"Nobody wants to cause you any trouble," I said. "I'd like nothing more than to just let you live your new life out here. But it's in my boss's interest to know what Savitch is up to on behalf of his son. It's better if you don't know why."

"I don't want to know," he said, shaking.

"Good. This fight isn't about you. It's between the Thornes and the Savitches. I promise. Mr. Thorne is just trying to confirm some things Lars Savitch told him. It's a matter where trust is at issue, Mr. Nadler. All you have to do is tell me the truth."

He shook his head. "Did he send you? Did Lars Savitch use my name?"

I weighed my answer. "Yes," I said.

"I knew it. I knew he wasn't going to be able to keep my name out of his mouth. You're telling me he's using me to flex his muscles for the likes of Killian Thorne?"

"Something like that."

"Fine," he said. "You tell your boss yes. I was loyal. I did what Savitch wanted me to. His influence extended that far."

"How?" I asked. "How far did it extend exactly?"

"What do you want me to say? Yes. You're right. I didn't go hard at Barclay and Savitch's son. I never did anything that would have implied sonny boy had unclean hands on this. I'm not proud of it. I don't know about any other witnesses. But yeah. You're right. I didn't exactly look that hard for any. But the jury got that case right. Andrew's guilty."

"How do you know that?"

"How could he not be? His blood was all over that girl. I'm not losing any sleep because I took a dive for an innocent man. I don't know why the hell Killian Thorne would be interested in undoing any of that now. I don't want to know. I want to be left alone. Tell Savitch, tell Thorne. Whatever business they've got together is none of mine. I've kept my word. Savitch did what he said he'd do. He paid my debts. He gave me a clean slate. I was going to retire my license anyway."

Nothing Nadler said surprised me. Not the content of it. But to hear him actually admit to being on the Savitch family payroll made me feel sick.

"That's all I needed to hear," I said.

"You'll tell Savitch? You'll tell Thorne?"

"You're a good soldier, Russ," I said. "I'm certain they'll both appreciate it. I just need one more assurance from you."

"What?" he snapped.

"I wasn't here. Neither of us were. Can you handle Doreen on that?"

"Of course," he said. "She knows the rules to this game, too."

"Good." I backed away from Nadler. Eric had already walked down the stairs. He was glaring at me.

Doreen came back out on the porch carrying a tray of lemonade.

"It's okay, Dor," Nadler said, rising. "They're leaving. They won't be coming back."

I gave Doreen a tight-lipped smile. Then Eric and I climbed back into the truck.

"What the hell was that?" Eric demanded as he drove back out to the highway.

"Just a hunch," I said. "A Hail Mary."

"It was risky," he said.

"But effective," I answered. "I just figured if Nadler could be bought so easily, he could also be bullied."

"What if Thorne finds out you've been throwing his name around?"

"He won't," I said. "And if he does, he won't care. Not about this. He'll know I must have had a good reason for it."

Eric grimaced. "I don't like it. You swore you're not in communication with him."

"I'm not. I don't even know where he is. Or ... if he's even alive, Eric. I swear. This was harmless."

He shook his head, but stopped giving me crap. We drove in silence for a couple of miles. Finally, when we came to a dead stop for a minor traffic jam, he turned to me.

"Dammit," he said.

"What?" Though I was afraid to ask.

"You're too good at this. I said I didn't like it. I don't. Actually, I hated it. But ..."

"But what?"

He smiled. "It was kind of brilliant, too."

Chapter 26

"SHE'S STILL PRETTY mad at you," Jeanie said. "Lord, if she didn't inherit your father's temper. Between her and Vangie ..."

"Vangie's an actual chaos agent," I said. "Emma had a good dad. Vangie didn't. Emma will calm down."

"Do you think she's right? That you should keep going for Andrew Doyle?"

I hadn't told Jeanie about my last couple of days on the Daria Moreau murder. I didn't want word getting out of the office. For one thing, Miranda would freak out about me working for free. For another, I didn't want to get Emma's hopes up about anything. But Jeanie, like my brother Joe, could always see straight through me.

She smirked. "You already have been."

"Jeanie ...I ..."

"What'd you find out?"

"Nothing we didn't already suspect," I said. "Nadler was on the take. He as much as admitted the Savitch family was behind it."

"Cass! That's huge. That's enough to maybe get Doyle's conviction overturned. Did you tell him?"

"No," I said. "For one thing, Nadler will never go on the record with it. He's afraid for his life. He actually reminded me a lot of Andrew. The Savitches have power over both of them. I tried to use my background as a wedge. It worked just enough to get Nadler to admit he took a dive. But it doesn't solve the critical problem."

"What do you mean?"

"I mean I can't prove Andrew's innocent."

"You don't have to. You only have to prove mistakes were made at trial. These aren't even mistakes. This is criminal."

I lay back on Jeanie's office couch. It felt like a therapy session. She sat in the chair beside me.

"That's not the point. The point is, there's still nothing tying Marcus to the murder."

"He was the last one seen with Daria. Nadler's fraud and Laneesha Dey's testimony should be plenty."

"Except it's not. Eric and I talked to Detective Messer. He was lead on the original investigation. He had a decent point. The physical evidence still implicates Andrew alone. He doesn't have an alibi for the window of time Daria might have died. He could have easily gone back out there later after most of the party guests left."

"That's for a jury to decide," Jeanie said. "They were never given that chance. They were fed false, unchallenged information from a sloppy prosecutor and a defense attorney who was actively trying to sink his own client. Who is now your client."

"That's debatable. And Andrew won't let me take any of this to court."

Jeanie growled in frustration. "Then you need to rattle the purse strings. Talk to Andrew's father. His wife. Bill Doyle needs to know what his son is putting him through on his behalf."

"What if he already knows?" I sat up.

"What?"

"What if Bill Doyle isn't the aw-shucks, Midwestern farm boy everybody thinks he is? We've assumed he's unaware of what the Savitches did for him and why. We've assumed he just didn't look a gift horse in the mouth when that business loan miraculously came through. We've assumed Andrew's just been taking the fall for Marcus. What if he's also trying to keep his own father out of jail?"

"What a mess," Jeanie said. "On one hand, I think you should raise hell and prove who really killed that girl. On the other hand, I'd like to close the book on the whole lot of them."

"Which puts you in the same square on the game board as I am," I said.

Miranda poked her head in. "Don't mean to interrupt the brain trust," she said. She was so deadpan it was sometimes hard to tell if she was being sarcastic. "But Cass, you've got a call. It's Bill Doyle."

Jeanie popped out of her chair. "That's a joke, right?"

"It is not," Miranda said. "He sounds pretty angry. Yelled at me to interrupt Cass no matter what she was doing. Which frankly made me want to just hang up on him. Maybe I should have. I still can. I thought I'd leave the final decision up to you."

"It's okay," I said. "I'll take it in here."

"Line one," she said, then slipped back out the door.

Jeanie had a landline on the table beside her. She reached over and pointed toward the blue speaker button. I gave her a thumbs up. Better to have her listen in than try to explain later.

"Mr. Doyle," I said. I heard rushing sounds, indicating he was behind the wheel.

"You wanna explain to me just what the hell it is you're doing?"

Jeanie made a fist and punched the air.

"No, actually," I said. I would only put up with his attempts to bully me so far. "I think it's your son who should do the explaining."

"He's shutting me out! Grace and I went over there yesterday for a scheduled visit and he refused to see us. He made a call to Grace later and told her you dumped him. She's so upset. She dropped Beckett off this morning and asked us to watch him so she could go for a drive and calm down."

"Mr. Doyle, I can't do anything about your relationship with your son. If ..."

"We paid you a lot of money, Ms. Leary," he shouted. "I've called in favors all over town. Humbled myself in a way that's not easy for me. I've never taken a handout in my life. I did it this time for Andrew. And for Beckett."

Jeanie blanched at his handout comment. It reinforced the theory that Bill didn't know where his loan money really came from. Or he was just a really good con man.

"And I told you from the very first day we met that no matter who signs my checks, Andrew is my client. My duty is to him and him alone."

"So honor it," Bill said. "He didn't kill that girl. I think you know it. So help him like we paid you to do."

He was stepping to the edge of a very tricky line. My duty to Andrew also extended to keeping his secrets. While I would have loved to tell his father just how uncooperative his son was being, I couldn't go into detail. I couldn't bring what I knew about Marcus Savitch into it. Andrew had explicitly told me not to.

"Mr. Doyle. I no longer feel I can adequately represent your son in light of his own choices. Any unused portion of his retainer will be returned to you along with a full accounting of my time. But any other information you'll have to get from your son. That's all I'm at liberty to discuss with you."

"And I told you he won't talk to me. He's shut down. Grace says he's refusing to go forward with anything. She thinks he's just going to lie down and spend the rest of his life in prison. I don't understand it. Neither does Grace. And Jenny? God. I haven't even broken any of this to her. She's not well, Ms. Leary. My wife is sick. She's fought back breast cancer two times. It's coming back. She needs something to hold on to if she's gonna fight this thing again. She needs to know her son has a future."

"I'm very sorry," I said. "Truly. But it's Andrew who needs to fill you in. I can't help you."

"You mean you won't," he said. "I thought I could trust you. I know all about you. I figured you'd fight dirty if you had to. Maybe you're in cahoots with Andrew's other lawyer. You all stick together."

"I'm not in cahoots with anyone. But I can't control what you believe. And I can't control your son."

"This isn't over," he said. "I'll get you disbarred if I have to."

"You can expect that check and accounting by the end of next week," I said, then had Jeanie end the call.

"Was that an act?" she said. "If it was, he's good at it."

"Maybe that's been the case all along," I said.

"Well, you should do what Andrew told you to do then. Walk away. Leave it alone. Don't let Andrew Doyle be your problem anymore."

From an ethical standpoint, I could make a clean break. From a moral one, I couldn't get Daria Moreau's face out of my damn head. Or Marcus Savitch. Eric's fears were valid. If he'd just learned he could get away with murder, odds are he'd try it again someday.

Miranda popped in again. "Sorry. You're popular today, Cass. I have Lee Cannon on the line. He also told me to interrupt you if you were in a meeting."

"You can take it in here too," Jeanie said. "I can make myself scarce."

"It's okay," I said. "Put him on speaker."

Miranda walked over to Jeanie's desk and hit the speaker button on her desk phone.

"Lee?" I said. "I'm here. My colleagues Jeanie and Miranda are too."

"That's fine," he said. Like Bill Doyle, it sounded like Lee was driving. "I'll make it quick. I got an answer on something I thought you'd like to have."

"I'm listening."

"Grant Reznick," he said.

"Okay? Am I supposed to know him?"

"He's currently in federal prison awaiting trial. He was caught up in the fraud sting I was telling you about. The one responsible for sending ringers in to take college and professional licensing exams."

I sat back down on Jeanie's couch. "Okay?"

"I'm gonna text you a mug shot. Maybe you can run it by your witness from the bar exam you've been looking into. They traced that fake driver's license number back to Reznick. He's not talking. Yet. But I'm pretty sure he's the one who sat for the bar in Marcus Savitch's place. If you want a sit-down with him, I can arrange it. Though I don't expect you'll get very far. Reznick's a good soldier. He knows getting caught was an occupational hazard. He's more scared of whoever he works for than doing time. He's probably getting a fat bonus for it."

I knew the look in Jeanie's eyes. Miranda's too. If I'd truly dumped Andrew Doyle as a client, what would be the point? Except that itch. The thing that made it impossible for me to walk away just yet. I had to know the truth.

"That's great, Lee," I said. "I really appreciate it. And yes. Where's Reznick now?"

"Not far. FCI Milan. I can get you in to see him as soon as tomorrow afternoon. Can you swing it?"

"I can," I said.

"I'll meet you there. I'm just as interested in what he has to say."

Lee ended the call.

"He's not going to tell you anything," Jeanie said.

"Maybe not," I said. My phone pinged with the picture text Cannon had promised to send through. I opened my screen. Jeanie and Miranda walked over so they could see the picture over my shoulder.

"Holy crap," Jeanie said. "It was barely even a stretch."

Grant Reznick had dark, broody eyes, thick brown hair, and an anvil-square jaw. He was movie-star handsome and I could understand why Brianne Folger found him so attractive when she sat near him during the bar. He also bore a slight resemblance to Marcus Savitch.

"You're going anyway," Miranda said. "Can we even bill for your time if you do?"

God bless her for staying on brand, at least.

"You can dock my pay." I smiled.

Miranda crossed her arms and scowled at me. "Don't laugh. Because that's exactly what I'm going to do."

Chapter 27

ERIC CAME with me to FCI Milan. Cannon met us there. As we walked through security, I received the text from Emma I'd been waiting for.

> Brianne Folger made a positive ID. Unequivocal. Grant Reznick is the guy she sat next to and tried to flirt with during her bar exam.

I showed the screen to Eric. "Did you have any doubt?"

"No," I said. "But it makes one less thing I've got to bluff about." He gave me his patented scowl. Though he might disapprove of my methods, he couldn't fault my logic.

Eric stepped forward and shook Cannon's hand as the three of us were ushered into a private visitors' room. I clipped my visitor badge to my blouse.

"What are we walking into?" Eric asked.

"He's kept his mouth tightly shut since he's been in here. I've talked to the field agent in charge of the case. He did me a favor by letting you in to see him, but it's not one-sided. If you can get the guy to talk. Name some names about who he's worked with. It would be appreciated."

"You don't have the ringleaders?" Eric asked. "You said it was a sting."

"We have some of the ringleaders. We want more. Particularly about who they're using to create the IDs. More about their onboarding. The test-taker arm of this is the least egregious thing we're after. I'm not at liberty to divulge more, but this is why Reznick's sitting here without an immunity deal already in place."

"You think I'll be able to turn him when your people haven't been able to?" I asked.

Cannon shot a look at Eric. He answered my question while holding Eric's gaze, not mine. "He knows who you are," he said.

"What do you mean?" I asked.

Cannon looked at me. "He knows who you used to work for. I'm not entirely sure he realizes you've left Killian Thorne's payroll. I didn't see the value in disabusing him of that belief."

"I don't like it," Eric said. "If rumors get out she's still in contact with Thorne, still involved with him, it makes her a target."

"I'm standing right here," I said. "I think I've proven more than once I don't need either of you to take care of me in this regard. I'm not afraid of Grant Reznick or who he works for. I'm here for what he can tell me about the weekend Daria Moreau was murdered. If I can pick up anything else useful, you're welcome to it. There are no cameras or recording devices in that room, I hope."

"None," Cannon said. "No one-way glass either. It's a lawyer's room. That's part of the favor I called in. You owe me."

I glared at him. "I thought it was the other way around. Though it's hard to keep track. Besides, if I get any usable intel about your operation, we'll call it even."

Cannon's phone buzzed with an incoming text. He glanced at it. "They're bringing him up now. I'll leave you to it."

He reached for the doorknob. "Eric," I said. "Go with him. I think this will go better if I meet with Reznick alone. If I find the need for backup, I'll let you know."

He opened his mouth with what I guessed would be a protest. But Cannon put a hand on his shoulder. "Come on. We've got some things to talk about anyway."

Talk about? I was about to ask what, but Eric didn't seem surprised. I heard the lock on the door behind me slide open. Before I could ask what Cannon meant by that, a guard ushered Grant Reznick into the room. Eric and Lee showed themselves out. A moment later, I was alone with Reznick.

He sat at the small, square table and sipped from a water bottle. He was even more handsome in person. His stint in federal prison had added a rakishness to his looks. A hint of rough stubble. Colder eyes. His hair had grown just a bit too long.

"They told you who I am?" I asked.

He put his water bottle down. "Yeah. But they didn't tell me what you wanted."

"I'll get to it then." I pulled a file out of my bag and set it on the table. I placed my palm on top of it. Let him wonder for a moment before I showed him what was inside.

"I have a client," I said. "His name is Andrew Doyle."

"Never heard of him," Reznick said.

"I wouldn't imagine you have. I wouldn't bring him up at all, but for the sake of transparency. You know I'm a defense lawyer."

"I said I know who you are," Reznick snapped. It lent credence to Cannon's guess that Reznick thought I still worked for the Thorne Law Group. I hadn't intended to use that bluff a second time. Because Eric was right. If too many people started spreading rumors about my association, it could stir things up I'd worked very hard to bury.

"Fine," I said. I opened my file and pulled out a copy of the bar exam seating chart. I spread it flat. Reznick looked at it, but didn't register a reaction.

"I don't want to waste either of our time. This highlighted seat here?" I pointed to the lower right of the chart. I'd circled Reznick/Savitch's seat in blue. "You sat here for the Michigan bar exam a couple of years ago."

No reaction.

"It's not a question," I said. "I'm not asking you to admit to anything I can't already prove. I know the ID you used popped in this investigation that put you here. I have an eyewitness who sat next to you. They've confirmed it was you from a photograph. So please don't bother denying you were there."

He said nothing.

"To be honest," I continued, "I don't care that you took a test for Marcus Savitch. As a member of the bar myself, of course it bothers me that Savitch is running around practicing law on a license he didn't earn. But I think that's probably the least of his transgressions to society."

"I don't have anything to do with Marcus Savitch," he said.

"I'm sure you don't anymore. You did your job. You were paid for it. You moved on with your life. Or tried to until all this happened. I'm sure part of that payment was to take the hit if you ended up in prison. My guess is you're actually earning a healthy bonus for keeping your mouth shut. Worst-case scenario, you're in here for a year, maybe? Then you get out. You've got a fat bank account and the gratitude of your employers. That's probably worth a lot more than the paycheck."

"Why am I here? You have all the answers."

"I don't," I said. "The thing is, I don't give a rat's ass about any of that. It's your life. But Savitch made a mistake that weekend. So far, I'm the only one who figured it out. Because while you were taking that test for him, he was sitting in a police interrogation room as a suspect in the murder of this woman."

I put a photo of Daria Moreau in front of him. His eyes flicked downward, but he didn't react.

"Before you say it," I said. "I know that's got nothing to do with you. But it has very much to do with Marcus Savitch. And his family. You're familiar with them?"

Just the slightest narrowing of his eyes, but I knew I had his attention.

"Savitch has made one too many mistakes," I said. "He's about to be exposed for them. His family knows that."

"You said you work for this Andrew Doyle. Why would the Savitches send you to talk to me?"

"This is my question for you," I said, ignoring his question. "I need you to tell me about your conversations with Marcus Savitch the week you sat for his bar exam."

"Why should I?"

"Because it could help you. I'm sure the terms of your employment prohibit you from talking about them. So you're not going to make any plea deals that involve ratting anyone out. But nothing would prevent you from telling me what you know about this girl, Marcus Savitch, and that weekend. And *that*, Mr. Reznick, is something the federal prosecutor might look kindly on when he or she considers a plea deal. You have a bargaining chip you didn't even know about."

I pulled out another photo of Daria Moreau. This one was taken at the crime scene. She was lying on the ground, her face waxen, her eyes bulging. She was about to be zipped up into a body bag and hauled to the morgue.

"I told you. I don't know this girl."

"Marcus Savitch did," I said. "He may not have mentioned her by name. But Savitch's phone was searched. There are two calls made to a burner phone just a few hours before this girl turned up dead. I believe he made those calls to you."

A bluff. But a reasonable one. Savitch made no calls from his personal cell that night. If he called Reznick at all, he had to have used a burner phone of his own. I had every belief Reznick's employers would have required it.

Nothing. No response.

"Did Marcus Savitch tell you he suspected this woman might expose his fraud?"

No answer.

"Look," I said. "You don't have to deny Marcus was your client. I already know it. I told you. You've been positively ID'd as the man taking his exam for him. It's irrefutable. You're caught. I want to know what the protocol was if your client feared you both might be exposed."

"She knew?" Reznick asked. "You're saying this chick knew Savitch's business?"

His curiosity seemed genuine.

"What was the play, Grant? Did Savitch have to confirm with you the night before or something? Is that why he placed a call to you?"

"I can't help you," he said. "I've never talked to Marcus Savitch in my life."

"Do you understand what I'm trying to do for you? If you help me with this, it will be points in your column with the U.S. Attorney."

"You got that in writing?"

"No," I said.

"You have no power over the federal prosecutor," he said. "So you *are* wasting my time."

"You said you know who I am."

I closed my file and stared into his eyes. I held his gaze. He finally looked away first.

"You want my help? It'll be on my terms, not yours."

"Which are?"

"Yes," he said. "I know who you are. You said you aren't working for the Savitches. Fine. Good. So you work for me."

"What?"

"You heard me. You take over my defense. You get me a deal that gets me out of here quicker. I know you're more than capable of it."

"First, you show me yours," I said. I couldn't believe I was contemplating it. I wasn't. Not really. This was a world I'd walked away from long ago. I would never go back.

"Fine," he said. "Yeah. I got a call. But not from Marcus Savitch. I never talk to the client. I get my instructions, I show up. I do my job. Period. Everything else is above my pay grade. But yeah. I got a call. Savitch was freaking out that weekend. I don't know why. Maybe it was because this girl knew something. Maybe not. I wasn't given a standby order."

"Which means ..."

"Which means it wasn't for sure I was supposed to show up for the test. It means the client could have been getting cold feet."

"Then what happened?"

He shrugged. "Then nothing. I proceed as planned, unless I'm told otherwise. I was never told otherwise. No idea what was going on behind the scenes. Maybe somebody talked the kid down. Maybe whatever was upsetting him got resolved."

He looked down at my closed file. Resolved. Murdering an innocent woman was a heartless resolution.

"Maybe the kid's old man intervened and got him to grow a pair. No idea. Told you. Above my pay grade."

It was nothing. Interesting. But nothing.

"Names, Reznick," I said. "Who was your contact? Who were you waiting for? A call from someone for a green light? You don't give me that. This conversation is over. Good luck to you, but whatever happens to you will be without my help or involvement."

Another bluff. But one for which I was certain of the outcome.

"Yeah," Reznick said with the same emphasis as if he'd spat in my face. "That's what I thought. You've got nothing for me."

He rose. "Door!"

I sat there as the door behind him opened. Reznick held out his wrists as the guard put cuffs on him and led him out.

A moment later, the door behind me opened and Eric and Lee walked back in.

"Did you hear any of that?" I asked. Despite everything Cannon assured me, I knew he'd been listening in.

"Yeah," he said. I could give him credit for not bullshitting me at least.

"Garbage," Eric said. "He's what they say he is. A good soldier."

"You think Savitch killed your victim based on that?" Lee asked.

"Do you?" I responded.

He scratched his chin. "He'd be my number one suspect."

"Yeah," I said. I slid my file back into my bag.

"You should have been a cop, Leary," Lee said.

"Thanks, I think," I said. "But I'm not quite ready to quit my day job."

I caught another strange look pass between Eric and Lee. Though my head pounded too much to ask about it ... I had the distinct feeling Eric and I were headed for a serious conversation.

Chapter 28

THEY WERE all downstairs or out in the yard. I stared at the ceiling, pulling the covers up to my chin. I'd been staring at that same ceiling most of the night. Eric slept blissfully unaware of the workings of my brain. How do men do that? Just lie down, put their head on a pillow, close their eyes, and pow. Lights out. Snoring within two minutes.

I was nowhere. Worse than nowhere. Technically, I didn't have a client anymore. I had a slam dunk reason to win Andrew Doyle a new trial, and no way to use it. Daria Moreau lay in a Canadian graveyard somewhere and as far as the truth about what really happened to her? It seemed those answers would stay buried right along with her.

I heard Emma's laughter coming from the yard. It was almost ten o'clock. A cloudless sky and eighty degrees out there already. A rarity for mid-June, but this was the first full week of those temps. It had gotten hot enough to warm the water to an acceptable temperature for swimming. So here they all were.

I forced myself out of bed and went to the balcony window. Jessa had baby Sean in the water, just getting his little toesies wet. He squealed with laughter as he kicked and splashed.

Emma sat on a lounge chair on the dock. Her boyfriend Byron sat next to her, dangling his own feet in the water. Joe and Matty had the fishing boat out, anchored just a few yards away, within yelling distance. The bluegill were on their beds. Tori and Vangie were on the porch in the shade. From the heavenly smells wafting up, Tori had made a breakfast casserole. I didn't see Eric. He'd probably gone up to the coop. Around this time every morning, he'd bring them a tray of whatever vegetables were left over from last night's dinner.

"Aunt Cass!" Emma called up. "Come on down!"

I waved to her. I loved this. Loved that my family would set up camp here regardless of where I was. It was my home. But it was for them just as much.

I went to the bathroom, scrubbed my teeth, twisted my hair up into a messy bun, and put on a bathing suit and cover-up. I couldn't find my favorite flip flops with the arch support, but I didn't mind. Barefoot would be fine today.

I made it halfway out the door when my cell phone rang. I was going to ignore it. Leave it right where it was on the charger. Everyone I cared to talk to was already here. But something made me turn back. The caller ID read Bellamy Creek Correctional Facility.

Shit.

I picked up the phone and sat on the edge of the bed.

"Yes?" I said.

"Hi," Andrew Doyle answered. His voice sounded small and far away.

"What do you need, Andrew?"

He didn't answer at first. I just heard his measured breaths.

"I don't know," he finally said.

"You're aware your father called me? He was pretty upset. I'd appreciate it if you told him not to do that again. I can't explain anything, you know that. But he needs to know why I'm not working on your case."

A lie. Why did I say that? Maybe it was because I was sick of the lies Andrew had been telling me since day one. Except for one thing. Maybe the only thing that mattered.

He didn't kill Daria Moreau.

"I'm sorry," he said.

"For what?"

"That I can't do what you want me to do."

"What *I* want you to do? I just don't understand why you don't want it. I don't understand how you think the decision you made is making things better? Your father clearly has no idea you're trying to protect him. He deserves to know. No matter what else he's done, he loves you."

"I know."

"So, why are you calling me?"

Again, silence. Just his breathing.

"Okay," I said. "Andrew, I need to go. I've got a houseful of people and frankly, I'm sick of this conversation. It never gets me anywhere. I told your father he can expect a final bill in about a week."

"I know you went to see Russ Nadler," he said.

"How?"

Andrew paused. "I got a call from Doreen. She was angry. She said she'd help Russ sue me for defamation. She sounded drunk."

"That's ... interesting," I said.

"What did he say?" Andrew asked. "What did Russ tell you?"

I debated blowing off the question. I wasn't going to be paid for getting it. But, screw it.

"He said exactly what I expected he'd say. That Marcus Savitch's family paid him off to tank your case. Though he'll never admit it in a way that could help you."

Andrew uttered a four-letter word that pretty much summed up my feelings on the matter, too.

"You can't tell me you didn't already know this," I said.

"No," he said. "I didn't. Not for sure."

"Does it change anything? Now, will you let me use the information I have to get you the hell out of there?"

I grew tired of his silence. Of his secrets.

"No," he said, but the word choked out of him. I knew he was crying.

"Why?" I demanded.

No answer.

"Fine," I said. "Maybe we shouldn't talk again. But you should know. I'm not going to sit on the information I have about Marcus's fraud against the state bar. I'm going to report it. I don't believe it's subject to privilege."

"Please! Please don't. It won't help anything."

"It'll help the State of Michigan," I said. "It'll help the partners at Carter Baldwin. It will help every client Marcus has ever worked with and those in the future. This is one his daddy won't be able to fix for him."

"He'll know it was me," Andrew said.

"He'll know it's *me*," I said. "And I'm not afraid of him."

"I'll sue you."

"Goodbye," I said. "Have a great weekend, Andrew."

"Cass, please. Just wait. Just let me ..."

I heard a scream from the lawn. It was Emma. Then a shout from Joe. I went to the window.

Joe and Matty had docked the boat. Matty was still aboard, pulling fish out of the live well and tossing them into the cage he'd tied to the dock. Joe was just below me, staggering sideways. When he turned toward me, I saw blood streaming out of his nose.

I dropped the phone and ran downstairs.

I HADN'T HEARD the car drive up. When I burst out of the French doors onto the porch, Tom Loomis's back was to me. He had his arm drawn back, ready to deliver another punch.

Joe blocked the blow, twisting Tom's arm hard. Tom dropped to his knees.

"The first one was free, asshole," Joe yelled. By this time, Eric and Matty were running toward them. Vangie pulled Tori away and got her inside the house. Jessa clutched Sean to her chest, but they were still in the water, safely out of the line of fire.

"You son of a bitch!" Tom yelled. "You couldn't leave her alone. You couldn't just let Katie and me be happy!"

"What is he saying?" Emma cried. She ran toward her father. Eric and Matty pulled Tom back out of Joe's reach. Tom struggled and yelled, his face purple, spit flying from his mouth.

I got in between Emma and the men. She tried to run toward her father. There was way too much testosterone flying around. I didn't want her anywhere near it.

"Enough," Eric said. "You need to get the hell out of here and cool off."

With a nod to Matty, he and Eric bum-rushed Tom back to his car. Matty got the driver's side door open. Eric shoved the man into the driver's seat, then leaned into the open window to say something to him. Matty strode back toward Joe.

As Joe took a step forward, Matty grabbed him by the shoulders, shoving him back hard.

"Enough!" Matty shouted. "What the hell did you think was gonna happen?"

"What?" Emma said. "Dad, are you serious? What is he talking about?"

Except she knew. Emma wasn't a fool. There was only one thing Tom Loomis could have meant by coming here and saying what he did.

I had half a mind to deck Joe myself. Behind me, Loomis's tires squealed as he slammed his car into gear and tore back up the driveway. Thank God.

Eric had a stern look as he walked back down and stood beside me.

"Sit down," I yelled at my brother. I grabbed a beach towel off the closest chair and shoved it under Joe's bleeding nose, tilting his head back.

He tried to push me off. "You're gonna suffocate me."

"Good," I said. "Serves you right. I told you this was gonna happen."

Emma stood next to us. Her face registered a range of emotions. Shock, fear, finally anger.

"You knew?" she said. "You all knew? How long has it been going on, Dad? How could you? After everything Katie put us through. You want her back? Are you sleeping with her? Why didn't you tell me?"

The last question was directed at me. It made me want to slap my brother. I knew I'd end up getting dragged into this mess somehow.

"Emma," he said, pushing the towel away from his face. It looked like the bleeding had stopped, but his nose had to be broken.

She put her hands up in a stopping gesture. She shook her head and walked right past us and into the house.

"Great," Joe muttered. "Friggin' Katie must have told him I was here."

"That's what you're worried about?" I asked.

"Stop it," he said. "All of you. You can save your judgmental eyes. This is none of your business."

"I'm sorry," I said. "Is that my porch you're bleeding all over?"

"Save me the lecture," he said.

"She's married, Joe," I said.

"So was Eric," he snapped back. On instinct and more testosterone, Eric took a step forward. I moved between them.

"Okay," I said. "Everybody just stand down. Christ. Joe, are you all right?"

He heaved a great sigh and leaned back against the porch railing. "I'm sorry," he said. "I didn't know he knew. I don't know what Katie's told him."

"Maybe nothing," Matty said. "You haven't exactly been discreet."

Joe started to shoot something back at our little brother. Vangie walked out carrying a package of frozen peas. She carefully put it on Joe's nose and nudged his head backward so he stared at the sky.

"What a mess," Joe muttered.

"It's not the end of the world," I said.

"It's just Saturday," Eric deadpanned. Matty caught my eye and we both struggled not to smile.

Vangie pulled the bag of peas away from Joe's nose. She put her thumb and forefingers on the bridge of it and gently felt her way down.

"Ow!" Joe yelled, then pulled her hand away.

"Pretty sure it's broken," she said. "But you should be fine unless a shard of bone gets jammed into your brain."

"How could we tell?" Matty teased.

Joe flashed him a middle finger.

Jessa brought Sean out of the water and wrapped him in a towel. Matty walked over to her and hoisted his son up, dripping wet, and put him on his shoulder. Sean broke into a big belly laugh. It appeared the commotion had amused him more than anything else. He hadn't uttered a single cry during the whole melee.

Tori came to the doorway and hollered. "Well, that was fun. Food's ready!"

I reached a hand down to Joe and assisted as he hauled himself to his feet. He and the others filed into the kitchen, ready to stuff their faces.

"Just another Saturday," I whispered, repeating Eric's comment. He put an arm around me.

"You good?" he asked. "I didn't want to wake you up. You looked so peaceful."

"Dandy," I said. I reached one hand up and touched the arm he had around my shoulder.

"Who were you talking to on the phone?" he asked. "Damn near everyone you know is here."

I smiled up at him. "I'll tell you later. Today, I'm just looking forward to a drama-free day with my family."

He rolled his eyes as we walked into the house and closed the screen door behind us.

Chapter 29

"Is she talking to you yet?" Jeanie asked. I'd spent my entire Monday catching up on clients I'd back-burnered during my work with Andrew Doyle. Tori came in earlier to file some withdrawals from the few active cases she still had in probate court. Jeanie would take those over. Miranda took a rare day off.

"Emma didn't come in today," I said. "She'll come around. She's mature enough to understand I'm not the bad guy here."

"I hate to say it, but Tom Loomis isn't either?"

I raised a brow. "As I recall Katie was still married to Joe when she started up with Tom. He doesn't exactly have clean hands."

"Well, it's their circus, anyway."

I picked up an empty bankers box off the floor. With the sharpie on the desk, I wrote Doyle/Moreau on the side of it. The five binders Emma had made for each of us in the office stacked perfectly inside of it. I fitted the lid over the box and taped it shut.

"So you're serious this time?" Jeanie asked. "You're cutting ties with Andrew Doyle for good?"

"I am indeed," I said, picking up another box and stuffing a few remaining files into it. The only thing left was the file I'd made with the items from Marcus Savitch's bar exam.

"This one hurts," she said. "I can't stop thinking about that poor girl."

"I know. But Andrew Doyle is a brick wall I can't penetrate."

"What about Eric?" she asked. "He got pretty invested in this one, too. Do you think he'll have a change of heart and come back to the office full time?"

I hadn't yet asked him about the substance of his private conversation with Lee Cannon. With all the drama with my brother, it just fell by the wayside.

"I'm trying not to pressure him," I said. "But he's going stir crazy. Stay-at-home chicken dad isn't gonna be enough."

Jeanie smiled. "Don't underestimate the power of chickens. Stay-at-home chicken dad sounds like a pretty terrific gig."

"Good news," I said. "Delilah turned out to be a hen. It was dicey there for a while."

Jeanie laughed and scooped up the bar exam documents. "Where do you want these?"

I looked around for another empty box. It looked like we'd filled them all. I took the papers from her.

"I don't know. I'm not sure whether I have a duty to report outside my duty to keep Andrew Doyle's secrets."

"Those aren't Doyle's secrets," she said. "They're Marcus Savitch's and he's not your client. Every day he shows up to that law office, he's committing a crime."

"I know. I don't think I'm going to let it slide. I just have to find a way to get the info about where it needs to go in the right way. Part of me thinks even if the partners at Carter Baldwin found out the truth, Marcus's family would figure out a way to handle it for him."

Jeanie leaned against the table. "Has it occurred to you that the partners already know? You said your friend told you he was more or less just breathing air in that building."

I rested my hands on the back of my neck. "I don't know. I just don't want to think about it right now. I want life around here to get back to normal. I want to stop thinking about the tragedy of Daria Moreau. Callous as that may sound. And I want you to hit me with a frying pan if I ever think about veering from my lane again with a post-conviction case I didn't try from the get-go."

"The check was good though." She smiled.

"And there really are more important things than money."

Jeanie's face dropped. She whipped her head around and put a finger to her lips. "Careful," she whispered. "Miranda has a way of knowing everything. Even when she's not here."

I laughed. I stacked the three bankers boxes and shoved them against the wall. I'd take them out to my storage unit later, though everything in them was also digitized. I was old-fashioned enough to want to keep physical copies of things for a while.

"All right, kiddo," Jeanie said. "I'm pooped. It's four o'clock. I'm cutting out early. You wanna come over? I made lasagna yesterday. Way more than enough for just me. It's always better on the second day. I was gonna bring it today but forgot."

My stomach growled. "I just might."

"Call Eric," she said. "If you can pull him away from the coop, bring him, too."

"Sounds good," I said. "I'll bring some dessert and some wine."

"White," she said. "You know red gives me hives."

I saluted her as she headed for the door. "Give me an hour? I just want to tie up a couple of loose ends here, grab a shower, grab Eric. Then we'll be over."

"Sounds good," she said.

I stood there for a moment, staring at the doorway after she left. Then I sank into the nearest chair and laid my head on my arms.

Daria Moreau. I meant what I said. I wanted her out of my head. I had two missed calls from her mother last week. I hadn't returned them. What could I say? Once again, privilege covered most of the things I knew. But maybe I could tell her enough. Encourage her to hire her own private investigator. But even then, I'd never be able to share any of my work product. If I couldn't get Andrew to change his tune, no one else would. At least not now.

I shot off a quick text to Eric, filling him in on dinner plans. He texted an okay emoji back. I asked him to grab a cheesecake from the country market a mile from the house and chill a bottle of white wine. He sent me back a picture of Marge. She'd been sold to him as a Wyandotte, but turned out to be a Crested

Cream Legbar. She stared at the camera with angry, golden eyes. She was the feisty one. Top hen so far. She liked to barricade the coop door after herding the rest of the flock up to bed for the night.

It started to rain a little. I stared at my phone. It did bother me that Emma hadn't returned a text to me in two days. She was hurting. She felt betrayed. When she found out Katie cheated on Joe, she rallied around him quickly. Not a moment of hesitation.

My fingers hovered over the keyboard. Four blue bubbles formed a wall of texts from me to her. A moment later, three gray dots appeared. She was forming a response. Then, two seconds later, the dots disappeared. I texted her again.

> " love you. I'm here if you want to talk.

Then I slipped my phone back in my bag. She'd either reach out or she wouldn't. I couldn't force the issue.

I heard the front door open downstairs. "You forget something?" I called down. No answer.

I went to the window to see whose car was in the front lot. It was a black sedan I didn't recognize. The hairs on my neck stood on end. I didn't have any appointments scheduled. Jeanie didn't either and Miranda was gone. We didn't get walk-ins.

"Hello?" I called out.

I grabbed my phone and walked out into the hall, standing at the top of the stairs. I couldn't see the reception area from here.

"Ms. Leary?" a male voice called up.

I slipped my phone in my pocket and headed down the steps. "I'm sorry," I said. "We're closed for the day. If you want to make an appointment, you'll need to call tomorrow and speak with my office manager."

As I reached the landing, the man's back was turned to me. He wore a well-fitting black suit, his thick brown hair swept back. Then Marcus Savitch turned to face me. One hand slipped casually into his pocket.

"Mr. Savitch," I said. "What can I do for you?"

His face changed from a neutral expression to a scowl. "Is it true?" he asked.

"What are you talking about?"

"Are you sticking your nose into my business?"

"Again, no idea."

I thought of the file on the table upstairs containing the evidence I'd collected about his fraud.

"I understand you've been running around asking a lot of questions about me. So I figured I'd show you the courtesy you haven't shown me and talk to you face to face."

"We did speak face to face," I said. "Remember? You gave me canned answers based on your statement to the police and your testimony."

"Canned answers?"

Was he dangerous? Was this the man who'd attacked Daria and dragged her to that slime-filled bog?

My eyes flicked to his shoes. I imagined them caked in the black mud and silt from the edge of the pond. Eric's words echoed through me. *They should have left tracks. There should have been traces of this stuff somewhere in the house. In the washing machine. The grass. The floor. Somewhere.*

"You're stirring shit up for no reason," he said.

"No reason?" Miranda kept a heavy crystal candy dish on her desk. I could throw it at him. The hallway to the kitchen was at my back. I could run there and grab a knife out of the block.

Instead, I pulled out my phone and opened the screen. Savitch didn't stop me.

"Do I need to call someone?" I asked. "Are you here to make threats?"

He took a step toward me. "I didn't do anything wrong. You just need to back off."

While I had my phone in my hand, I pulled up my camera roll. I had a photo of the seating chart as well as Grant Reznick's mugshot.

"Marcus," I said. "You're at the end of the road. I've already reported you to the state bar."

His eyes widened. Whatever he was expecting me to say, it wasn't that. He took another step forward and I thought about Russ Nadler and Grant Reznick. How easy it had been to convince them both I was still in Killian Thorne's service.

"I know what you did," I said. "I think it's time you finally tell the truth."

He shook his head. "You think I killed Daria? Is that what Andrew's been telling you?"

"Lucky for you, I can't tell anyone what Andrew's been telling me. Not without his permission. But what I know about you didn't come from Andrew."

"You've got nothing. Because there is nothing. I didn't kill Daria. I had nothing to do with whatever happened to her."

"But you did tell Andrew to lie to the cops, right?"

"I've already told you everything I know and everything I did."

It was my turn to advance on him. "Then why are you here? Were you just planning to ask me nicely to break attorney-client privilege? You should know all about the rules on that, right? Because you're an attorney too."

I pulled up Reznick's mugshot and showed my phone screen to Marcus. He looked at it, but kept his expression cold.

"He's talking, Marcus," I said. "I'm actually glad you're here. It saves me a trip out to your office. His name is Grant Reznick. He's currently sitting in federal prison in Milan, awaiting trial for fraud, and about a half a dozen other charges. He's been offered a deal. Sold you out. He admits he took the bar for you. You and maybe a dozen others across four states. See, it was pretty easy to put together that you couldn't have been in two places at once. You couldn't be sitting in Detective Messer's interrogation room and at the Breslin Center at the same time."

He started to sweat, but he didn't move.

"There's an eyewitness willing to testify. She was supposed to be *your* seatmate for the bar. She picked Mr. Reznick out right away. I mean, he's pretty handsome, right? She'll confirm it was Reznick in your seat, not you. That's a pretty big secret. One that could cause you a lot of trouble if it got out. Daria knew that, didn't she?"

"This isn't what you think," he said. Marcus looked genuinely scared. His face turned white and he took a step back.

"This feels like the kind of secret you might have wanted to kill for."

I turned my phone back toward me and hit the first number from my recent calls. Eric answered almost immediately. I put the phone on the desk beside me, hitting the speaker button. Marcus stared at it, his face filled with terror.

"Detective Wray?" I said.

Eric hesitated before answering. "Speaking."

"I have Marcus Savitch here in the office with me. You wanted me to let you know the next time I talked to him. He ..."

Savitch grabbed the phone and clicked off the call. Not five seconds later, I felt the vibration on my smartwatch. Eric and I both had a GPS app that alerted when the other left the house or came home. Eric had to have been right next to his truck, keys in hand, ready to head to the store as I asked. He would now be on his way here.

"What did you tell that guy?"

"Do you understand what happens if you get caught cheating on the bar? You're done ever being able to practice law. So that's over. I'm assuming you'd rather not go to jail."

"I didn't do anything. This is nothing. I can pass the bar. That was all my father's idea."

"Sure," I said. "You can tell that to the feds. But I'd hurry. See, Grant Reznick has his heart set on using you as a bargaining chip. But if you get to the cops first and tell your story, maybe you could flip this. They're pretty interested in knowing who

Reznick's clients were. You can't save your career, but you might be able to save your freedom."

"Call him back," he said. "Call that detective back. You've got it wrong. You don't know who you're dealing with. You don't know who I have behind me."

I stepped forward. "You actually walked into *my* office and said that? Well, I'd say just like the bar exam, you haven't studied. I mean, you know my name. A simple browser search would probably tell you what you need to know. Grant Reznick figured it out pretty quick. Why do you think he was so willing to talk to me when he'd kept his mouth shut for over a year? Or Russ Nadler for that matter?"

"What's he saying?"

"Forget that. Think about why he'd be saying it. I imagine your family paid for his silence, too. Right? And yet I waltz in and he starts talking."

Savitch was white as bone. "I didn't kill Daria. Call it off."

"No," I said. "See, it's you who needs to call it off."

"What are you talking about?"

"If you want me to make this go away, then call Andrew Doyle. Take off his muzzle. If you really didn't kill Daria, you have nothing else to lose. I mean, your ability to practice law, sure. But it could be handled quietly. You can take some cushy job in your dad's company and go about your life. Which is probably what you wanted in the first place."

"I don't know what you're talking about."

"Enough," I said. "This demeans us both. You've been blackmailing Andrew for two years. He won't act in his own best interest because of it. So, tell me again that you didn't kill Daria Moreau."

"I didn't! I swear to God. I never touched her."

Was he so far in denial he believed it himself?

"Then let Andrew go. If you're really innocent, nothing will happen to you. But Andrew doesn't deserve to be in prison for something he didn't do either."

"He did it! Are you really that stupid? Andrew killed her. Not me."

"Then why are you choking him into staying quiet?"

He shook his head and backed away. "You have no idea what you've done. I don't care who you work for, lady. You can't mess with me. You can't mess with my family."

"Then. Why. Are. You. Here? Did you think you could bully me too? Here's how this goes. I can be reasonable. To be honest? I don't give a crap one way or another whether you have a law license or not. You're not hurting anyone. The partners at Carter Baldwin are smart enough not to let you get near real clients. Your incompetence is protecting you from your lack of license. But if I report you, that'll make headlines. That will damage your father's reputation and put you both in the middle of a federal investigation. So here's what you're going to do. You're going to back off."

I grabbed a piece of paper from the desk and wrote down a number. I thrust it at Marcus. He took it. "You're going to call that number," I said. "Ask for a call from Andrew. When you talk to him, you're going to let him off the hook. You're going to give him permission to do whatever he has to do to clear his name. Since you claim you didn't kill Daria either, you have nothing to worry about. And I'll keep your secret. I won't report you to the Attorney Grievance Commission. You can carry on with your life and your lies. Are we clear? I expect a call from Andrew within the next twenty-four hours telling me you talked to him."

The front door burst open behind him. Eric was breathing heavily, his eyes wild. He had his service weapon clipped to his belt, but no badge, of course. Marcus didn't seem to notice. He took a step away from Eric and toward me. Eric moved with the power of a tsunami and backed Marcus into the wall with an arm like steel across his chest.

Marcus put his hands up in surrender. "I'm not here to hurt anybody. You need to chill out, man. I was just asking questions."

Still wild-eyed and half feral, Eric looked at me. "More or less," I said.

Eric pushed against Marcus, then let him go.

"Time to leave, son," Eric said. "I catch you near her again and I won't be as polite."

Marcus straightened his jacket. If he were a dog, he'd have his tail between his legs. He didn't hesitate. He ran out the front door.

Eric turned to me. "Are you okay?"

"I'm fine," I said. "Thanks for that. He just showed up."

"Go get your stuff," Eric commanded, still in full-on cop mode. "I don't want you here or driving anywhere alone tonight. We'll get your car later."

"Yes, officer," I said.

Eric narrowed his eyes. Too soon, I realized. He wasn't calm enough to joke.

I went upstairs, grabbed my bag, and came back down.

"Thanks for coming to my rescue," I said, going up on my toes to kiss him on the cheek.

He let out a still-feral growl, then put an arm around me as we headed for his car.

Chapter 30

Two DAYS LATER, and I still had no calls from Andrew Doyle. That was the bad news. The good news was currently sitting cross-legged on my office carpet, sorting through discovery material for a felonious assault case set for trial next month. My client had finally fought back against her abusive husband. But the man was a county commissioner and I couldn't get the prosecutor to drop the charges so far.

"He should resign," Emma said. She rose from the floor, holding the worst piece of evidence against my client. A photo of her husband's bloodied face after she hit him with an aluminum bat.

"That's the county's problem," I said.

"He's really gonna put this poor woman through a whole trial? Even if we lose, there's no way this a-hole comes back from this."

Emma had finally come back to work yesterday. She'd said nothing about Joe or Katie. She just dove back in as if last weekend hadn't happened. I took her lead. But as she put the photo back in the discovery pile, she took a seat in one of the office chairs in front of my desk, gripping the armrests. Her cheeks flushed, which meant she was nervous. Which meant ... we were about to get into it. I sat down next to her.

"I'm sorry," she said. "I know it wasn't your fault. I know you were just trying to protect me by not telling me about my dad and Katie."

"No," I said. "I don't think you need protection from that. You're a grown woman now. But I don't think it's fair of either one of you to put me in the middle of this. Joe knows how I feel. But in the end, it's none of my business. To some degree, it's none of yours either."

Her eyes flashed. "How can you say that?"

"*Because* you're a grown woman now. You haven't always made the best relationship decisions either. That's not judgment. My record isn't exactly spotless in that regard. I'm just saying we're all human. And my brother is going to have to sort this out himself. If our opinions mattered to him, he never would have let Katie cross his threshold again."

"She's been trying to call me," Emma said. "I blocked her number."

"As is your prerogative. I'm just really glad you're not blocking me."

She blinked rapidly, staving off tears. Then she leaned over and gave me a hug. "I just don't want to see him hurt. Katie did a number on him. On me too. If he gets back together with her, how in the world are we all going to be civil when he starts bringing her to family stuff again?"

"One thing at a time," I said. Though I had the same question. Lord, my sister Vangie might actually try to scratch Katie's eyes out over Thanksgiving turkey if it came to that. Mercifully, we hadn't even hit the 4th of July.

"I see you boxed up Doyle's files," she said, deftly changing the subject.

"No reason not to," I said. "Miranda's prepping a final bill. Grace Doyle is supposed to show up to pay it in person."

"Why?"

"Probably to try to convince me not to bail on her husband."

"You're not bailing on him. He bailed on you. Are you gonna tell Jacqueline Moreau?"

I shook my head. "It's not my place."

"How do you know she might not want to hire you herself? There wouldn't be a conflict of interest, would there?"

I thought about that for a second. "Probably. I wouldn't be able to use or disclose anything Andrew told me or that I found out during the course of my representation."

"She signed a waiver. She gave you permission to dig into her daughter's medical records."

"But I'm still no closer to proving Marcus Savitch killed Daria."

Miranda jumped in on the intercom. "Grace Doyle's here," she said. "Do you want her in your office or in the conference room?"

I surveyed the mounds of paperwork Emma and I had left all over the floor, couch, and coffee table.

"Conference room," I said.

"I'll have her up in a minute. The bill's in an envelope on the table in there." Miranda hung up.

"You wanna sit in on this one?" I asked Emma.

"Sure."

I stood, checked my hair in the mirror on the back of my door, then walked over to the conference room. Miranda had already set up bottled water along with a blank legal pad and cup of pens. I'm not sure what she thought I planned for this meeting. Did she think Grace Doyle could somehow play on my heartstrings and get me to change my mind?

Grace came up a moment later. She was alone this time. No baby Beckett.

"Thanks for seeing me," she said. She wore a fuzzy gray cardigan and a long denim skirt. It seemed too hot for late June. But it was a little chilly in the conference room. The air conditioner always blasted the strongest in here.

Emma offered her a water. Grace took the seat at the end of the table. She looked small and tired. Like she hadn't slept in a week. Maybe she hadn't.

"Have you spoken with Andrew?" I asked.

"He's not well," she said. "He wouldn't let me call you. He said you're through with him."

There was no accusation in her tone, just defeat.

"That's not exactly accurate. But like I told your father-in-law, I can't represent your husband if he refuses to cooperate with my plan of representation."

"I know. I know. He's completely immovable. I thought we had a chance. A small window. But something happened. He won't tell me what."

I pursed my lips. There wasn't much I could say. Though it occurred to me there were a few things I could ask.

"Do you know if he's had any other visitors?" I said. "Or phone calls?"

"What do you mean?" Grace asked.

"I'll be blunt. Marcus Savitch paid me a visit the other day. He wasn't very happy about the work I've done on Andrew's behalf. He was very defensive and threatening."

The color drained from Grace's face. I wondered if Marcus had cornered Grace like that, too. Andrew swore she didn't know about his deal with Marcus Savitch. It was entirely possible Grace pieced it all together for herself.

"Did he hurt you?" she asked. "Did Marcus hurt you?"

Emma blurted the question that immediately popped into my brain too. "Did he hurt you?!"

Grace looked shocked by the question. "What? I didn't say that."

"Grace," I said, feeling that headache coming on. "If you know something about Marcus, now's the time to say it. Though, at this point, it doesn't even really matter anymore. Not if Andrew won't let me do my job."

I slid Miranda's final bill across the table. Grace looked at it. She picked her purse up off the floor and pulled out a checkbook. Without hesitation, she wrote the check and slid it back to me.

"You didn't have to come all this way to do this," I said. "You could have paid online."

"I wanted to see you one last time. To thank you for how hard you've tried. Plus, it's on the way to Bellamy Creek. I saw Andrew early this morning. I came straight here after. And I just ... I know you were the last resort. I'm trying to accept it. Accept the fact that my husband is never getting out of prison. If you can't help him, nobody can."

Her argument made a certain amount of tragic sense.

I put my hands flat on the table. Part of me wanted to reach across and take her hand. This woman had been loyal to Andrew when he hadn't deserved it.

"Nobody can," I said to her. "I'm sorry I couldn't do more."

"I know. But Andrew's different. I'm worried."

"Different how?" Emma asked.

Grace shrugged. "He's saying goodbye. He's never done that before. Today, he told me not to come back."

"He'll come around," Emma said. "He sounds depressed."

"It's not uncommon," I said. "Inmates like Andrew, those facing a life sentence, they can go through stages of grief. If you love him, if you're committed to him, just give him some time."

"No," she whispered. "This was final. I know Andrew better than anyone else. You understand? We met in kindergarten. He's not a depressed person. He was always the optimist. I was the one who needed cheering up. I was the pessimist. Cass, I don't think my husband is going to survive. I talked to a family liaison at the prison. A social worker. I asked how to request my husband be put on suicide watch. He's doing crazy things. I think he's been provoking other inmates. Dangerous ones. Trying to get himself hurt until he can work up the courage to hurt himself."

"I'm sorry to hear that," I said.

Grace buried her face in her hands. "He didn't do this," she said. "That's the whole thing. If I believed he killed that girl, I could almost accept all of this. I would probably still love him even then. Isn't that crazy?"

I had no answer for her.

"I know it's crazy. But I've said it a million times. My husband isn't a killer. He didn't kill Daria. Or leave her in that filth. Or try to cover it up after the fact. Just none of it. And there's nothing I can do?"

She wanted answers. Maybe she wanted my permission to let go.

"No," I said. "You can try to be there for him if you still love him. If Andrew's made up his mind, there is no hope of him ever getting out. I'm sorry." It was blunt. I learned long ago to never say never. But I also sensed this woman badly needed closure and a reason to move on with her life if her husband had given up on himself.

She didn't cry. Grace Doyle found some inner strength. If I had to name it, she almost seemed relieved. I understood that in a way, too. I'd experienced it myself where it came to Andrew Doyle. You can only try to help someone so much. But if they won't accept it, you have to walk away for your own mental health.

"Okay," she said. "Then I'll do what he asked. I won't go to see him. I'll try to move on without him. I'll stop telling Beckett he'll see his father soon."

"I really am sorry, Grace," I said. I extended a hand to hers. She got to her feet and shook it.

"I'll walk you out," I said.

She moved like a zombie. Her expression had gone completely blank. For a moment, it was like she forgot where she was.

When we got outside to her car, she absently fumbled for her keys. When she found them, she stared at them. Then, she snapped back to the present.

"Drive safely, okay?" I said.

She nodded. "Cass, I wasn't going to say anything. I wasn't going to ask. Because I know Andrew's done his number on you, too."

"His number?"

"He has that way of sucking people in. He's always been like that. Like a sick puppy you find on the side of the road. A broken boy. You want to help him? You think you can fix him. But in the end, he always goes cold."

"Then you really do have to let go," I said.

"I know."

"What do you mean? Something you didn't want to ask me?"

She met my eyes. "He asked me to ask you. Right before I left this morning. He asked if you'd come to see him one more time. He said he wanted to thank you in person. And apologize. You don't have to. I would completely understand."

She waved her copy of the bill in the air. "This is the end of it. Your obligation. I'm sure you have a ton of other clients you've pushed aside over the last few weeks."

"Yes," I admitted.

"Well, anyway. He asked me to give you this."

She pulled another sealed envelope out of her purse and handed it to me. It had my name written on the outside.

"I don't know what it says. He wouldn't tell me."

"Okay," I said. "I mean, okay, I'll read it. I'm not agreeing to go back to Bellamy Creek."

"Cass," she said, touching my arm. "Don't. God. Does that sound awful? I'm the one who begged you to take his case in the first place. I'm just ... I don't know. I'm so tired. Don't listen to anything I say."

She let go of my arm and got into her car. Grace Doyle had a sad smile on her face as she drove away.

I stood there in my office parking lot, the sun beating down on my skin. I tore open the end of the envelope she gave me. In scrawling handwriting, it read:

"Cass, please. I've put you back on the visitors' list. I'm ready to admit what I did."

Miranda walked out and stood beside me. "You have a check for me?"

When I didn't respond, she took the piece of paper out of my hand. I opened my mouth to tell her that wasn't her check, but Miranda had read it before I could. She set her jaw and handed Andrew's note back to me.

"You're going up there to see him, aren't you?"

I wanted to tell her no. I wanted to tear up that letter and never speak Andrew Doyle's name again. But those seven words on that page sliced through me.

I'm ready to admit what I did.

Miranda sighed. "You're free tomorrow afternoon."

Chapter 31

THE NEXT DAY, three things happened in thirty minutes that changed the course of Andrew Doyle's life. The second thing had been percolating in the back of my mind for weeks. I just hadn't fully understood it. But the first thing happened the moment Andrew walked into the visitors' room.

He took a step, saw me at the table, and halted. There was no denying his expression. He was surprised. Maybe even shocked.

"Weren't you expecting me?" I asked. "Did I get the time wrong?"

"No," he said. "I just ... no."

"Sit down," I said. "I don't intend to be here long. So just tell me what you have to tell me."

"Me? I don't know what you're talking about."

Now I was completely confused. I had his note folded in my pocket. I took it out but kept it in my palm.

"Have you gotten any phone calls or visits from Marcus Savitch?" I asked.

His face fell. "You're really bringing him up to me again?"

Either my threats to Marcus made no impact, or Andrew was lying to me. Again.

"He came to see me," I said. "You didn't know that?"

"No! I didn't. Why? What did he say?"

Now I knew he wasn't lying. Andrew wasn't that good of an actor. But there was something else about him as he sat down. He winced and stiffened, as though he were in pain.

"What happened to you?" I asked.

His face turned to stone. "Nothing. What did Marcus say?"

"Stand up," I said. "Lift up your shirt."

"Mind your own business."

He looked like hell. Even worse than the first time I saw him. He'd lost weight. It looked like his hair was falling out. The bruises I'd seen on his face had faded to a light yellow. But he was still clearly hurt.

I ignored his protests and went over to his side of the table. I grabbed his shirt and started pulling it up. He surrendered.

What I saw sent a chill through me. He'd been beaten. Badly. He had bruises all around his torso. On his back, he had one with definite tread marks. He'd been kicked, stomped on. Probably had broken ribs.

"Am I wasting my breath asking you what happened?" I asked.

"Yes."

I gave a resigned sigh as I sat back down on the other side of the table. "So this is what it's going to be. You're not going to live long. You have no protection in here. If anything, you're a huge target. If anyone finds out about your connection to Marcus Savitch, they might see that as a prize. If you're a problem with Marcus's family, somebody might think they can curry favor by taking you out."

"How would anyone ever figure that out?"

"You know I talked to Nadler. If he spilled his guts to me, he could do it with someone else."

"You didn't answer my question. What did Marcus want?"

"What do you think he wanted?" I yelled. "He wanted to make sure you got the message that you were supposed to keep your mouth shut. Sacrifice yourself for him. That's the deal, right? In exchange, your father gets to keep his freedom and his livelihood. Marcus gets to stay out of prison for killing Daria. And you lose everything."

"What did you say?"

"I told him where he could shove it. If he's innocent like he's claiming, then he shouldn't have anything to be afraid of if you get a new trial. And I told him if he doesn't release you from your little contract, I'm reporting him to the state bar."

Andrew rested his forehead against his closed fists. I flung his note at him.

His eyes snapped open. He kept them locked with mine as he picked up the note. Slowly, he unfolded it and read it. Something went through him. Obvious surprise. But he recovered quickly and put the note on the table. There could be no mistaking his shock or what that meant.

He hadn't written it.

My mind raced. Images. Statements. Impressions. Everything I'd been staring at and studying about Andrew's case whirled around in my head like a cyclone.

Andrew didn't write that note.

I'm ready to admit what I did.

Grace's words.

Whatever happened out in that grotto, it wasn't something that would have pushed him to the edge.

He wouldn't leave her to rot in some scummy pond with fetid water like some rotting fish.

Laneesha Dey's words.

I turned to walk back to the patio. That's when that little grotto or whatever was in my line of sight.

I closed my eyes and remembered what I saw when Eric and I walked the crime scene. The little hollow in the hill formed by that massive fallen tree. It made me feel like I was walking through pictures in a storybook. I described it to Eric as a fairy cove.

I desperately wanted the trial evidence log in front of me. The answer was in it. The answer had been right in front of me. Only, it didn't make sense.

I felt like I'd floated outside my body. I asked a question, but my voice sounded so far away. Like I was watching the scene play out from high above.

"What do you want to admit to, Andrew?"

He pressed his thumbs into the corner of his eyes. He kept shaking his head. Then finally, he settled and met my stare.

"I did it, okay?"

"Did what?"

"I killed Daria. I'm sorry. But I killed her. It was me."

Rage bubbled up inside me.

"No," I said, snatching up the note. "She wrote this, didn't she?"

He feigned confusion, but it was no good.

"Grace," I said. "She wrote this note."

"No," he whispered.

"She wrote this note because she knows who really killed Daria. Doesn't she, Andrew?"

"No."

"It bothered me," I said. "When my associate and I went out to the crime scene. We walked the grounds. I saw the birdbath where Daria hit her head. There was this beautiful hollowed-out spot on the hill. Laneesha Dey called it a grotto. *Grace* called it a grotto. I walked the trail to the edge of that boggy pond. It ruined my shoes. Beyond repair. I wouldn't even put them on when we got back to the car. Same with my associate. There were thick, muddy footprints out there when they found Daria. But they didn't lead back to the house. They just … stopped. They never found muddy shoes. My associate wore pants. The hems of them ended up caked in mud too. But you didn't have muddy clothes. Neither did Marcus nor Kade."

"Stop," he said.

"It's impossible. Nobody can cover their tracks that well. There should have been some mud from the bog tracked back to the house. Something. Only there wasn't. Because Daria's killer never walked up to that house. She never set foot in it."

He reared back like I'd shot him in the chest at the word "she."

"No more. That's enough!"

Adrenaline pumped through me. I was partly talking to Andrew, but mostly to myself. "She was there. Grace was there. She said you'd never have left Daria in that filth. In that muck. The grotto. Only ... how could she know? How could she know unless she'd been out there too? She wasn't at the trial. She didn't see pictures of the crime scene. Unless you told her. Unless you described that scene in great detail. But you couldn't, could you? You couldn't because you'd never been out there either. Not past the birdbath or the trail to the pond. Because you didn't kill Daria. You didn't drag her body into that bog. Grace did."

He was crying. Sobbing. But he didn't deny anything I said.

"Why?" I asked. "How?"

"You can't," he said. "You can't prove it."

"But I can," I said. "Why did she write this letter? Why did she send me back out here to talk to you?"

"No. Just ... no."

"This wasn't a message for me, was it?" I said. "This was a message for you. Instructions. I don't understand it, Andrew. Make me understand?"

Grace was there with Andrew's parents that first day in my

office. For months, she'd begged me not to give up on Andrew. Why would she do that?

"You're not protecting Marcus," I said. "You never have been. You've been protecting Grace all this time. It was your parents who forced the issue of hiring me. Because they don't know what really happened either. They don't know who Grace is. She had to play along. She had to play the part and stand by her man. The dutiful, grieving wife."

"She didn't mean it," he whispered. "It wasn't her fault. It was my fault. It's always been my fault."

"Tell me what she did. Dammit, Andrew. She isn't the one you should be protecting. It's Beckett. Don't you get that? If he's your son, he needs you."

"He *is* my son!" he shouted. And I knew he was. Beckett was the spitting image of his father.

"Andrew," I said. "What will I find if I subpoena Grace's phone records? You know they can track her movements. She was at the Colby House on July 24th, two years ago, wasn't she?"

"Walk away. Just stop."

"I don't think you really want me to. I think the burden of this secret has been killing you. And you don't deserve to die like a dog in here. And that's what's happening. Every time you get beaten, it's worse. I can't protect you from it. Only the truth can."

"It was an accident!" He nearly screamed the words. "She didn't mean to do it. It was still my fault. I drove her to it. I led her on. Grace was always loyal. Always there for me. She wanted to wait for me while I went to law school. I told her not to. I told her to go on with her life. But I *was* her life. And that

Christmas, when I came home for break, I was just feeling so overwhelmed with everything. My last semester. The bar. Carving a path for myself. She was comforting. She was comfortable."

"You slept with her," I said. "Is that it?"

He closed his eyes and nodded.

"You slept with her, but you had feelings for Daria. Strong ones."

He dropped his chin.

"How did Grace know about where you were staying? How did she know about the party?"

"She wanted to surprise me," he said. "She drove all day to surprise me. We talked on the phone a few weeks before that weekend. Maybe even two months before."

"That's when you told her," I said. Andrew's phone was searched. But a call from weeks before to Grace wouldn't have tripped anyone's radar. If the cops had even looked back that far.

"Yes."

"She drove up to surprise you. What happened, Andrew? Did she see you with Daria?"

"I didn't know."

"She saw you with Daria. Then she confronted Daria. Alone. It got violent."

"It was an accident. I know it was."

"An accident," I said, shaking my head. "My God. Andrew, Grace killed Daria and dragged her body away. She didn't call for help. She didn't call the police. She just left. She slipped away before you or anyone else knew she was there. Didn't she?"

"You can't tell anyone. This is privileged."

"No," I said. "Not this time. I'm not your lawyer anymore, remember?" That was a blurred line, but I wagered Andrew wouldn't go researching it.

"She has to confess or I'm going to the cops myself. You're not protecting Beckett. And none of this is fair to Daria or her family. If you ever cared about her at all, there's only one way forward. I think you know that."

"It was my fault," he croaked.

"No. It wasn't. You may have been a shitty boyfriend, but you're not a murderer. Grace has been manipulating you. She's not a good person, Andrew. Do you get that? She's capable of murderous rage. She covered up her crime. She bullied you into keeping her secret. And Marcus? Where does he fit in all of this?"

"He thinks I think he killed Daria."

"Of course," I said. "And he knows he's not innocent. He knows he has a bigger motive to kill Daria than you did. If someone had found out at the time, Marcus would have been arrested instead of you, right?"

"It doesn't matter. He helped my family."

I let out a bitter laugh. "I guess you're a pretty good manipulator yourself. You've had Marcus fooled for years. You've had him paying you off for nothing. It serves you for people ... for me ... to think Marcus was the real killer. That's how you've protected Grace the most."

"I can't do it anymore," he said.

"No, you can't. What was this?" I picked up the note.

"Like you said. A message. She came to me yesterday. She said it was over. Since you quit, everything could just go back to normal. I told her you still weren't satisfied. That you talked to Nadler. That you had enough evidence to get me a new trial. She knows that means you might find out the truth."

"So what? She gives me this note as her final assurance that you'll keep her secret? I won't let go, so you're supposed to admit you killed Daria so I back off once and for all?"

"Yeah," he said.

"Beckett isn't safe with her."

"She didn't mean it," he said. "I know she didn't go out there to kill Daria. It just happened. It was an accident. You can still help me, Cass. If I tell the truth, you can help Grace. You put all of this together. I know you could see to it that the cops know Daria's death was an accident. It wasn't murder."

I shook my head. "God. Maybe if the two of you had told the police that in the first place. This would be over."

He was silent. The depth of Grace's treachery made my stomach turn.

"She's been playing you since the beginning, Andrew. Of course, she was there for you when you came home after that weekend. Right by your side. Keeping you close. Finding out what the police suspected. Getting pregnant."

His eyes went wide. "No. That's not how it was."

Of course it was. Andrew was just too blind to see it. It was hard to feel sorry for him. Every act he'd committed had hurt someone else. He'd pressured Daria. Made her feel so uncomfortable she lashed out at him. Scratched his face. Marcus was no saint, of course. But Andrew had known he wasn't a killer all this time. He said nothing.

"When did you find out?" I asked.

"What?"

"Your parents said you were fighting for your innocence in the beginning. Right up until the eve of trial. Then you just gave up. You stopped acting in your own defense. That's when you found out, isn't it? She confessed to you. Or you found out on your own. She told you she was pregnant. That you had to protect your unborn child by taking the fall for this. Right?"

"Henry," he croaked.

My mind spun. Henry. Henry. "Henry Barber? The witness who saw you with Daria at twelve forty-five? The one who died before the trial started?" It felt like my veins had filled with lava.

"He was sick," Andrew said. "He already knew he had cancer that week. We were supposed to take the bar."

"He died two weeks before the trial started," I said. "Did you ..."

"No!" Andrew shouted. "Don't even say it. No. I didn't hurt Henry. But he called me. He knew he was on his deathbed. We'd been friends in law school. Not close, like I was with Kade, Marcus, and Daria. But he was a good guy."

"He's one of the few people you actually invited to the party," I said.

"Yes. He told me he felt guilty. He didn't really believe I hurt Daria. It weighed on him that he had to provide testimony he knew would help convict me. He wanted my forgiveness before he died. Can you believe that? He's dying and yet he's thinking about my miserable problems. That's what I mean about him being a good guy. So I went to see him. After his deposition. I told him I didn't blame him. He just said what he saw. And it was the truth. I *did* argue with Daria. It got heated. I've never lied about that. But Henry told me something else. Something he didn't think was significant enough to mention in his testimony. He only casually mentioned it to me that last time we met. But he said someone was looking for me that night. Just before he saw me with Daria."

"Grace," I said.

"I felt pretty sure, yes. He described her. I didn't know she was there."

"You confronted her," I said.

"Yeah. I was angry. She never told me she was there. And I knew there was only one reason she'd lie about it. She was so upset. Hysterical. She told me what happened. It was an accident. And I knew it was my fault. I *did* lead her on. I was going to leave her for Daria if Daria would have had me. I caused this. Grace was defending herself. It was an accident. But it was my fault."

"She told you she was pregnant," I said.

Andrew nodded. "I could not have my son born in jail."

"But you were willing to give up your life with him."

"No!" he shouted. "No. It wasn't supposed to come to that. I didn't do this. I swear to God I thought I'd be acquitted. I didn't

318

know Marcus got to Nadler. And then Marcus came to me. He threatened to ruin my family or save them. I thought I would go through this trial, then I'd be free of it all. I could protect Grace and my son from my failings and save my father, too. It all just got so messed up. I did what I thought I had to do. I had no choice."

I couldn't hear another word. He had every choice. He could have taken the hint and left Daria alone. He could have told the truth as soon as he learned it. He could have told me the truth the first time I met with him.

"What's going to happen?" he asked. "Cass, please. You can help Grace like you were going to help me."

The thought of it made my stomach twist. But I knew I could use it to save Andrew from himself. More importantly, I could get Daria Moreau and her family the true justice they deserved. "All right," I said. "I'll do what I can to help Grace. That doesn't mean I'll represent her. But you will do exactly as I tell you. It's non-negotiable."

"Fine. Yes! Please. Tell me what to do."

"You're going to do exactly what Grace told you to," I said, waving the note in front of him. "I'm taking this to Detective Messer. Today. He'll have a warrant to search Grace's phone. It's going to prove she was at that party that night. And when Detective Messer shows up, you're going to give him a formal statement detailing everything you just told me. Everything that really happened. Until then, I'm leaving instructions with the warden before I go. You'll have no phone privileges until you hear from me again. If Grace shows up, she won't be allowed to see you. If I find out you talked to anyone after I leave here other than Tim Messer, I'm out. Do you understand?"

"No. I know."

"Good. And you're doing this for Beckett."

He nodded. But as I walked out of that room, I knew Beckett's father was only slightly less miserable than his mother.

I composed myself as best I could. All these weeks. All these years. All these secrets. As I walked out into the sunlight, I took out my cell phone and punched in Detective Tim Messer's number.

Chapter 32

WITHIN TWENTY-FOUR HOURS, Andrew kept his word and gave a formal statement to Detective Tim Messer. Forty-eight hours later, Messer served a subpoena on Grace Doyle for her cell phone records. Now, seventy-two hours later, I kept my word.

"Nice call," Eric said as Kieth Slater walked into the interrogation room at the Ingham County Sheriff's Department. Messer agreed to let Eric and me sit behind the one-way glass and watch the whole thing. Kieth Slater had been Eric's lawyer, long ago, when he too faced an uncertain future behind bars. He's who I would call if I ever needed defending of my own.

"He owes me," I said.

That might not technically be true. It might be the other way around. In any event, Slater sat beside Grace Doyle. I don't know how I expected her to be. Maybe I thought she'd pretend to be scared. Maybe she *should* have been scared. If anything, she sat there with calm confidence as Messer informed her of her rights for the video recording he made of the interview.

"Who's here with you today, Ms. Doyle?" Messer asked.

"Mrs. Doyle," she corrected him. Messer didn't respond. "This is my lawyer."

"My name is Kieth Slater," Slater said. "I'm here representing Grace Doyle."

Messer went through the housekeeping questions. Grace turned herself in voluntarily and of her own free will. She understood she could stop the interview at any time.

"Ms. Doyle," Messer said. "You know I came to your residence the other day to serve a subpoena for your cell phone records. I have the preliminary results from that search. I made a copy for your lawyer."

Slater took his copy and scanned it. I knew the results were no surprise to him. Grace didn't even pick up her copy.

"Ms. Doyle, your cell phone records put you in the vicinity of Colby House in Williamston, Michigan on Sunday, July 24, 2022. You were there for an hour before leaving the premises and heading back to Walkerton, Indiana. I need you to tell me what happened that night."

She looked at Slater. He gave her a small nod. The door opened behind us. A young woman walked in. She quickly and quietly introduced herself as Maisie Runyon, assistant prosecutor for Ingham County.

"I went to see Andrew," Grace said. "To surprise him. He was studying for the bar exam but I knew how nervous he was. I thought I could help calm him down."

"You're saying Andrew Doyle had no idea you were heading up to East Lansing?" Messer asked.

"No."

"You didn't text him, didn't call him beforehand?"

"You have my cell phone records," she said. "I believe they speak for themselves."

Maisie Runyon raised a brow and wrote something on her notepad.

"Fine," Messer continued. "What happened when you got to the residence?"

"I looked for Andrew. There were so many people there. I didn't expect that. I couldn't find him. I remember asking someone if they'd seen him. But the people at that party were strangers. Someone directed me to where the drinks were. I walked out of there and looked around. I saw Andrew. But he wasn't alone. He was talking to this woman. It was just the two of them on a path further into the woods."

"Who was the woman?" Messer asked. "I need you to say it."

"Daria Moreau," she said.

"Did you know Daria before that night?"

"No," she said. "I mean, I knew she was a friend of Andrew's. I'd heard the name. But no, I'd never met her."

"So you didn't know she was Daria Moreau that night?"

"No," she said. "That's true. No. I only knew she was talking to Andrew. It was later I found out who she was."

"Okay. So tell me what happened?"

Grace looked at Slater. He leaned in and whispered something in her ear.

"He's telling her to say no more and no less than what happened. Facts only," I whispered to Eric.

"I was shocked," she said. "Andrew looked ... intimate with this woman. He had his hands on her arms. They were shouting. I couldn't hear what they said. But Andrew looked really upset. He ... he leaned in and kissed her."

"He kissed her? How?"

"On the mouth," she said.

"Did Ms. Moreau reciprocate?"

"It looked that way. Yes. I was so upset. You have to understand. Andrew and I were together. We'd been on and off again since high school. But since that past Christmas, we had most definitely been on."

"Ms. Doyle, you understand we've searched your phone. There are no calls or texts to Andrew from you or from him to you for about six weeks prior to Daria Moreau's murder. And yet you're saying you were in an intimate romantic relationship with him?"

"You don't have to answer that," Slater said. "As my client told you, the records speak for themselves. You can ask her what she did that night. That's all."

"Fine," Messer said. Runyon scribbled furiously on her notepad.

"Their exchange was clearly passionate," Grace said. "Until Daria pushed Andrew away. I saw her slap him."

"And then what?"

"That's it. I was devastated. Andrew was with another woman. He was cheating on me. That was obvious."

"So, what did you do?"

"I ran. I felt sick to my stomach. Then I actually got sick to my stomach. Dizzy. I thought I was going to pass out, so I just sat under a tree for a little while. To try to collect my thoughts."

"Do you remember how long you sat there?"

"No. A while, I think."

"Could it have been as long as a half hour?"

"Maybe. Yes."

Henry Barber, in his deposition, said he saw Andrew and Daria arguing at twelve forty-five. Laneesha Dey saw Marcus arguing with Daria at 1:13 a.m.

"What happened, Ms. Doyle?"

"I got up. It was my intention to leave. Just go. But I got turned around. It was dark. I was in the woods. I kept walking in circles. When I came out, I saw Daria out there again. Standing not far from where she'd been kissing Andrew. I was not thinking straight at all. My heart was broken. Just ... shattered. And she'd slapped him. As strange as this sounds, I felt protective of him. Even then. If he loved her, how could she do that? Then ... she saw me. She was shocked. I was shocked. I was crying. I mean ... sobbing."

She started to sob now. Slater slid a tissue box over to her.

"Do you need a break?" Slater asked. Grace put a hand up and she blew her nose.

"No," she said. "I'm okay. Let's get this over with."

"Please continue," Messer said. "You said Daria was crying."

"Uh huh. And I came upon her. You know. I'm crying too. And I just snapped. Just ... unloaded. I told her to leave Andrew alone. That he was mine. I can't remember everything I said, but it was along those lines."

"What did she say?"

"Nothing. I don't remember. I mean, she was yelling back at me. But I don't think she was making sense. She asked me who I was. I remember that. And that just sent me. Like Andrew hadn't even told her about me? Then ... she got in my face. Advanced on me. She was about my height, and thin, but she scared me. She had this wild look in her eyes. I saw her slap Andrew. She drew her hand back, like she was going to hit me too. So I just lashed out. I shoved her back, you know. To protect myself. Then ..."

She broke down in tears again. It took her a moment to recover.

"Then," she continued. "She just fell. Lost her balance. Went kind of sideways. I reached for her. I swear. I tried to grab her to keep her from falling. But it happened so fast. She went backward and hit her head on the edge of the birdbath behind her. It sounded so awful. I'll remember that. Just a crunch. Then she was on the ground."

Messer took a beat. He had his back to us so I couldn't read his expression. But Slater looked up. He seemed to stare straight through me even though I knew he couldn't see me.

"What did you do then, Ms. Doyle?" Messer asked.

"I just ... I panicked. Daria wasn't moving. There was blood pouring out the back of her head. And she wasn't moving. She was just staring at me, but her eyes were gone. I was in shock. I didn't know what was happening. I didn't know what to do."

"What did you do?" Messer pressed on.

"I ... I ... I don't know."

"You don't know?"

"I blacked out," she said. "I can't remember."

"But you told Ms. Leary you remembered the bog. The muck where you dumped Daria Moreau's body. Andrew never told you about that. He couldn't, because he'd never been back there. But you were. So which is it? Were you lying to Cass Leary, or are you lying to me now?"

"All right," Slater said, ending the interview exactly when I would have.

"I don't remember," Grace yelled. "I swear. I don't remember."

"She's lying," Eric muttered. Maisie Runyon got up, gathered her pad, and left the room. A moment later, she walked into the interrogation room. She whispered something to Messer. He nodded, reached forward, and turned off the mics so we could no longer hear what was going on in the room.

"She's a liar," Eric fumed. "She knows exactly what she did. I think your friend coached her pretty well. She's describing second degree at worst. She can't possibly think the prosecutor will let her off with that flimsy story."

"I don't think Slater would coach her," I said. "I think Grace Doyle has known exactly what she's been doing since day one. This is just her fallback plan. She's not describing second degree, Eric. She's trying to establish it was self-defense."

"Christ," he muttered. "Good luck getting a jury to believe any of that."

He stood with his hands on his hips. "I can't stomach this anymore. Are you ready to go?"

The door opened and Messer walked in. He had the same scowl on his face as Eric did.

"I assume you heard that load of crap?"

"What else did you expect her to say?" I asked.

"Maisie's not going to go for it. She's signing off on the charging document. Second degree. Obstruction. Evidence tampering. Everything we can throw at her."

"What about Andrew?" I asked. "His story holds water. He didn't know Grace was there. There was no communication between them. What Grace did, she did alone. There's no evidence my client helped Grace try to hide that body."

"He's your client again?" Messer asked.

"For now."

Maisie Runyon walked back into the room. "We'll support your motion to reverse his conviction," she said. "As long as Mr. Doyle continues to cooperate in the case against his wife."

"There should be no conditions to his release," I said. "Andrew didn't kill that girl. As I was saying to Detective Messer, you have no evidence he did anything to aid Grace Doyle in the commission of this crime. All he did was keep her secret once he found it out."

"Which makes him an accessory after the fact. And he wasted taxpayer resources. And he denied Daria Moreau's parents the justice they deserved."

"I'm not saying he should win any Man of the Year prizes. But you know he doesn't deserve another day in prison. And you know once I file, I'll win. No matter what he's done, he's been in prison for almost two years. Every judge in the state would easily give him credit for time served. It's a no-brainer."

Runyon's face was sour. But she nodded. "Our office won't fight you on that. Again, though, I expect his full, continued cooperation. You tell him that."

"I think we're done here," Eric said.

He was right. I'd seen all I needed to see. With any luck, Andrew Doyle would be a free man inside of forty-eight hours.

Eric and I walked out of the observation room just as Grace was brought out in handcuffs. She had a strange smirk on her face as she passed me. Eric saw it.

"She's a damn psychopath," he said.

"I'm not sure. She's at least a malevolent narcissist."

"You didn't buy any of that, did you? That she acted out of blind rage and jealousy?"

"No," I said. "Everything she did after Daria's head hit that concrete, and everything she's done over the last two years was calculated. Cunning. And terrible."

Kieth Slater walked out. He gave me a grim smile and let the police lead his client down to booking.

"I don't know if I should say sorry, or you're welcome," I said as Runyon and Messer disappeared down the long corridor.

"Yeah." Slater smiled. "I'm not sure yet if I should thank you."

"You'll get press out of it," I said. "No way this case doesn't make national news."

"Eric?" Slater said. He extended a hand to shake Eric's. Eric was rigid. He had mixed feelings about Kieth Slater. Some of it was basic testosterone. Some of it was because Slater reminded him of a very dark time in his life. A time I hated to even think about.

"Well, thank you," I said to Slater. "I don't know if my client would have cooperated if you hadn't been willing to come on board. And whether she realizes it or not, Grace Doyle won the lottery with you."

Slater smiled. "Thanks for the endorsement. This is gonna be a fun one."

"Will she take a plea deal?" I asked. "For all their bluster, I can pretty much guarantee the prosecutor will want one. They aren't going to want to admit how wrong they got this one. I know Messer won't want to."

"Don't be so hard on him," Slater said. "Messer's a good detective." He directed that last bit at Eric as much as me.

Eric gave a tight-lipped nod. "He is," he agreed. "I've told Cass more than once. With the same evidence, I probably would have arrested Andrew Doyle, too."

"Of course you would," Slater said. "And Cass, you know I'm gonna want a conversation with him myself. If we can't work out a deal for his wife. He'll have to be a witness against her at trial."

"He knows," I said. "He'll be available. He's finally come to his senses. He wants to be there for his son."

"Good," Slater said. "Well, I better get back to my client. It was good seeing you both again."

Eric and I headed for the stairwell. It had been a long day. I couldn't believe I'd actually pulled any of this off. At Andrew's request, I had some phone calls to make. He hadn't wanted his family to know what was happening until I knew for sure he'd be getting out.

———————

As it turned out, Bill and Jenny Doyle were waiting for me when I got back to the office.

"Terrific," Eric muttered. "You up for this?"

"I don't have a choice," I said.

"Why do I half feel like this isn't good news?" he said. "I just feel ..."

"Wrecked," I finished his sentence for him. "Yeah."

"They're up in the conference room," Miranda said. She had her purse over her shoulder and an umbrella in hand. It was past five. Time for her to go home.

"Thanks," I said.

"I tried to tell them you'd just call them on your way home. They insisted on coming in."

"It's okay," I said. "This shouldn't take long."

"You want me to wait?" Eric asked.

"No," I said. "Just drive home. My car is still out back. I'd rather drive it home than leave it here, anyway."

Miranda yawned as she held the front door open for Eric. He kissed me on the cheek. "See you at home."

Then Eric and Miranda left and locked the door behind them.

I looked up at the stairs. I was beat. Cooked. But I owed Andrew's parents some good news.

Bill was pacing as I walked in. Jenny sat against the far wall, her purse in her lap. Bill froze when he saw me.

"It's good news," I said. Bill's whole posture deflated with relief.

"Grace has admitted to just about everything. The prosecutor is cooperating on Andrew's release. Hopefully, by this time tomorrow, he'll be under your roof."

Jenny let out a choked cry. Bill's eyes welled with tears. He crossed the room in two strides and pulled me into a hug.

"Thank you," he said. "God. I never thought this day would come."

"He may still be charged with something," I said. "He's kept this secret from the cops and from you for a very long time."

"She lied to us," Jenny said. "All these years. We did everything for her. Brought her into our home. And we didn't do it for her. We did it for Beckett. But I have treated Grace like a daughter."

"I know," I said. "It's a betrayal."

"That's the least of what it is," Bill snapped. "That woman is a murderer. A conniver. A succubus. I never want her to see Beckett again. Do we have that right? Can we do that?"

"To an extent," I said. "He's just a baby. His mother is going to prison. Maybe for the rest of her life. If Andrew wants it that way, he can get a court order denying her access to him. He can't be forced to bring him to prison to visit her."

"Good," Jenny said. "That's what we want too."

"For now," I said. "Let the courts decide what to do with Grace. Just hold your grandson close. And be there for Andrew. It might be an adjustment for him when he comes home."

"I want to kill him," Bill said. "Does that make me a bad person? Everything we've done. Have suffered. He could have ended it. He could have chosen Beckett over Grace. He could have chosen us over Grace."

I still couldn't tell them that he had. Part of Andrew's choice ensured Bill Doyle's financial security. Would it break him if he knew? I was glad I didn't have to make that decision. It was Andrew's call whether to keep that last, horrible secret.

"He loves her," Jenny said. "In spite of all of it. Andrew still loves Grace. She doesn't deserve it. But part of me is proud of him. It was wrong. It was twisted. But he tried to protect his family."

"You're a good mother," I said. "Andrew will need you to be. Beckett will need you to be. Regardless of what she's done, all Beckett will know is that he lost his mother. So go home. Be with your grandson. Hold him tight. Kiss him a lot. Then help him get to know his father."

Jenny cried as she stood up and hugged me. "Thank you," she said. "This never would have happened without you. We know that. We'll always know that."

"You're welcome," I said. We said our goodbyes and the Doyles walked out of my office arm in arm.

I sank into my desk chair. I wanted to curl up and sleep for six years. I wanted to go home. But there were two things left to do.

I flipped open my laptop and went to my email. A single letter sat in drafts. I clicked on it. It contained the letter I wrote to the

Attorney Grievance Commission along with an attached .zip drive. Inside that .zip drive was a copy of Marcus Savitch's timestamped police statement, an affidavit from Brianne Folger, a copy of the fake ID Grant Reznick used for Marcus's bar exam (one more gift from Special Agent Lee Cannon), and a copy of Marcus's actual driver's license. The letter explained everything. I hovered my mouse over the big blue button, hesitating for just a moment. Then I hit send. It was done.

That left just one last thing. One more person who deserved to be freed from the shackles of Andrew Doyle's secrets. I hoped it would bring her some small measure of comfort. But I knew nothing ever really could.

I sifted through my desk until I found a scrap of paper with a telephone number on it. I picked up my cell and punched it in. I closed my weary eyes and took a breath. Jacqueline Moreau answered on the second ring.

Chapter 33

"Oooooʜ!" Sean rested the back of his towhead on my chest. I loved the weight of him. He pointed skyward with one chubby index finger, waiting for the next round of fireworks. We were getting to the finale.

"Aaaaaah!" he shouted as purple and green burst over the lake, leaving its mirror reflection in the calm water. That was immediately followed by a red, white, and blue shell. The barrages popped off once a second after that, bathing the sky in a bright glow.

Tori walked up and took the empty lounge chair beside me. We lined up in the yard along the seawall. She handed Sean a fresh juice box and me another hard cider.

"Thanks," I said.

"Again, again!" Sean squealed.

"I think that's it, buddy," Tori said. She was showing now. She shifted uncomfortably in the chair.

"How's your back?" I asked. At times, she had to be in excruciating pain. After surviving a horrific car crash when she was pregnant with Sean, she'd had to have several vertebrae fused together.

"It's okay if I don't sit too long," she said. "It's gonna get worse when this little guy gets bigger." She placed a flat hand over her stomach. Her mouth dropped open. I couldn't stop my smile.

"You're sure?" I whispered. Joe, Matty, and Eric stood at the end of the dock, judging the fireworks display. Vangie and Jeanie were up on the porch, putting on more bug spray. Emma and Byron sat a little further down the yard from us, but still within earshot. Jessa was right beside Emma. I knew she thought of Emma as her cool cousin. She wasn't wrong.

Tori smiled brightly. "We found out two days ago. Matty wants it to be a surprise. Don't say anything."

"Not a word," I promised her. So I was getting another nephew. I hugged Sean a little tighter. He made an exaggerated groan.

"You're squeezing my guts, Auntie Cass," he said.

"Too bad," I told him. "I get to."

"I gotsta pee!" he abruptly announced. I let him go immediately. Tori sprang into action, scooping him up and running for the house. Potty training had been more of a war with that one.

Joe was almost to the yard, close enough to witness the emergency. "He's just like his dad," Joe said. I smiled. He was right. Our mother had the devil of a time getting Matty to go. He was strong-willed in every regard.

"Remember the summer of naked?" I said. Joe barked out a laugh and sat in Tori's vacated chair.

"I forgot about that," he said.

"Mom kept Matty naked from the waist down for three months. If you put underwear on him even once, he'd wet himself. But he was civilized enough not to pee on the floor for some reason."

"Little shit," Joe said, sipping his beer.

"Always." Down at the end of the dock, Matty was pointing out something across the lake to Eric. Whatever it was made Eric laugh heartily. Beside us, Emma and Byron got up and walked hand in hand up the driveway toward the trail in my woods. Joe tracked them, frowning. Byron had been nothing but sweet to Emma. But Joe wasn't thrilled about their dozen-year age difference.

"You okay?" I asked, sipping my cider.

We hadn't talked much since Tom Loomis tried to break Joe's face not far from where we were sitting.

He hesitated, taking another swig from his beer bottle then picking at the label.

"I'm sorry," he said.

I shook my head and smiled. "No, you're not."

Still looking at his beer bottle, he smiled wide. "Yeah. Maybe not. But you're never gonna mind your business, are you?"

"As soon as you start minding yours." I clinked my can against his beer.

"Fair point," he said. "And not that I need your permission, but I told Katie it's over."

"Oof. How'd she take it?"

"About how you'd expect. She freaked out. But I think she's trying to hold her marriage together."

I raised a brow. "She's got an interesting technique on that."

Joe laughed.

"Well," I said. "For what it's worth, I'm glad. She's no good for you. She's been jerking you around for years. Time to move on. You got out clean. You don't owe her anything. I can't believe I'm saying this, but if you're in the mood to hook up with an ex, Josie would have been a better choice."

Josie Banfield was Emma's biological mother. She and Joe had a complicated history and had been far too young to be parents. Joe had full custody of Emma by her first birthday. When Joe didn't respond, a little trill of fear went through me. He wouldn't meet my eye.

"Do not tell me," I said.

He took the last sip of his beer and said, "Okay."

I decided not to ask. I didn't want to know. Mercifully, Matty called out to Joe anyway.

An hour later, everyone started turning in. I'd have a houseful tonight. Sean crashed in the downstairs guest room and Tori didn't want to move him. She and Matty scooted Sean into the middle of the bed and camped out.

Joe took the living room pullout. Jessa took the upstairs guest room down the hall from the primary suite. I think Emma and Byron took the third and fourth bedrooms upstairs but that was mostly so Joe could stay in denial. I had no doubt Byron would end up with Emma sometime in the middle of the night.

Whether her father liked it or not, she was a grown woman. Vangie took the loft bedroom. Marbury and Madison were mildly annoyed with the development as they thought of that as their room. Vangie didn't mind sharing the bed with them.

I was beat beyond beat as I finished brushing my teeth and slid under the covers. Eric was already there. He patted the space beside him and curved around me.

"It was a good night," he said. "You and Joe are talking again?"

I yawned. "Yep. He says he dumped Katie."

"Good," Eric said.

My phone had been on its charger since yesterday afternoon. I intended to stay off all screens for most of the weekend. But I could see four missed texts on the home screen. I picked it up.

"Who the hell is that from?" Eric asked, looking over my shoulder. "Everybody you know is under this roof except for Jeanie."

"She was okay to drive?" I asked.

"She only had one sangria," Eric answered. "Emma made them kinda weak at that."

I sat up. The texts were from Kieth Slater, the lawyer I'd gotten for Grace Doyle. I quickly scrolled through them.

"Slater got Grace to take a plea deal," I said. "Voluntary manslaughter, obstruction, misuse of a corpse. But not murder."

"Wow," Eric said. "That's a gift. I'm not sure how I feel about that."

"The prosecutor knows she'll have problems at trial. It's a long shot, but there's room for reasonable doubt on the elements of murder. A jury might believe her story that it was an accident. Plus, there could be politics involved. Andrew Doyle did time for a murder he didn't commit. But Grace will do twenty years at least," I said. "Possibly more if the judge decides to tack her time consecutively. But I know Slater. He'll have negotiated that too. But...she'll eventually get out. She's in her late twenties. She won't raise Beckett, but she's going to get to have a life.

It left a bitter taste in my mouth. It would be a hard pill for the Moreaus to swallow. But at least the truth came out.

"It's those three men," Eric said. "They may not have killed Daria, but they sure mucked things up enough to make it hard to prosecute her real killer."

"They're not getting off scot-free," I said. "Andrew spent two years in prison. It's going to take a long time for him to rebuild his life. If he really can. He'll never be a lawyer now. He won't pass character and fitness."

"That's something, I guess."

"I got a call from the AGC two days ago," I said. "Obviously Marcus Savitch has been stripped of his license. He's going to be charged."

"I'm sure Daddy Savitch will figure out a way to keep him out of jail."

I put my phone back on its charger. "Maybe. I'm just glad to be done with the lot of them."

Eric kissed me. "You did a good thing. A great thing, actually. Any other lawyer would have given up on that case a long time ago. You found the truth. Even if Grace Doyle gets paroled someday, this has to bring some closure to the Moreaus."

I hoped he was right. "I didn't do this alone," I said. "I kinda liked having you by my side again." I turned to face him. Eric's face was unreadable. Then he leaned in to kiss me. I was tired, but had a stir of energy anyway.

"I liked being by your side again too," he said. "There's something I wanted to talk to you about."

I sat up on one elbow. "I was wondering when you would. Are you gonna tell me why Lee Cannon wanted to talk to you so badly a couple of weeks ago?"

He traced a finger from my shoulder down my arm, leaving a trail of goosebumps.

"It was about a job," he said. "And yeah. That's the thing I wanted to talk to you about."

I felt my throat go dry. "You want to be a cop again, don't you?"

He gave me an owlish gaze. "Would you hate that?"

"I would hate you not being happy," I said. "I would worry about you."

"You don't have to. I don't want to be a cop again. I mean, it's not something you can really stop being. But no, I'm not interested in wearing that kind of badge again. But I still have my security clearance with the Marshals service. From all the task forces I've been on. So ... Cannon and I were talking about me becoming a special investigator for the Feds. FBI, DOJ, OPM, the marshals too. I'd be running background checks. More high-profile stuff. Federal judges and appointees. New agents. That kind of thing."

"That sounds ... kinda fun actually."

"It pays pretty well too," he said. "And I can do it mostly from home except for the interviews. But I'll make my own schedule."

"The flock will like that," I said. "Me too."

"But," he said, "I did like working with you. It scratched an itch. Like I said, I can't turn off my detective brain. Ever. So yeah. Maybe sometimes. If you're working on something I can get behind, like the Doyle case."

A rush of excitement went through me. I rose up and straddled Eric's lap and pressed my hands against this bare chest.

"And I won't bug you to work on any client you hate. I promise. It'll always be your call."

He slid his hands around my waist. "And you have to listen to me. If I tell you something's too dangerous, you'll back off. Starting with no more pretending to still be a mob lawyer."

I bit my lower lip. "Okay. On that anyway. But you also have to trust my judgment."

He gave me a sort of harrumph, but didn't challenge me. I leaned down to kiss him. It felt good. He would be my professional partner again. Sometimes.

I melted into him, fitting against him like we'd been born for each other. I often thought we were. It was past one in the morning, but one of my neighbors lit off another firework. It flashed in Eric's eyes. Above us, in the loft bedroom, Marby started barking to wake the dead.

"Dammit dog!" we heard Vangie yell.

"Shut your hole!" Joe shouted up at her from downstairs.

Sean let out a horrendous wail at the disturbance. "Nice job, Joe!" Matty shouted.

I heard giggling from the room down the hall where Emma was supposed to be sleeping. Then a loud shoosh from Byron, clearly at her side.

On the other side of the door, Jessa yelled, "You're all nuts!" Then she slammed her door so hard the pictures on my wall shook.

Under me, Eric quaked with quiet laughter. "It's *your* family, not mine," he whispered.

I gently grabbed his jaw. "Except I didn't get to pick them. You're here by choice."

"Damn straight," he said, pulling me back against him.

He was my choice, too. One I would make again and again.

KEEP READING to learn more about the next book in the Cass Leary Legal Thriller series.

This time, murder becomes family matter when Cass's former sister-in-law is the prime suspect in a grisly crime. Katie Leary knows she'll need the best lawyer in town for any hope of clearing her name. Cass knows she should walk away, but she can't ignore her brother's pleas for help. The trouble is, the further Cass digs, the more she realizes it's her brother who might get buried.

https://www.robinjamesbooks.com/tblbm

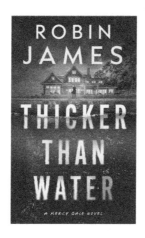

Newsletter Sign Up

Sign up to get notified about Robin James's latest book releases, discounts, and author news. You'll also get *Crown of Thorne* an exclusive FREE bonus prologue to the Cass Leary Legal Thriller Series just for joining.

Click to Sign Up

https://www.robinjamesbooks.com/subscribe/

About the Author

Robin James is an attorney and former law professor. She's worked on a wide range of civil, criminal and family law cases in her twenty-five year legal career. She also spent over a decade as supervising attorney for a Michigan legal clinic assisting thousands of people who could not otherwise afford access to justice.

Robin now lives on a lake in southern Michigan with her husband, two children, and one lazy dog. Her favorite, pure Michigan writing spot is stretched out on the back of a pontoon watching the faster boats go by.

Sign up for Robin James's Legal Thriller Newsletter to get all the latest updates on her new releases and get a free bonus scene from Burden of Truth featuring Cass Leary's last day in Chicago.https://www.robinjamesbooks.com/subscribe/

Also By Robin James

For the most up to date Booklist, visit

https://www.robinjamesbooks.com/books/

Mara Brent Legal Thriller Series

Time of Justice

Price of Justice

Hand of Justice

Mark of Justice

Path of Justice

Vow of Justice

Web of Justice

Shadow of Justice

Edge of Justice

With more to come...

Cass Leary Legal Thriller Series

Burden of Truth

Silent Witness

Devil's Bargain

Stolen Justice

Blood Evidence

Imminent Harm

First Degree

Mercy Kill

Guilty Acts

Cold Evidence

Dead Law

The Client List

Deadly Defense

Code of Secrets

The Best Lawyer

With more to come...

Mercy Gale Mystery Thrillers

Thicker than Water

With more to come...

Audiobooks by Robin James

Cass Leary Series

Burden of Truth

Silent Witness

Devil's Bargain

Stolen Justice

Blood Evidence

Imminent Harm

First Degree

Mercy Kill

Guilty Acts

Cold Evidence

Dead Law

The Client List

Deadly Defense

Code of Secrets

The Best Lawyer

With more to come...

Mara Brent Series

Time of Justice

Price of Justice

Hand of Justice

Made in the USA
Middletown, DE
20 July 2025